Special Edition
Books 1-3

Special Edition
Books 1-3

Belinda Ray

SCHOLASTIC INC.
New York Toronto London Auckland Sydney
Mexico City New Delhi Hong Kong Buenos Aires

Charm Club: Angel, ISBN 0-439-56011-X, Copyright © 2003 by 17th Street Productions, an Alloy company. All rights reserved. Published by Scholastic Inc.

Charm Club: Unicorn, ISBN 0-439-56012-8, Copyright © 2003 by 17th Street Productions, an Alloy company. All rights reserved. Published by Scholastic Inc.

Charm Club: Fairy, ISBN 0-439-56013-6, Copyright © 2004 by 17th Street Productions, an Alloy company. All rights reserved. Published by Scholastic Inc.

 Produced by 17th Street Productions, an Alloy company 151 West 26th Street New York, NY 10001

12 11 10 9 8 7 6 5 4 3 2 1   6 7 8 9 10 11/0

Printed in the U.S.A.   23

ISBN 0-439-85199-8

First compilation printing, January 2006

CONTENTS

ANGEL

CHAPTER
One

"Okay, class," Mrs. Wessex said in her usual cheery voice. "Clear off your desks. It's time for our vocabulary test."

Several students moaned as they placed their books on the floor, but not Anna Lee. She didn't mind tests. Back at her old school, all of Anna's friends had envied her amazing memory. She could read something just once and have it memorized. It was a skill that made studying for tests—and acing them—pretty easy.

Everyone had considered her the smartest student in the class, but Anna had been pretty popular at her old school, too. She got invited to all of the birthday parties, received a ton of cards on Valentine's Day, and was even voted "Most Spirited" at last year's fourth-grade field day competition. But that was back at Jackson

Intermediate School. Elizabeth Cady Stanton Middle School was completely different.

Here no one seemed to have noticed how smart Anna was or how well she did on tests. Or if they had, they didn't care. As for birthday parties, she hadn't heard about any yet, and the only title she'd earned so far was "the-new-girl." Or, as Anna saw it, "the-new-girl-with-no-friends."

"All right," Mrs. Wessex said, adjusting her glasses. Anna had Mrs. Wessex for both English and social studies. "Is everybody ready?" She looked around the room and smiled pleasantly at Anna. Then she raised her gaze slightly. Matt Dana, the boy who sat directly behind Anna, had his hand in the air.

"Yes, Matthew?" Mrs. Wessex called.

"I need to sharpen my pencil," he replied.

A few girls giggled. Anna rolled her eyes. Matt Dana *always* needed to sharpen his pencil.

In the three days that Anna had been attending Elizabeth Cady Stanton Middle School, Matt Dana had asked for permission to sharpen his pencil approximately ninety-six times. Secretly, Anna believed that if she turned around quick and caught him by surprise, she'd see him chewing the tip off just so that he could get up and sharpen it again.

"Quickly," Mrs. Wessex told him. Matt sprang to his feet and headed for the pencil sharpener at the front of the room. "Walk, please," Mrs. Wessex warned him, and he slowed his sprint to a shuffling jog.

Lead-eater, Anna thought as he passed her desk.

"All right," Mrs. Wessex went on. "While Matthew is taking care of that, I need someone to help pass out the tests." Twenty arms shot into the air, but Mrs. Wessex ignored them all. "Anna—could you come up here, please?" she asked.

Anna swallowed hard. Why did teachers always do that? Call on the one person who hadn't raised her hand? Ugh. The only thing worse than being the-new-girl-with-no-friends was being the-new-girl-with-no-friends-standing-up-in-front-of-the-whole-class.

"Anna?" Mrs. Wessex repeated.

Reluctantly, Anna rose from her chair. On the other side of the room, Lauren Graham whispered something to Maria Mancini, and they both giggled. Anna's cheeks burned. Were they talking about her?

Just ignore them, she told herself. She wasn't going to let a few giggles intimidate her.

"Five per row," Mrs. Wessex said, handing Anna a stack of papers.

"Okay," Anna said with a nod. Then she turned and began counting out papers for the girl at the front of the first line of desks. Her name was Theresa Allen, and she wore her long brown hair in cornrows that spilled around her shoulders.

Anna thought about asking how long it had taken to make all those tiny braids and who had done it for her—and how they stayed in place when she washed her hair—but instead she just handed Theresa the tests. "Here."

"Thanks," Theresa said with a wide grin. Then she leaned forward slightly. "I like your shirt," she confided quietly.

"Me, too," Carrie Weingarten whispered from the next desk back. Carrie was Theresa's best friend. The two of them were practically inseparable.

More than once Anna had walked down the hall behind them, watching Carrie's bright red curls bouncing up and down as Theresa's thin brown braids swayed from side to side. They were always talking and giggling, and they seemed really nice.

"It's really cool," Theresa added. "Where did you get it?"

Anna's almond-shaped eyes widened. She

glanced down, having completely forgotten what shirt she was wearing. It was a simple white peasant blouse—nothing special, really—but her grandmother had embroidered tiny red flowers around the wide cuffs and square neckline.

Anna felt a smile creep onto her face. She was just about to say "thank you" when the girl at the head of the next row spoke up.

"*Hel-lo*? I'd like to take my test *this year*, if you don't mind," Sharon Ross said. All the kids around her giggled—especially Kimberly Price, who seemed to think that everything Sharon said was hilarious.

"Anna—please don't dawdle," Mrs. Wessex instructed her.

"Sorry," Anna said. She felt her cheeks go red again, and she was so flustered, she forgot all about thanking Theresa and Carrie. Instead, she lowered her eyes and started toward Sharon's desk, counting out another five tests.

Unfortunately, in that same instant, Matt Dana finished sharpening his pencil and turned to sprint back to his seat. In less than two strides, he crashed into Anna, sending her and all the test papers—except for the five she'd already handed out—flying.

"Hey!" Anna yelled, trying to regain her balance. But before she knew what had happened, she found herself lying on her stomach on the red-and-white-tiled floor, with Matt Dana sprawled across her legs and papers fluttering down all around her. Everyone in the room howled.

"All right, settle down, everyone," Mrs. Wessex said. The laughter began to subside as Mrs. Wessex knelt next to Anna. "Are you okay?" she asked.

"I guess," Anna said, scowling at Matt.

"I didn't mean to," he protested.

"Wow, that's the first time I've seen someone fall down handing out tests," Sharon said, causing another surge of giggles in the classroom.

Anna narrowed her eyes. "I didn't *fall*. He—"

"All right, all right," Mrs. Wessex interrupted. Anna glared at Sharon. She'd made it sound like Anna was a klutz, when really Matt was to blame. Why wasn't anyone laughing at *him*?

Anna tried to stare Sharon down, but Sharon's gaze was unflinching, and Mrs. Wessex shifted, blocking Anna's view.

"How about you, Matthew?" Mrs. Wessex asked. "Are you hurt?"

"No," he said. "I'm fine."

"Okay, then," Mrs. Wessex said, offering each of them a hand. "Why don't the two of you return to your seats? I'll take care of the tests."

Anna stood up slowly, aware of a tender spot on her right knee. She was sure to have a first-rate black-and-blue there by the end of the day. Limping, she returned to her desk. No sooner had she sat down than she felt a tap on her shoulder.

"Hey, I'm sorry," Matt Dana whispered. Anna sighed. He sounded sincere, but she couldn't help it—she was still upset. He could apologize all day long and it wouldn't make a difference.

Thanks to him, she was no longer the-new-girl-with-no-friends. She wasn't even the-new-girl-with-no-friends-standing-up-in-front-of-the-whole-class. Now she was the-new-girl-with-no-friends-who-had-fallen-flat-on-her-face. It wasn't exactly a step in the right direction.

CHAPTER

Two

During recess and lunch, Anna laid low. It was pretty easy to do. No one missed her in the kickball game, no one missed her in the circles of friends laughing and talking, and no one missed her at any of the tables in the cafeteria.

In fact, aside from one of the lunch ladies, no one even spoke to her until she was on her way back to class.

"Hey, Anna!" Sharon Ross called out as Anna was opening her locker. "Did you have a nice *trip*?"

"Good one," Kimberly Price hooted, slapping her friend's hand. Anna closed her eyes and tried to ignore their laughter, but it was no use. She was tired. Tired of being new, tired of being alone, and tired of being laughed at.

It had only been ten days since she'd left

Doncaster, California, but it felt like years had passed. The sunny beaches with their warm sand and big blue waves seemed worlds away from New Hampshire, this land of gray skies and cold spring rain. And the fact that she hadn't managed to make any friends yet didn't help.

At Anna's old school, she'd had plenty of friends. Fifteen kids had come to her going-away party! If only she could be back there now. But she was stuck here, in Newcastle, New Hampshire. Alone. And so sick of it, she felt like crying.

"Anna?"

Anna felt her shoulders tighten. She pressed her eyes closed and fought back the tears, bracing herself for the next joke. Sharon could tease her all she wanted, but Anna wasn't going to cry. She wouldn't give Sharon—or Kimberly—the satisfaction.

"*Anna,*" the voice repeated. "Come on. You're going to be late for class."

Slowly, Anna looked up, surprised to see Carrie Weingarten standing beside her. *Smiling.*

"Oh . . . um . . ." Anna glanced around. She and Carrie were the only ones in the hallway.

"Let's go," Carrie said, tugging Anna's elbow.

"Uh . . . okay," Anna stammered. She grabbed her math book and followed Carrie's bouncing mass of curly red hair down the hall to Mr. Kane's room.

"I hate being late for math," Carrie confided as they walked. "Whenever I am, Mr. Kane always says something embarrassing like, 'I'm glad you could find the time to join us, Carrie,' and then everyone stares at me and I feel so stupid."

Anna snorted. "Try falling on your face in front of the whole class."

"Ooh—that's right," Carrie said with a wince. "I almost forgot. But that wasn't your fault. And besides—you handled it really well."

"I *did*?"

"Yeah," Carrie said with a shrug. "You just got up and went back to your seat like it was no big deal. I would've died of embarrassment."

Wow, Anna thought. Carrie didn't seem to think she was a total loser—she actually thought Anna had handled the situation well. And she realized it hadn't been Anna's fault.

Anna wished she had more time to talk to Carrie. It seemed like they reached Mr. Kane's room way too soon.

"Thanks for joining us, ladies," he bellowed

as they entered. Carrie shot Anna a sideways glance, and Anna smirked. Sometimes teachers were *so* predictable. "Go ahead and take a seat."

Anna hurried toward the back of the room, following Carrie's lead. When Theresa saw Carrie approaching, she moved a red jacket from the chair next to hers. Thankfully, there was another free seat at the table for Anna. It was next to Matt Dana, but Anna tried not to let that bother her. After all, he hadn't *meant* to make her look like an idiot in front of everyone. And at least now she knew that not *everyone* thought she was.

"Hey, Anna," Theresa said as Anna sat down. "Where were you at recess? I wanted to ask you about your shirt. You never told me where you got it."

"Oh, right," Anna said. "We sort of got interrupted." She stole a look at Sharon Ross, surprised to see that Sharon was staring right back at her. What was her problem, anyway? Anna turned back to Theresa. "I got it at this shop in Venice Beach, but my grandmother did the embroidery."

"Cool," Theresa said. "I really like it."

"You lived near Venice Beach?" Matt Dana asked, looking up from whatever he was working on in his notebook.

"Sort of," Anna started. "I mean—"

"Okay, people, listen up," Mr. Kane called out. He was moving about the room, handing work sheets to each table. "Today we're going to have a little contest," he said. "I've given each table the same set of work sheets, and we're going to see which group can work together to finish theirs the fastest."

Anna glanced at the others and raised her eyebrows. It sounded like fun.

"The winners," Mr. Kane continued, eyeing each table in turn, "will get a special prize at the end of class."

Theresa grinned. "I like prizes," she whispered, and for a moment, Anna forgot all about being the new girl. She loved games and contests of all sorts, and math was her favorite subject. She smiled back at Theresa and Carrie. She even smiled at Matt Dana.

The class was silent as everyone watched Mr. Kane for their cue to start. As the second hand on the clock approached twelve, he put his hand in the air. "Okay . . . go!" he said, lowering his arm like he was starting a race. Anna reached out a hand, but not fast enough. Theresa quickly grabbed all the work sheets.

Back at Jackson Intermediate, Anna would

have been the one to take charge, and all of her friends would have expected her to—but not here. Here no one thought of her as a leader. In fact, no one really knew anything about her, which meant she was going to have to prove herself all over again.

Anna sighed. She was already sick of this starting-over business, and she hadn't even been at it that long. Still, she wished she could just skip ahead. Or fast-forward to the good part. *The part where I fit in and feel comfortable and have plenty of friends and things to do and parties to go to and—*

"All right, let's see what we've got," Theresa mumbled, flipping through the papers. "Metric measuring. There are sixteen things to measure in the classroom—we should split those up and each do four," she said, setting that work sheet aside. "Then there's graphing—"

"I'll take that one," Matt Dana said, and before Theresa could reply, he snatched it out of her hands and went straight to work on it.

"O-*kay*," Theresa said, glancing at Carrie and Anna with a shrug. "So that leaves two work sheets—one on figuring out the areas and perimeters of a bunch of shapes and one on . . . *oh, no.*" She grimaced as she looked at the last paper.

"What is it?" Carrie asked.

"Adding, subtracting, and multiplying fractions," Theresa said with a groan. "I hate fractions."

"I'll do it," Anna offered. She'd always found fractions easy.

"Are you sure?" Theresa asked.

"Yep," Anna said with a nod, and, following Matt Dana's lead, she snatched it from Theresa's hand and set to work.

"Okay," Carrie said, "but don't worry if you don't finish them all. Theresa and I will split up these other problems, and when we're done, we'll help you with the fractions."

"Or Matt can help when he's done with the graphing," Theresa suggested. "Right, Matt?"

"Sure," Matt said without looking up. He had already plotted out half of the points on his graph paper, and it looked like his final picture was going to be some kind of bird.

"Okay, Anna?" Carrie asked.

Anna nodded again, but she was barely paying attention. She'd already finished the first two problems on her sheet, and she was determined to get the rest done on her own, too.

After about fifteen minutes, Matt Dana set down his pencil and looked up. "Great horned owl," he said, showing the picture to the rest of the group.

"Awesome," Theresa said. "Now can you help Anna finish the fractions?" But before he could answer, Anna set down her pencil as well.

"Done," she said.

"What?" Carrie asked, her hazel eyes as wide as nickels.

Theresa squinted. "You're kidding," she said.

Anna couldn't help smiling. "Nope. They're all finished." The rest of her group stared at her silently. "They were easy ones," she added modestly.

"Easy *fractions*?" Theresa said. "Is there such a thing?" Anna shrugged. She didn't know what to say. If she made it sound like they had been too easy for her, the others might think she was conceited. Thankfully, Matt broke the silence.

"Come on. Let's get measuring so we can win this thing," he said. "I'll take the first four problems, and you can start on five through eight."

"Okay," Anna said. She took out her ruler and set off to measure the tissue box, an electrical outlet, and the length and width in centimeters of her desk and her social studies book. By the time she had completed her first measurement, Theresa and Carrie had finished their work sheet and began their measuring, too.

They finished quickly, and with ten minutes left in class, Theresa arranged all four work sheets in a neat stack and ran up to give them to Mr. Kane. She beat Sharon Ross by just five seconds.

"So did we do it?" Carrie asked when Theresa returned to her seat. "Did we win?"

"I don't know," Theresa said. "Mr. Kane said that since our group and Sharon's group finished so close together, he was going to check all the answers and see who got the most right."

Anna glanced over at Sharon's table and gulped. Sharon's brown eyes were trained on her with the intensity of a cat stalking its prey. What was *with* that girl?

As other students handed in their work sheets, the classroom began to buzz with excitement. Everyone wanted to know which group had won, and Mr. Kane had made it clear that even the late finishers had a chance if the first groups done had made too many errors.

Finally, with only three minutes to go before the end of class, Mr. Kane stood up from his desk. "Okay!" he said. "We're down to two groups." A hush fell over the classroom. "We've got Sharon, Kimberly, Jeremy, and Billy . . . and Theresa, Carrie, Matt, and Anna."

Carrie reached out and grabbed Theresa's hand. Then she reached across the table and grabbed Anna's, too, squeezing it hard. Anna squeezed back. She wanted to win—partly because it would be fun to be part of a winning team, but mostly because it would feel so good to beat Sharon after all of her rude comments and mean stares.

"Both groups have gotten every answer correct so far, and all I've got left to look at are the fractions," Mr. Kane told them. "So . . . Lauren, why don't you take the work sheet from Sharon's group, and Maria, you take the one from Theresa's group, and I'll read the answers out loud. Ready?"

Maria and Lauren sat up straight, each of them aware of the responsibility they'd been given. "Ready," they said at the same time.

As Mr. Kane called out the answers, they made large *C*s for "correct" next to each problem. Anna leaned forward and watched Maria closely, sighing with each *C* but dreading that the next mark she made would be an *X*.

"I know ours are right," Sharon told her group. "I did them all myself."

Theresa, Carrie, and Matt shot nervous glances at Anna, and Anna bit her lip. She was pretty sure her answers were right, too, but she wasn't about to say so. It sounded pretty arrogant. Plus, there was always the possibility that she had missed one, especially since she had been trying to finish them so fast.

But when Mr. Kane had read the last answer, Anna could see that her paper was covered with nothing but *C*s.

"What's the total, ladies?" Mr. Kane asked.

"These are all right," Maria said. Matt Dana offered his hand to Anna for a high five, and she slapped it.

"How about yours, Lauren?" Mr. Kane asked.

"One wrong," Lauren said.

Carrie and Theresa squealed.

"Let me see that!" Sharon demanded.

"One-half plus one-third is five-sixths," Lauren told her, pointing at the problem in question.

"One-third?" Sharon said. "I thought it said *one-eighth*. Mr. Kane, that's not fair," she protested. "I didn't get it wrong—I misread it."

"Well, next time you'll just have to be more careful," Mr. Kane told her. "But right now, I'd like to present our winners with their prizes." He walked over to Anna's table and gave her, Theresa, Carrie, and Matt each a certificate good for a free ice cream or milk shake at Ed's Soda Shoppe, a local ice cream place.

"Cool," Matt said.

"Awesome work, everybody," Carrie told the group. "Especially you, Anna," she added.

"Yeah," Theresa agreed, grinning across the table. "Will you be in our group next time we have a contest?"

"Sure," Anna replied. Did they actually think there was a chance she would say no? Maybe they hadn't noticed that she had no friends. Then again, maybe that was about to change.

Theresa and Carrie seemed really nice, and they *had* invited Anna to work with them again. Maybe today was the day Anna was finally going to make some friends at her new school.

CHAPTER
Three

Or maybe not.

Anna was putting on her jacket when she heard familiar voices nearby.

"Do you know what's better than black raspberry chocolate chip ice cream in a sugar cone?" she heard Carrie say.

"No—what?" Theresa's voice replied.

"*Free* black raspberry chocolate chip ice cream in a sugar cone," Carrie replied, and the two of them giggled. They were just a few lockers down, but there were enough people in between that Anna could sneak glances without being noticed.

"I'm so psyched we won the math contest," Theresa said.

"I know," Carrie answered. "That was awesome. But did you see Sharon's face when Lauren said she got one wrong?"

"Oh, my gosh," Theresa said. "She was so red, I thought she was going to burst into flames."

"Or tear Lauren's arm off getting her paper back," Carrie added. "You know, I think that's the first time Sharon's lost one of those contests in over a month."

Wow, Anna thought. *No wonder she was giving me death glares all through social studies.* Then again, getting death glares from Sharon wasn't anything new. Anna had been receiving them since her very first day at ECS.

The first one had come right after she'd spelled *tintinnabulation* correctly to win a mock spelling bee in English class. Sharon had left out an *n* on her turn.

The second death glare had been given later that same day, when Anna had been the only one to solve a logic problem Mr. Kane had written on the chalkboard. Since then, they'd been coming steadily—three yesterday, four today, and if the pattern held, she had five to look forward to tomorrow.

So death glares were old news for Anna. But speaking to Carrie and Theresa was something new. And thanks to the math contest, Anna had an easy opening so she could talk to them again soon.

All she needed to do was to walk over and ask them where Ed's Soda Shoppe was. It was a totally legitimate question—she had a free ice cream certificate to use. And once they told her where it was, it would be easy enough for Anna to ask if they wanted to go with her to get their ice cream.

It was a perfect plan, and Anna was ready to put it into action. She just needed to finish packing up her books. She was shoving her social studies homework into her notebook when she heard Carrie speak up.

"Hey, Resa—do you want to go to Ed's *today*?"

Anna peeked around the side of her locker door and watched nervously. If they decided to go today, that might make things even easier.

Theresa shrugged. "I don't know. Are you in the mood for ice cream?"

"Are you kidding? I'm *always* in the mood for ice cream," Carrie said.

"Oh, yeah, I forgot," Theresa said with a laugh. "Sure, why not?" She slammed her locker shut, hefted her backpack onto her shoulder, and stood waiting for Carrie.

Anna took a deep breath. In another minute, they'd be coming her way and she could ask them about Ed's and see if she could tag along.

"Hey," Carrie said as she closed her locker, "maybe we should see if Matt and Anna want to come. I mean, we did win the certificates as a team—maybe we should celebrate together."

Anna's heart jumped into her throat. She had to be hearing things.

"Yeah—that would be cool," Theresa agreed. "Let's ask them."

Ask them? Anna thought. Maybe her luck was finally changing.

"Hey, Theresa! Carrie! Hold up!" Sharon Ross called. Anna's heart fell. It was uncanny how Sharon could be heard so easily above everyone else.

Anna glanced over to see her racing down the hall.

"Hurry up, Kimberly!" Sharon shouted over her shoulder. "We're going to miss the bus." Kimberly Price shuffled along behind Sharon, carrying a backpack that was almost as big as she was.

Oh, yeah, my luck's changing, Anna thought. *For the worse.*

"Okay, let's go," Sharon said as soon as she and Kimberly had reached Theresa and Carrie.

"Sharon got *Make It Real* on DVD," Kimberly

gushed, "and we're going to watch the second ending."

"That sounds cool, but . . ." Carrie's voice trailed off, and she shot a nervous look at Theresa.

"We're going to Ed's," Theresa finished for her.

"*Ed's?*" Sharon asked with a bit of a sneer. Carrie stared at the floor, but Theresa held Sharon's gaze.

"Yeah—have you seen Matt or Anna?" she asked. "We were going to invite them along—you know, since they were on our team."

"How could I forget?" Sharon grumbled. "But you *can't* be serious."

"Why not?" Theresa asked.

"Are you kidding?" Sharon said. "Anna Lee is a total loser. She's so quiet. And boring. And did you see the way she fell all over herself in English class? She's such a klutz, she'd probably spill her ice cream on you."

Klutz?! Anna was two seconds away from slamming her locker and storming over there when Carrie spoke up.

"*Sharon,*" she said.

Anna froze. It sounded like Carrie was going to defend her. If she did, Anna would know for certain that she had made her first friend.

Come on, Carrie, she wished. *Tell her to quit it.*

"What?" Sharon snapped. "Didn't you see her?"

Anna peeked around her locker door just in time to see Carrie shrug and stare at the floor again. Thankfully, Theresa came to her rescue.

"Come on, Sharon—it wasn't that bad," she said. "It wasn't even Anna's fault. It was Matt's."

Yeah, thought Anna. *You go, Theresa.*

"It was *not*," Sharon argued. "She stepped right in front of him. 'How many papers, Ms. Wessex?'" she mimicked in a meek, high-pitched voice. "'Five? I'm not sure I can count that high—aahhhhhoooooops!'"

Anna didn't have to look to know that Sharon was imitating her.

"That was perfect!" Kimberly squealed.

Anna waited for Theresa to speak up—to tell them that it wasn't perfect and that it wasn't funny, either. She waited . . . and waited . . . and waited. Nothing. Finally, she sneaked a glance in their direction, and what she saw made her jaw drop. Theresa was smiling, and so was Carrie. And even though they weren't exactly laughing, they did look amused.

"Why was she sitting with you in math class, anyway?" Sharon asked.

Anna was beginning to wonder the same thing. If they really liked her, they'd tell Sharon to stop making fun of her—wouldn't they?

"I guess because we walked to class together," Carrie said. She was speaking so quietly that Anna had to strain to hear her.

"Well, I guess you won't make that mistake twice," Sharon joked as Kimberly chortled. Their voices were plenty loud.

Anna was stunned. How could someone be so mean? Sharon barely even knew Anna. Why did she hate her so much? *And why weren't Carrie and Theresa saying anything?*

"Actually," Theresa started, her voice almost as quiet as Carrie's now, "we invited her to be on our team next time, too."

Anna sucked in her breath. There was still hope. There was still a chance that Theresa and Carrie wanted to be her friends.

"You *invited* her?" Sharon repeated. *"Why?"*

Because they like me, Anna thought. *Go on, tell her.*

But it was silent. And the longer the silence dragged on, the worse Anna felt. How hard was it to explain that they wanted her on their team? Or that they didn't think she was so bad? Or that maybe—just maybe—she was even kind of cool?

"I don't know," Theresa finally answered. "I guess because she's smart."

"You think she's *smart*?" Sharon sneered.

"Yeah," Carrie said. "I mean, she always gets the right answers when Mr. Kane calls on her in class. Even for the hard stuff."

That was it? Anna's shoulders slumped forward. She felt like she'd been punched in the stomach. Two minutes ago, she'd believed she was on the verge of making friends, but now she knew the truth. They'd only wanted her to help them win the contest.

"Whatever," Sharon said. "She's still a loser. And anyway—we have to go if we're going to make the bus."

"But what about Ed's?" Theresa asked.

"We can go there after the video," Sharon said. "If we see Matt on the way to the bus, you can invite him. He's cool. But forget about Anna. There won't be any math contests at Ed's." Theresa and Carrie—and of course, Kimberly—giggled.

"All right. Let's go," Theresa said.

As the four girls moved toward her, Anna tried to make herself invisible. She practically dove into her locker. If she could have fit inside, she would have closed the door and stayed there.

And why not? It wasn't as if anyone would have missed her.

Anna walked home in the mist, wishing she had brought the umbrella her mother had tried to give her that morning. When were these gray days going to end, anyway? It had been cold and rainy ever since Anna and her family had arrived. Back in California, all the flowers were already in bloom, but spring still seemed to be at least a month away here in New Hampshire.

By the time Anna reached her house, her short black hair hung heavily at the sides of her head, dripping onto her neck and shoulders. She swung open the wooden front door and stepped inside, hanging her jacket on its wall peg and removing her shoes.

"How was school, honey?" her mother called from the kitchen.

Anna answered the same way she had the last two days. "Fine."

"Did you learn anything new?"

Let's see . . . I'm lame and a total loser, thought Anna, but she knew that answer wouldn't go over well with her mother. Mrs. Lee would either lecture Anna on the importance of maintaining a positive attitude or, worse, get out her

Talking to Your Preteen book and start asking Anna questions like, "Are you starting to feel confused about boys, honey?"

No, thank you, Anna thought. It was easier to just answer her mother's questions and get them over with.

"Ummm," Anna murmured as she walked into the kitchen. She had to come up with something. Her mother wouldn't accept no for an answer. Every day she insisted that Anna and her older brother, Kim, come up with at least one new thing they'd learned that day.

"I know," Anna said finally. "One-half plus one-third is five-sixths."

"Very good," her mother replied. "But didn't you know that before?"

"Not really. I mean, I could have figured it out before," Anna said, "but now I have it memorized. That's new."

Her mother stopped chopping vegetables and squinted at her. "I guess it is," she agreed after a moment. Then she picked up a potato and started to peel it. Slivers of potato flew into the sink as she worked.

"Where's Kim?" Anna asked.

"He went to play baseball with some friends," Mrs. Lee answered without looking up. *Friends?* Anna thought. Kim had already made friends? And enough for a baseball team?

"What about Gran?" Anna asked.

"Volunteering at the soup kitchen with that seniors group she joined," Mrs. Lee replied.

Anna shook her head. Even her *grandmother* had new people to hang out with. Apparently, Anna was the only loser in the family. She sat and watched her mother peel another potato. *Another exciting afternoon,* she thought. *Boy, is Kim going to be sorry he missed this.*

Finally, her mother set down the last of the freshly skinned potatoes and turned to her. "Are you okay, Anna?" *Uh-oh.* She had that concerned, furrowed-eyebrow look going. "Would you like something to snack on? Some apple? Carrot sticks?"

"No, thanks," Anna said. "I'm not really hungry. I think I'm just going to get started on my homework." She snatched a round carrot slice and a few cherry tomatoes from the salad her mother had made and ducked out before the strange questions about boys and body changes could start flying.

Phew, Anna thought, starting up the stairs. *That was a close one.* She ran her hand along the handrail as she climbed. It was just a thin bar attached to the wall, and its white paint was peeling.

In her old house, there had been a solid oak banister that ran the full length of the stairs, curving outward at the bottom. Anna used to love to slide down it. So did Kim, up until about a year ago. Now that he was fifteen, though, he considered himself too old for that kind of stuff. Not that it mattered. The banister was back in California, along with everything else Anna liked.

She plodded to her room, which was down at the end of the hall. The pale blue carpet that covered most of the upstairs was kind of cushy on her feet, but Anna preferred the hardwood floors of her old house.

As she passed Kim's room, she noticed that he'd found time to hang his DANGER ZONE: NO ENTRY sign on his closed door. Last night, she'd heard him tacking up posters and stuff, too. He didn't seem to be having any trouble settling in. And by now, he probably had a decent amount of dirty laundry on the floor, which meant that his room here was probably starting to look pretty much like his old room in California. Anna's, however, was still plain.

Its white walls depressed her. It seemed so

sterile, so devoid of personality. She hadn't taken the time to put up any of her old posters or unpack any of her books yet, so it didn't even feel like *her* room. It could have been anyone's, and right now it just felt like one more place where she didn't belong.

"How pathetic is that?" Anna muttered as she dropped her backpack on the floor. "Even *at home* I don't feel at home."

If only she could have stayed in Doncaster—at least to finish out the school year. Having to move away from all her friends was bad enough, but having to move in the middle of the year was even worse.

She'd begged her parents to let her stay with one of her friends—just until summer—but they wouldn't even consider it. They told her the family was staying together and that was that. End of discussion.

Kim had been kind of upset about the move, too, but it didn't seem to be bothering him anymore. He'd been lucky. The boy next door, Dylan McPhetres, was his age, and they'd hit it off right away. And now it sounded like Kim had made even more friends. He seemed to be doing really well with all of the recent changes. A lot better than Anna was, anyway.

She couldn't stop thinking about the fact that in just ten days, she'd gone from being kind of popular to being completely friendless. She'd been forced to leave the house she'd grown up in and move into one where she felt like a guest. She'd left behind a town where she knew every single shortcut and where to get the best pizza, to come to this place, where she couldn't even find the local ice cream parlor.

And she'd gone from an intermediate school, where the fifth graders ruled, to a middle school, where she was at the bottom of the ladder all over again. But the hardest part was having no friends. No one to talk to all day and no one to hang out with after school.

Friends. Like Caitlin and Leah.

Anna walked over to her bureau and opened a medium-sized box that was sitting on top of it. She took out an old diary, a few animal posters that were folded up, and finally, a small wooden jewelry box.

Inside, the box was lined with red velvet and separated into several compartments, but Anna's favorite part was the secret storage area. The top shelf lifted out to reveal a sunken area where Anna kept her most valuable jewelry—like the necklace Caitlin and Leah had given her as a going-away present.

When the three girls had been younger—they'd known each other since they were six—they'd really liked angels. They'd had angel posters on their walls, angel stickers on their notebooks, and matching angel T-shirts. They seemed to have outgrown their angel phase sometime around third grade, but when Anna was getting ready to move, Caitlin and Leah had pooled their money to buy her an angel necklace.

Anna held the gleaming silver chain in her hand and ran her thumb over the cool metal links. Then, flopping down on her bed, she spread the necklace out in front of her and examined the five tiny angel charms that dangled from it.

Guardian angels, Anna thought. She knew Caitlin and Leah had given her the necklace as sort of a good-luck charm. Unfortunately, it didn't seem to be working—not that good luck could really improve her situation, anyway. What Anna needed was to fit in at this new school. But after hearing Sharon, Kimberly, Theresa, and Carrie making fun of her, it didn't seem like she ever would.

And why not?

Anna scowled at the necklace. "Because I'm a loser," she said, poking the first angel with her index finger. "And a klutz," she added, prodding the second one. "And I'm boring and way too quiet," she continued, jabbing the third angel and then the fourth. "And that's why I'm never going to have any friends." On the word *friends,* Anna gave the fifth angel the hardest poke of all.

"Hey—watch it!" a strange voice suddenly exclaimed. Anna's mouth dropped open as the tiny form rolled backward slightly, then shot up into a standing position. And as it did, the charm changed from shining silver to full color, as if a wave of water had splashed over it and washed off its metallic finish. Plus, the angel had nearly doubled in size; she now stood a full inch and a half tall!

"Sheesh," the angel cried in a little voice. "What an attitude! I can see I've got a lot of work to do here."

Anna gaped as the small figure shook her head rapidly, like a wet dog after a bath. A tiny shining halo wiggled back and forth, finally settling in a crooked position. "Whew!" the angel exclaimed. "Crossing over always makes me so dizzy. They say you get used to it, but I don't know. Hey—you got anything to eat?"

CHAPTER
Four

"Oh, no," Anna whispered. "I've lost it. *All this time alone has made me crazy.*"

The angel cocked her head, tipping her crooked halo to the other side. "Crazy, shmazy," she said, dusting off her white blouse and pleated plaid skirt. "If you're crazy, I'm Jiminy Cricket, and last I checked, my legs weren't long and green."

Anna blinked rapidly. The little . . . *angel*—or whatever she was—had come completely free of the necklace, and now she was standing on Anna's bed, wearing what seemed to be a private-school uniform. She even had white knee-highs, although they were mostly hidden by her bulky black combat boots.

Combat boots? Anna narrowed her eyes. "What kind of dream is this?" she muttered.

"Angels don't wear combat boots and . . . skull-caps," she added, noticing the dark blue knit hat that covered most of the angel's straight red hair and rested just above her eyebrows.

"Says who?" replied the angel. Anna jumped. If this vision was a figment of her imagination, why did it keep talking back to her?

"Uhhh," Anna moaned. It was all she could manage with her mouth still hanging open. She touched her hand to her forehead, but it didn't feel hot. "Maybe I didn't eat enough at lunch today," she wondered aloud. "Or maybe—"

The angel clicked her tongue. *"Hel-lo?"* she said. "I'm still in the room. And I'm *re-al.*"

"You can't be," Anna replied, shaking her head. "It's not possible."

"Yeah, whatever. Possible, impossible, here I am. Go ahead, pinch yourself. Heck, pinch *me.*"

Anna reached out and grasped the angel's tiny arm between her thumb and forefinger.

"Ouch! Not so hard, Gargantua! You're, like, a hundred times bigger than I am. Have a little sensitivity!"

"You told me to pinch you," Anna said.

"Yeah—*pinch* me. Not squeeze the life out of me!"

Anna blinked. *"Sor-ry."*

The angel waved one hand. "Aw, forget about it," she said. "Hey—where's my . . . ?" Suddenly, she started turning in circles, looking all around the bed.

"What?" Anna asked, but the angel didn't answer. She just shook her head and walked over to the necklace.

"Ack. I hate it when this happens."

Anna watched as the angel reached down and grabbed a small silver stick with a ball at the end that was attached to the necklace. She planted her feet on the chain on either side of it and pulled with all her might.

"Urgh," the angel grunted as she tugged upward.

At first, it looked like she was fighting a losing battle, but on her fourth try, the stick came loose and the angel toppled over backward, landing in a heap.

"Are you okay?" Anna asked.

"Oof. I think so. This down comforter makes for a pretty soft landing—way better than the pepperoni pizza I landed on the last time I left my wand behind."

"Ewww," Anna sympathized.

"Yeah, it wasn't pretty. But I'm not here to talk to you about pizza. I'm here to talk to you about . . . oh, man." The angel wrinkled her nose.

"What?" Anna frowned.

"Oh, nothing," the angel replied. "It's just that . . . well . . . I'm here to talk to you about friends, which technically makes me the . . . oh, I can't even say it."

Anna slid off her bed and knelt on the floor so that she was eye to eye with the angel. "Say *what?*"

The little sprite shook her head and rolled her eyes. "All right, here goes: I'm here to talk to you about friends, which technically makes me . . . *the friendship angel.*" She practically groaned the last three words.

"The *friendship angel?*" Anna repeated. "Are you kidding me? That's got to be, like, the corniest thing I've ever heard. What do you do? Fly around sprinkling magic dust on people to make them play nice?"

"Magic dust is for amateurs!" the angel snapped.

"Whoa—sorry," Anna said. "I didn't realize friendship angels were so *sensitive,*" she added with a giggle.

"All right, all right," the angel replied. She put her hands on her hips and tapped her foot. "Are you just about done?"

"Yeah, I guess," Anna said. "I mean, I wouldn't want to upset you or anything. You might wave your wand and make me friendly." She giggled again, but the angel just scowled at her.

"Uh-huh," she said, still tapping her foot. "Good one. Got any more?"

"Ummm," Anna murmured, pretending to think it over. "I guess not. That's it."

"Good. Then let's get down to business."

"We've got business?" Anna asked. "What kind of business, friendship angel?"

"Would you stop calling me that?!" the angel demanded, stamping her foot.

Anna laughed. This little person might not be real—although Anna was becoming more and more convinced that she was, with every passing minute—but still, Anna had to admit . . . she was pretty entertaining.

"All right," Anna said. "What should I call you? I mean, do you have a name? Other than . . . well, you know."

"Oh, right. Sorry. I guess I never really introduced myself, did I? I'm Zadie."

"Zadie. Wow—that's a cool name."

"Yeah, I guess," Zadie replied. "Until you tack 'the friendship angel' onto the end of it."

Anna laughed again. "Well, don't worry. I

won't. But, um . . . what's all this friendship stuff about, anyway? Is that your job or something? To go around making friends with people?"

Zadie exhaled heavily. "*No-o.* Actually, this is my first friendship assignment. The last time I was in your world, I was on dream patrol—you know, planting ideas in people's heads while they sleep. And before that I had to help this woman finish a book she was writing. Boy— that was a tough assignment. Writers are such procrastinators."

"Jeez," Anna said. "That sounds kind of cool—especially the dream stuff. I'd like to plant a few ideas in my mother's head while she's asleep. Maybe I could get her to give me a bigger allowance—or buy me a CD player for my room. Then I could convince my brother to let me use his MP3 player, and I could burn a bunch of—"

"Earth to Anna!" the angel called, cupping her hands around her mouth.

"Huh? Oh," Anna said, turning back to the angel. "I guess I was getting a little carried away. But wait—I still don't get it. Why are you here?"

"*Hel-lo?*" Zadie said. "Figure it out. I'm the friendship angel, right?"

"Yeah."

"And I popped off *your* necklace, right?"

"Uh-huh," Anna agreed.

Zadie cocked her head. "Okay. Will everyone in the room who has *no* friends please raise her hand," she said, pretending to address a crowd of people.

"Hey!" Anna protested, catching on. "I have friends!"

"In this state?" Zadie asked.

"Well . . . *no*," Anna admitted. "But what are *you* supposed to do about that? Bonk people on the head and make them think I'm cool?"

"You *are* cool," Zadie said.

"Yeah, right. That's why I sit in my room playing with my jewelry every afternoon— because I'm so cool, I can't decide who to hang out with."

Zadie shook her head. "There's that attitude again. If you want to make friends, you're going to have to lose that."

"You mean I should *turn my frown upside down?*" Anna scoffed.

"Ewww, no way," Zadie said, wincing. "Because then that little dimple above your lips would be on your chin, and that would just look freaky."

In spite of herself, Anna had to laugh. "Yeah,

I guess it would," she agreed. "But then what am I supposed to—"

A knock on the door stopped Anna midsentence.

"Anna?" her mother's voice called. "Are you all right? Who are you talking to in there?"

CHAPTER
Five

"Quick—hide!" Anna said.

With one swift jump, Zadie launched herself onto Anna's head. She ran a few circles, trying to figure out which way to go, and finally slid down a strand of hair in the back. "Ouch!" Anna cried.

"What did you say?" her mother asked through the door.

"Nothing," Anna said. "I mean . . . come in."

Her mother stepped into the room and glanced around. "Were you talking to someone?" Mrs. Lee asked.

"No. Why? Who would I be talking to?" Anna blurted.

Her mother squinted at her. "Are you feeling all right?"

"Yeah. Fine. Perfect. Why?" Anna said. She

knew she was talking way too fast, but she couldn't seem to slow herself down.

"Anna," Mrs. Lee said. "What's going on? I know I heard voices in here."

"Ohhh, voices," Anna repeated, stalling for time. "Right. That was just me. I was . . . practicing a poem I have to read out loud. For English. Tomorrow." That seemed to settle her mother down a little. Her gaze had changed from seriously worried to only half suspicious.

"That sounds interesting," Mrs. Lee said. "What poem?"

"Huh?"

"What's the *name* of the poem you're working on?"

"Oh, it's—" At that moment, Zadie must have lost her balance because Anna felt two quick footsteps at the nape of her neck and then a sudden tug on the fine baby hairs that grew there. "Ow! Quit it!"

"Anna?" Mrs. Lee said. Her seriously worried face was back.

"Oh, no, I mean—that's it," Anna stammered. "That's the name of the poem. 'Ow—Quit It.'"

"The poem is called 'Ow—Quit It'?" Mrs. Lee asked, folding her arms across her chest.

"Yeah," Anna said. She cleared her throat. "It goes, 'Ow—quit it . . . you're messing up my hair. Ow—quit it . . . you . . . shouldn't be back there." She smiled hopefully at her mother, who was still scrutinizing her with narrowed eyes. "It's about . . . a cat. Talking to a flea," Anna said.

"Hey—that was good," Zadie whispered.

"Thanks," Anna said. Her mother stared. "For listening, I mean. Thanks. It's . . . good practice for me. To get used to an audience, you know?"

Mrs. Lee nodded silently, and Anna held her breath. She couldn't tell if her mother was buying the whole poem thing or not.

"Well," Mrs. Lee said finally, "it's a very strange poem, but I guess your teacher wouldn't have assigned it if there weren't some value in learning it."

"Right," Anna agreed. "She wouldn't have. Mrs. Wessex is a really good teacher, and you're right. She wouldn't make me memorize a poem unless it was a good poem, and 'Ow—Quit It' is a really good poem. Really."

Zadie tugged Anna's hair again. "I have two words for you," she hissed. "Shut. Up. The more you talk, the weirder you sound."

Anna winced a little, but she managed to keep quiet.

"I see," Anna's mom said. Anna forced a smile and tried to look natural while her mother studied her face, but it was hard. She felt like an overripe piece of fruit that her mother was trying to decide how to handle. Should she throw it out or keep it for one more day?

"Well, I hate to interrupt you in the middle of your homework," Mrs. Lee said, "but quite frankly, I think you need a break. Come on—we're going to the mall."

"The mall?" Anna echoed.

"Yes. The mall. I need curtains for the house, and you're going to help me choose some."

"All right!" Zadie cheered from Anna's neck. "I love the mall. I hope there's a big food court. I could really go for some pizza."

"Pizza?" Anna said.

"No, we're not getting pizza," Mrs. Lee replied. "I've already started dinner. But we might be able to get a small snack—if there's time. Now get ready and meet me downstairs," she said, turning to leave.

"Yahoo! Giant pretzels, here I come!" Zadie shouted, but Anna couldn't share her enthusiasm.

"Please. Curtain shopping with my mom?" she muttered. "That's supposed to cheer me up?"

"Oh, and Anna," Mrs. Lee said, popping her head back into the room. "Do something about your hair. It's a mess."

CHAPTER
Six

"Ooh, these are nice," Mrs. Lee said, running her hand down the length of a set of red gingham curtains.

Anna rolled her eyes. She had thought spending the afternoon alone in her room was as lame as she could get. Now she knew she'd been wrong.

"Thanks a lot," she muttered, speaking into her jacket pocket. "Things weren't bad enough before. Good work."

Zadie poked her head out of the top of the pocket and glanced around. "Are you kidding? This is *way* better. We're at the mall!"

Whoopee, Anna thought.

"What do you think of these for the kitchen, Anna?" Mrs. Lee asked, still holding on to the red-checked curtains.

Anna shrugged. "I don't know," she said. "They're okay, I guess."

"Just *okay*?" her mom questioned. "I think they'd really go nicely with the black-and-white tile."

"I think you should get them," Anna said. She really didn't care what kind of curtains her mother bought. She just wanted to get out of there.

"I like them," Zadie said, but her voice sounded louder this time. Suddenly, Anna realized why.

Somehow, when she hadn't been paying attention, the tiny angel had managed to climb up onto her shoulder, where she was now perched.

"What are you doing?" Anna snapped as loudly as she could in a gritted-teeth whisper.

"Scoping out the scene," Zadie replied matter-of-factly.

"Are you *crazy*? Do you want everyone to see you?"

"Oh. Don't worry about that," Zadie said with a wave of her hand. "You're the only one who can see me. I'm invisible to everyone else."

"You're what?"

"Invisible," Zadie repeated.

Anna shook her head. "If no one else can see you, why did you have to hide on my neck and pull my hair before?"

"I don't know." Zadie shrugged. "You said 'hide,' and I guess I just forgot."

"You forgot?" Anna practically shouted.

Mrs. Lee whipped her head around. "What did you say, Anna?"

"Huh? Oh, um . . ."

"You're hot," Zadie coached her. "Tell her you're hot."

"Um, you're hot," Anna said. "I mean, *I'm* hot."

Mrs. Lee narrowed her eyes again. It was becoming her regular expression.

"Good," Zadie said. "Now tell her you need something to drink."

"You—I mean *I* need something to drink," Anna said.

Her mother sighed and placed the back of her hand to Anna's forehead. "I don't know what's gotten into you today, Anna. You're acting awfully strange. But . . . you do feel a little warm."

Anna did her best to look innocent. And hot. And to ignore the inch-and-a-half-tall person on her shoulder chanting, *"Oh, yeah, you know it, we're goin' to the food court. Oh, yeah, you know it. . . ."*

Mrs. Lee opened her pocketbook and pulled out a five-dollar bill. "Here. Go get yourself a drink and something to eat—something *healthy*—and meet me at the main entrance in . . ." She paused to check her watch. "Forty-five minutes. Okay?"

Anna nodded. "Okay."

With Zadie still cheering, Anna moved from the curtain shop—where she'd felt smothered in ugly fabric—into the bright, high-ceilinged expanse of the mall. To her surprise, she actually began to feel a little better. She walked to a planter in the center of the huge open area and stopped, looking left and then right.

"What do you think?" she said, trying not to move her lips.

Zadie stood tall and squinted in each direction. "Left. Definitely left," she said. "Trust me—I have excellent mall sense."

"Okay," Anna said, and she started down the east wing of the mall.

She had passed two shoe stores, a camera store, a candy shop, and a couple of trendy clothing stores when Zadie suddenly jumped up and started pointing.

"Oh! Let's go in there! Please, please, please, please!"

"The arcade?" Anna asked.

"Yeah! I see Storm Ranger! I play it all the time on the TruView back in my dorm room. Please—can we go play?"

Anna glanced into the dark cavern filled with blinking lights and beeping sounds. "I don't know," she said. "I've never really been all that good at video games."

"You don't have to be," Zadie said. "It's just for fun."

"Yeah, but . . ." Anna studied the crowded game room. The last time she'd been in an arcade had been with her brother. He'd played one game for a half hour on one quarter, and she'd blown through all of her money in less than fifteen minutes. It hadn't exactly been exhilarating.

"Oh, come on," said Zadie. "Just one game."

"I don't know, Zadie. Video games aren't really my—"

"Great!" the angel exclaimed. She ran down Anna's arm, speared the five-dollar bill with her wand, and ran with it—like it was a giant flag— all the way over to the change machine.

"Hey! Wait!" Anna yelled, chasing her money across the terra-cotta-tiled floor. She nearly bumped into an elderly couple and had to stop to excuse herself. Otherwise she would have caught Zadie. Unfortunately, by the time she reached the entrance to the arcade, her five-dollar bill had been turned into twenty-five golden tokens.

"Zadie! My mom's probably expecting change," Anna snapped.

"Does *she* like video games?" Zadie asked. Anna scowled at the angel and scooped up her tokens.

"Come on," Anna said, and she started to walk away.

"What?! Do you mean to tell me that you've got all those tokens and you're not even going to use one?" Zadie demanded. "You're killing me!"

Anna stopped and sighed heavily. "Fine," she said. "One game. Where is it?"

Zadie clapped and beamed. "Right there," she said, pointing to a machine surrounded by people.

"*Zadie*," Anna whined. "The line for that game is huge. We'll never get a turn."

The words were barely out of Anna's mouth when a blue light on the other side of the arcade began flashing and a loud siren started to wail.

"Someone beat Robo Warrior!" one of the boys yelled, and they all ran over to see who the new champion was.

Anna shot Zadie a sideways glance. "Okay, that was weird," she said.

Zadie just shrugged. "Game's free," she said. "Better hurry." Anna studied her small friend for another minute, then slowly—reluctantly—walked over to the newly vacated machine.

"Storm Ranger?" Anna said, raising her eyebrows.

"Yeah, kind of a lame name," Zadie admitted, "but it's really cool. See, you have to fight your way through a series of villains to get to the evil Dr. Sphere, who's turned the world into a wasteland of chaos with his SD3000 Storm Maker."

Anna frowned.

"Okay, so it *sounds* lame, too," Zadie said, "but it's really fun. I promise. Go ahead—put your tokens in."

"All right," Anna said, and she dropped two tokens into the slot. A red START GAME light began flashing, and Anna was just about to hit it when she noticed all of the other controls.

"Zadie! There are like a gazillion buttons here! I can't do this."

"Don't worry—I'll coach you," the little angel said, and she jumped on the button to start the game.

"Great. Maybe I'll last an extra ten seconds," Anna said. She grabbed the joystick with her left hand and poised her right hand above all of the colored buttons. She never understood why people wasted their money on this stuff.

"Get ready," Zadie commanded. "And three . . . two . . . one—here comes the first brute!"

As unenthusiastic as she was about the game, Anna couldn't help getting into the background music. It was a funky melody with a steady, driving beat that kept getting faster and louder as she played. In spite of herself, she felt her shoulders tense, and butterflies took over where her stomach used to be.

"Quick! Green!" Zadie yelled, and Anna smacked the green button as fast as she could.

"Great—now red! Blue! Joystick up! Now left! Yellow! Yellow! Move right! Awesome kick—do it again! And blue! You've almost got him! Red! Red! One more! Yeah!"

Zadie was jumping up and down on the screen so frantically that Anna forgot how much she hated video games and started to laugh.

"Don't get too relaxed," Zadie cautioned her. "The first guy's easy. Here comes number two!"

Anna readied herself at the controls as another enemy warrior approached. Once again

Zadie shouted out commands, and Anna executed them flawlessly until the second opponent had been reduced to dust as well.

"All *right*!" she said, a huge smile spreading across her face. Who'd have thought that crushing the cronies of chaos could be so much fun?

By the time Anna had defeated her sixth rival, Zadie had switched from yelling out specific commands to just plain yelling. Anna didn't really need advice anymore—she was doing fine on her own. What's more, she was really beginning to have fun! She didn't even mind that a few people had gathered around to watch her.

"Cool," she heard one of the onlookers say when she beat enemy number seven, and she couldn't help smiling. It felt good to be kicking butt at this game, and it didn't even matter that she was doing it alone.

"Smash him!" Zadie yelled.

Well, *almost* alone.

Finally, at the entrance to Dr. Sphere's fortress, Anna met her match. He . . . she . . . *it* was a two-legged, forty-foot-tall reptile with a plated back, twelve-inch claws, two heads, and a clubbed tail. Even Zadie wasn't sure how to tackle that one, so Anna just did what she could and at the very least went down fighting.

"Whew." Anna sighed as GAME OVER flashed on the screen. "That was fun."

"Major fun," Zadie agreed. "And you were awesome. You made it two levels farther than I ever have, and hey—look! You got your name in the top ten!"

Anna gazed down at the screen, and sure enough, it was asking her to enter her name. "Cool," Anna said. She used the joystick to choose letters until she had spelled ZADIE, then she stuck out her pinky for an angel high five.

"Thanks!" Zadie said. "Let's see where you placed." As the two of them were waiting for the screen to show the top ten high scores, Anna felt someone tap her on the shoulder.

"Hey. You're pretty good at that."

Anna turned around to see Matt Dana standing behind her. "Oh. Thanks," she said. "That was my first time."

"Whoa? Really?" he asked. Anna nodded. "Nice job. You're number six," he said, pointing at the screen. Anna turned back to see ZADIE glowing in bright green letters halfway down the list. And then she noticed the other high scores. Numbers one through five and seven through ten were all filled in with the same name: MATTYD.

"Wow. I did *okay*, but it looks like you've got me beat," she said.

Matt shrugged. "I come in here a lot," he said. "Was that really your first time playing Storm Ranger?"

"Yeah," Anna said with a laugh. "I'd never even heard of it before."

"Huh—you must be a natural," Matt said.

"Or maybe it was just beginner's luck," Anna offered. "If I play it again, I probably won't even get past the first screen."

"Maybe," Matt said, "but I doubt it. You looked like you knew what you were doing. You'll probably have all my high scores wiped out by the end of the week."

Anna jingled the tokens in her pocket. "Yeah, right. And it'll only cost me about fifty dollars."

Matt laughed. "Hey—in math class, you said something about Venice Beach. Does that mean you're from California?"

"Yeah, but not that close to Venice Beach. We just went there on weekends and stuff. I lived farther south, near San Diego."

"Cool. Were you right on the coast?"

"Mm-hm." Anna nodded.

"Ever go surfing?"

"A couple of times," Anna said. "It was a lot of fun."

"I bet. I'd love to go, but it's hard around here. The waves aren't as big, and there just aren't that many places to try."

"Yeah, my brother was pretty bummed about that when my parents told us about the move. He was really into surfing. But then I think he found some kind of East Coast surf club online, and it listed a few spots around here where the surfing is actually supposed to be okay."

"Huh. I'll have to check that out. Think you could get me the URL?"

"Sure," Anna said with a shrug.

"Cool. Meanwhile, I guess I'll just keep skateboarding."

"You skateboard?" Anna asked.

"Yeah. You?"

Anna shook her head. "No way."

"What do you mean, 'no way'? If you've surfed, you can probably skateboard. It's the same idea."

"Uh-huh. Except that if you fall off a surfboard, you land in the water. If you fall off a skateboard, you fall on the *pavement*. That's enough of a difference for me."

"So you wear pads," Matt said. "And a helmet."

"I don't know," Anna said. "I like sports that don't require body armor. You know, like eating ice cream." She grinned, pulling the gift certificate she'd won in math class out of her back pocket. "Where is Ed's, anyway?"

"It's actually here in the mall," Matt said. "And I have my certificate, too. Do you want me to show you where it is?"

"Sure," Anna said. She had just started out of the arcade behind him when she heard a tiny voice yell, "*Hel-lo?* Dreamy conversation with your new buddy, but aren't you forgetting something?"

"Oh!" Anna gasped.

"What's up?"

"I, um . . . think I left some money back there," Anna lied. She ran over to the Storm Ranger machine, scooped up the disgruntled angel, and raced back. "Just a few tokens," she said, "but I didn't want to leave them."

"That's cool," Matt said. "All set?"

"Yeah. All set," Anna said.

They walked down the mall corridors, continuing in the same direction Anna and Zadie had been heading before they found the arcade.

"Told you I had good mall sense," a muffled voice yelled from inside Anna's jacket pocket.

And after just a few more clothing stores, a giant sports place with four escalators, a coffee shop, an electronics store, and a bookseller, they hit the food court.

Zadie peeked out of Anna's pocket and started sniffing the air. "Pretzels—I smell pretzels," she said. "And pizza!" She hopped up to the top of Anna's pocket and teetered on the edge.

"Zadie—what are you doing?" Anna hissed.

"I'm busting out my beat box," the angel said. She stuck her hands under opposite armpits with her thumbs sticking out and started making percussion noises with her mouth. Then, to Anna's amazement, she started *rapping*.

> *"I wanna eat right now!*
> *When I'm at the mall, I like to chow down!*
> *My name is Zadie,*
> *They say I'm a lady,*
> *But I still know how to get crazy—"*

Anna planted her index finger on Zadie's head and pushed her back down into the pocket.

"Hey!" Zadie's muted voice protested. "I wasn't done!"

"You are now," Anna whispered.

"Fine. I get it. A human comes along and it's

bye-bye, Zadie. *Nice.* Well, I'm going to score some food—I'll meet you at the ice cream place." And with that, she jumped from Anna's pocket and ran across the floor.

Anna watched her go. She looked just like a little piece of paper being carried along by the drafts of air from people's shuffling feet. *I hope she doesn't get squished,* Anna thought. But she figured an angel who could cross from one world to another without getting injured could probably navigate the mall.

"Here it is," Matt said as he and Anna approached what looked like an old-fashioned soda shop. There was a long red counter with stainless steel sides and matching bar stools, and the three people working behind it all wore white jackets and paper hats.

"Cool," Anna said. "Do you know what you're getting?"

Matt nodded. "My usual," he said, and stepped up. "Mint chocolate chip in a plain cone, please," he said, handing over his gift certificate.

"Make that two," Anna said, presenting hers as well.

"You like mint chocolate chip?" Matt asked.

"It's my favorite," Anna said. "Back in Doncaster—that's where I lived in California—there was this ice cream place that had *green days.*"

"Green days?"

"Yeah, it was this special deal they had a few times a year—on St. Patrick's Day, the first day of spring, and . . . I guess the other one was sometime in the middle of summer or something. Anyway, on green days you could go in and get any flavor of ice cream that was green for half price. It was really cool."

"That *is* cool," Matt said.

"They did other colors, too," Anna said. "Like pink on Valentine's Day, brown whenever it was raining."

Matt scrunched his eyebrows together. "I get the pink," he said, "but what does brown have to do with rain?"

"I don't know. Maybe because rain makes mud?" Anna guessed.

"Yeah." Matt nodded. "I bet that's it." He and Anna took their ice-cream cones from the woman behind the counter, thanked her, and headed toward a table at the center of the food court. Anna licked her ice cream, pleased to find that mint chocolate chip tasted as good here as it did in California. She and Matt were just about to sit down when Anna heard someone calling Matt's name.

"Matt! Matt! Over here!"

I know that voice, Anna thought with a sense of dread.

"Matt! Matt Dana!" the voice called again, but Matt didn't seem to notice.

"Um . . . I think someone's trying to get your attention," Anna said.

"Huh?" Matt glanced around. "Oh." He turned in the direction of the voice and spotted Sharon Ross, waving madly. She, Kimberly, Theresa, and Carrie were sharing a table.

Matt turned back to Anna. "Do you want to sit over there?" he asked.

No, no, a thousand times no, Anna thought. But what was she going to say? *I can't—none of your friends like me?* Yeah, right. She might as well just tattoo an *L* on her forehead for *lame.*

"Sure," she said. She followed Matt as he made his way through the maze of tables and chairs.

"Hey, Matt," Sharon said. "It's so cool that you came for ice cream at the same time that we did. Here, have a seat." She pulled over a chair from a neighboring table and placed it next to hers. Anna looked for another seat, but no one had bothered to make room for her.

"You guys know Anna, right?" Matt said.

"Yeah," they all murmured.

"Hey, Anna—nice job on those fractions

today," Theresa said. "You really carried our team." Anna tilted her head slightly. She noticed Sharon glaring at Theresa and wasn't quite sure what to make of the whole situation. Was Theresa trying to upset Sharon? More important, was Theresa really trying to be nice to Anna, or would she just start laughing behind Anna's back again as soon as she was gone?

"Thanks," Anna said. "It really wasn't that big a deal."

"Free ice cream is a *very* big deal," Carrie disagreed, and everyone chuckled. Except Sharon. Even Kimberly was smiling until she realized Sharon wasn't amused. Again, Anna was puzzled. They didn't *seem* to hate her. Okay, so maybe Sharon did—but the others didn't.

"Hey, Anna, why don't you take that chair," Matt offered. "I'll grab another one."

It was a nice gesture, and Anna appreciated it, but the last thing she wanted was to sit next to Sharon. She looked around for another possibility, but Matt insisted. "Really. Go ahead. That's cool, right, Sharon?"

"Sure," Sharon said with a smile. Anna just about fell over.

"I'll be right back," Matt said, and he headed off in search of a chair.

"Okay," Anna said.

She glanced at Sharon. The smile vanished, and her face once again looked like it had been chiseled from stone. She had obviously wanted Matt sitting next to her, and Anna . . . well, she probably wanted Anna back on the other side of the country. But what else was there to do?

Anna swallowed hard and walked toward the chair. Maybe, just this once, Sharon would be willing to call a truce. After all, she seemed to really like Matt, and Anna had come over with him.

As Anna edged along the table to her chair, she gave Sharon a weak smile. "Bad luck on the math work sheet, huh? Those numbers were pretty blurry. I had a hard time reading some of them, too." It was a lie, but she thought it might soften Sharon up a little.

"No big deal," Sharon said with a shrug. "I've had enough free ice cream this month already."

Anna nodded. "Yeah, I heard that you usually win those—aaaaaghhhh!"

There was a bang and a thud, and suddenly, for the second time that day, Anna was on the floor. Only this time she was covered in mint chocolate chip ice cream.

"Sharon!" she heard Carrie yell.

"I didn't mean to," Sharon said.

"Did you pull out her chair?" Theresa asked.

"No—I just bumped it a little," Sharon said. "I told you she was a klutz."

"I am *not* a klutz," Anna said through gritted teeth.

"You mean you did that on purpose?" Sharon asked.

Anna looked down at her white shirt and her jeans. There were light green splotches all over them as well as on her hands and probably even her face.

"Are you okay?" Carrie asked. Anna nodded.

"Good," Kimberly said. "Because—" The corner of her mouth curved into a smirk. "I don't think I can keep from laughing much longer." And suddenly she burst out giggling, which got Sharon started, too. And it wasn't long before Theresa and Carrie had joined in.

"I'm sorry, Anna," Carrie gasped between giggles. "But you look so funny!"

Just then, Matt returned with his chair. "What happened?" he asked. The four girls were laughing so hard that no one could answer him, and Anna couldn't handle it any longer. She stood up, shook the ice cream from her hands, and hurried away.

"Anna! Wait," she heard Matt calling after her, but she wasn't stopping for anything.

"Oh, no! What happened?" a tiny voice

screeched. Anna just shook her head and kept walking. Zadie sprinted ahead, scaled a fake tree, and jumped onto Anna's shoulder as she passed by.

"I knew you were going for ice cream," Zadie said, "but I had no idea you were such a messy eater."

"I'm not," Anna said through clenched teeth. "This girl Sharon, who *hates* me, pulled my chair out from under me and I dropped my cone."

"Ooh! That's low. Which one is she?" Zadie stood on Anna's shoulder, staring back at the table where Anna had been sitting. "She's the blonde, right? Let's go get her. We'll give her a piece of your mind!"

Anna shook her head, and a few fresh drops of ice cream hit her neck. Gross. It was in her hair, too. "No. We won't," she said. "I'm through listening to you. If I had just stayed in the curtain shop with my mother, this never would have happened. I'm covered in ice cream, I feel like an idiot, and I want to go home."

"Yeah, but you can't just let her get away with that," Zadie protested.

"I can, and I did," Anna said. "If you want to go find her and tell her off, be my guest. But you're on your own. I'm outta here."

CHAPTER
Seven

"Sorry," said the boy behind Anna in the lunch line. He and his friends—a few seventh graders—were horsing around, and one of them had pushed him into her.

"It's okay," Anna murmured. At least she was still standing—for once. But Anna wasn't about to let her guard down, even though it had been a pretty uneventful day. So far.

She hadn't been tripped, knocked over, or publicly humiliated, although she had heard Sharon saying something about how she'd never be able to eat mint chocolate chip ice cream again. But no one else had said a word.

At one point, during English class, she thought she saw Carrie and Theresa trying to get her attention, but Anna had refused to look their way. They had probably just wanted to laugh at her some more.

The lunch line moved forward, and Anna reached for a tray from the shining silver cart. As she did, she felt the brown paper lunch sack she was holding in her other hand begin to tear. Thankfully, she managed to set it on the tray before the whole thing split open, scattering whatever her mother had packed for her everywhere.

"That was lucky," she muttered to herself. "Maybe I'm finally going to have a day where nothing goes wrong."

"Phew! At last, some fresh air!" a familiar voice squeaked. *Or not.*

"Oh, no," Anna groaned. She glanced down to see Zadie peeking out through the hole in the paper bag. "What are you doing here?"

"Nice to see you, too," Zadie said. She crawled out of the sack and jumped down to Anna's lunch tray. "Hey," she said, sniffing twice. "Something smells good. What's for lunch?"

"You're *always* hungry, aren't you?" Anna murmured. "It's pizza, but I'm just getting fries. My mom packed my lunch."

"Yeah, I know," Zadie said, wincing. "I've been hanging out with it all morning. *Tuna.* Ick. You should definitely get the pizza."

"Whatever," Anna muttered. "How'd you get in there, anyway?"

"Well, after you refused to bring me to school with you," Zadie sneered, "I sneaked down to the kitchen and jumped into your lunch bag when your mom wasn't looking."

Anna slid her tray along the metal counter. "Why?" she asked. "Why couldn't you just stay home like I told you?"

"Because you need me," Zadie said. "And you need a slice of that pizza, too. Make it pepperoni, 'kay?" Anna shook her head, but she did order the pizza. Tuna wasn't exactly her favorite, either.

"All right," Zadie said, scurrying up Anna's arm. "You do the lunch line thing, I'll find us a seat. Hmmm . . ." Zadie scanned the cafeteria from her perch on Anna's shoulder.

"Definitely not at that table," she said. "Too many teachers, and you don't want to look like a brownnoser. And you can't sit over there, either, because it looks like those older girls are saving all the seats. Huh. This isn't easy, is it?"

"Tell me about it," Anna said. "I usually just sit at that little table in the back corner."

Zadie checked it out. "Okay, two things: First, there's no way you're sitting alone today.

And second, you're getting really good at talking without moving your lips. Have you considered becoming a ventriloquist?"

"Oh, yeah. That would send my popularity rating through the roof," Anna scoffed.

"It's just a thought," Zadie said. Then she did a little jump. "Ooh! I've got it. See that table over there—third one back? That's where we're sitting today."

Anna set some fries on her tray, then moved into line at the cash register. "Third one back?" she repeated, searching for the table Zadie had chosen. "Are you kidding?" she said when she spotted it.

One side of the long, rectangular table was packed with girls—among them Carrie, Theresa, Kimberly, and Sharon. On the other side of the table was a group of boys, including Matt Dana. In the middle were plenty of spare seats, but Anna had no intention of sitting in one of them.

"It's okay," Zadie said. "The seats are attached to the table. There's no way anyone could pull yours out—I already checked."

"Forget it," Anna said, moving forward in line. "If I go over there, Sharon will do something to make me look stupid, and I'm not going to set myself up for that."

"What if Sharon left?" Zadie asked.

"She's not going to leave," Anna said. "She's eating lunch."

"Yeah, but what if she did leave?" Zadie persisted. "Then would you go over there?"

Anna scowled at the angel. She was really becoming an annoyance. "Sure," Anna said. "If Sharon just got up and left, sure. Why not? I'd run right over and make friends with the whole darned table. But she's *not* leaving."

"We'll see about that," Zadie said. Anna just rolled her eyes. *Tomorrow I'm locking her in my jewelry box,* she thought.

Anna paid the cashier and waited for her change. Meanwhile, Zadie was dancing around on her shoulder, waving her wand and chanting something that sounded like:

Heckle, deckle, pickled ear,
Now make Sharon disappear!

She circled her wand in the air twice and pointed it in Sharon's direction. Nothing happened.

"Shoot me now," Anna muttered.

"What's that, honey?" the cashier asked.

"Oh. Nothing," Anna said, taking her change. "Just—thanks."

"I don't get it," Zadie said. "That should

have worked." Anna grabbed a small paper cup and began filling it with ketchup. "Shoot!" Zadie exclaimed, examining the ball at the tip of her wand. "That's the problem. It was set on *Ask again later.*"

Anna squinted at the tiny wand. "Oh, my gosh," she said, eyeing the tiny sphere. "Is that a Magic 8-Ball?"

"Yeah—isn't it great?" Zadie asked. "Kind of hip, kind of retro. And it works really well, too—when it's set right." She shook her wand and checked the message in the transparent window of the Magic 8-Ball. "*It is doubtful,*" she read. "That won't work."

Zadie jiggled the wand again and came up with *Don't count on it.* "Darned thing," she muttered, giving it another shake. "Ha! There. *Signs point to yes.* That'll do it."

She started her crazy dance again and yelled out another spell:

The second try will save the day.
Now make Sharon go away!

Again she circled the wand above her head and thrust it toward Sharon. Again nothing happened.

"Zadie," Anna sighed. "Couldn't you just—"

"Please excuse the interruption," a voice said

over the intercom. "Could Sharon Ross please come to the office. That's Sharon Ross to the office. Thank you."

Anna's jaw dropped. If her tray hadn't been resting on the condiment table, it probably would have dropped, too. She watched as Sharon got up and left the cafeteria. Then she stared at Zadie.

"Told you it would work," the angel said with a smug smile. "Now, go on. Sit down."

Slowly, Anna picked up her tray and began walking toward the table. But the closer she got, the worse her stomach felt. "I . . . *can't.*"

Zadie groaned. "Fine. Have it your way. Go sit at that little table, all alone."

Anna knew the angel was disgusted with her, but she just couldn't bring herself to sit with the others. What if they started laughing at her again?

She quickened her pace, determined to walk by before anyone saw her, but unfortunately, she didn't speed up quite enough. Just as she was passing the table where Matt and the others were seated, Zadie grabbed a fry and chucked it—like a javelin—right at Matt Dana's head.

"Hey," he said when it hit him on the cheek.

He looked up, trying to determine where the renegade fry had come from, but the only person nearby was Anna.

"Anna!" he called. "Over here."

Anna stopped dead. "Tomorrow you're staying home," she hissed at Zadie. Reluctantly, she walked over to Matt's table.

"Hi," she said quietly. She was just about to apologize for the fry when he broke in.

"Hey, Ryan," he said to one of the other boys. "This is Anna. The one who made it to level nine on Storm Ranger yesterday."

"Cool," Ryan said. "You must play a lot. The farthest I've ever made it is level seven."

Anna straightened up. "Actually, it was my first time," she said.

"No way!" another boy exclaimed.

"Are you serious?" Ryan asked.

"Yeah," Anna said. "But like I told Matt—I probably just got lucky, you know? I mean, I doubt I could ever do it again."

"Wow," a few of the guys said. Anna smiled, remembering how it had felt to get so far in that game in front of all those people. She really had done well, hadn't she? And she still had twenty-three tokens to use. Maybe she would wipe out a few of Matt's high scores after all.

"Hey," Matt said, interrupting her thoughts. "Where are you sitting?"

"Ummm . . ." Anna hesitated. She didn't exactly want to admit that she was planning to sit alone.

"Because there's plenty of room here," Matt offered, nodding toward the empty seats.

"Oh. Uh . . . okay," Anna said. She couldn't help wondering why he was being so nice to her.

"Maybe he thinks you're cool, or maybe he's just a nice guy," Zadie said, reading her mind. "Who cares? Just sit down."

Anna took the angel's advice and set her tray down next to Matt's. As she did, Carrie and Theresa both looked over.

"Hi, Anna," Theresa called. She raised her hand to wave and accidentally knocked over her juice glass. "Oops," she said, standing it up again quickly. A bit of punch had spilled on her cookie, but that was all. "See—you shouldn't worry about the ice cream," Theresa told her. "I'm always doing stuff like that. *Without* Sharon's help," she added.

"Yeah." Carrie laughed.

Anna blinked rapidly. Did that mean Theresa and Carrie knew that Sharon had been lying and that she really *had* pulled out Anna's chair? She looked over at their smiling faces and felt a sense of relief. Maybe there was a chance the three of them could be friends after all.

"So, Anna, what did you think of the Toxic Ogre?" Matt asked as she took her seat. "You know—the one right outside Dr. Sphere's fortress?"

"Oh, right," Anna said. "He was creepy. Didn't he have two heads?"

"Yeah—that's because of the mutation," Ryan put in.

"The *mutation*?" Anna said with a giggle, and the boys began to give her the lowdown on the game. They told her some of the same stuff Zadie had already mentioned, but they also had a lot of other information. In fact, they actually made the game seem even more interesting.

Anna was so into the conversation that she didn't even notice when Sharon walked back in. Until she spoke.

"Can you believe it?" Sharon said. "There wasn't even a message. They said the announcement must have been a mistake."

"Whoa—wicked witch at three o'clock," Zadie chirped. Anna tensed a little. She tried to focus on Matt, Ryan, and the others as they described more of the villains, but she kept one eye and one ear on Sharon, too. Just in case.

"That's weird," Kimberly said.

"Hey, what's she doing here?" Sharon said, and Anna didn't need three guesses to figure out who she was talking about. "This is *our* table," Sharon went on. "She can't just—"

"Matt invited her," Carrie broke in.

"And if he hadn't, we were going to," Theresa added. "Carrie and I think she's nice." Anna could hardly believe her ears. Were they actually standing up to Sharon? *For her?* It certainly sounded that way. And to Anna's surprise, it seemed to be working. Sharon sat back down and started eating without another word. And only *one* death glare.

This must be my lucky day, Anna thought. She reached into the paper bag her mother had packed for her. The sandwich might be tuna, but there was usually something yummy for dessert. Anna grabbed a small, square plastic container and pulled it out to reveal chocolate . . . crumbs.

"Oh, yeah," Zadie said. "I meant to tell you—your mom makes *awesome* brownies. Let's snag some more when we get home. And hey— how about sharing some of that pizza?"

CHAPTER
Eight

"Matt! Over here," Jeremy Gray shouted.

Anna watched as Matt kicked the soccer ball to Jeremy, who dribbled it a few feet before crossing it back. Then wham! Matt took a perfect shot, and the ball went soaring right into the net.

"Nice one, Matt," Ryan said, giving him a high five. Anna was impressed, too. It seemed like Matt was good at everything. Math, video games, sports. And it was becoming more and more obvious that he was really popular, too.

At first, Anna had pegged him as a bit of a loner, and in a way, he was. He didn't seem to care much about what other people thought, and he clearly liked to hang out alone from time to time—like yesterday, at the arcade. But it was also clear that he had plenty of people to hang out with if he wanted.

Plus, even though he was kind of quiet, whenever he *did* talk, everyone listened—Sharon Ross in particular.

"Okay, everybody," Ms. Gilbert said. "Let's count off by twos."

When everyone was done, she ordered the twos to one side of the field and the ones to the other. Anna, who was a two, was glad to see that she had ended up on Matt's team.

"Anna—cool," he said as she walked over. "Are you as good at soccer as you are at video games?"

"Not even," Anna said. And she wasn't kidding. Gym had always been her least favorite class, unless they were playing games like dodgeball— she was pretty good at stuff like that. But soccer? Forget about it. She'd rather have answered her mother's embarrassing preteen questions.

"Don't worry," Matt said. "I'll set you up."

"What about me?" Sharon said. "I'm on your team, too. Will you pass me the ball?"

"Oh, hey, Sharon," Matt said. "Yeah. Sure."

"Cool," Sharon said, "because I was the high scorer on my traveling team, you know. All you have to do is cross it to me just outside the circle and I guarantee I'll get it in."

"All right," Matt said, but he didn't actually sound all that impressed.

"Anna," Sharon said, touching Anna's forearm like they were old friends, "I never got to talk to you after you fell and spilled ice cream all over yourself yesterday. Are you okay?"

Anna narrowed her eyes. What was this about? "Yeah, I'm fine," she said.

"I'm really sorry for laughing," Sharon said. "You just looked so funny. I hope you can forgive me."

"Uhhh . . ." Anna felt like she was in the twilight zone. Sharon Ross, asking for forgiveness? Please.

Before Anna could answer, Ms. Gilbert blew her whistle. "Everybody on Matt Dana's team grab a red pinny. Jeremy's team will be blue. Let's go!"

Anna took the opportunity to break away from Sharon and her freaky personality disorder, but Sharon barely even noticed. She was already talking Matt's ear off.

Well, that was bizarre, Anna thought. She reached into the mesh bag and grabbed her red pinny. She was about to walk away when she spotted Zadie, reclining in a miniature lawn chair on the sideline.

"Knock 'em dead," she said, raising a candy bar in the air.

"Where did you get that?" Anna asked, but Zadie just shrugged.

"How's the Wicked Witch of the West?" she asked.

"Weird," Anna answered. "She's acting all nice to impress Matt Dana."

"Is it working?"

Anna squinted. "I don't think so."

"Yahoo!" cheered Zadie. "Score one for the nice guys!"

"Zadie," Anna chastised.

"Hey, Anna," Theresa called as she and Carrie bounded over. "Are you a two?"

"Yeah," Anna replied.

"Cool, so are we," Carrie said.

Anna smiled. "Awesome." She was psyched to be playing with Matt, but she was even more psyched to be on a team with Carrie and Theresa. The three of them had sat together in math class again—Matt had sat with Ryan and Jeremy instead—and Anna had really enjoyed talking with them. They were nice and funny, and they actually seemed to like her.

The only drawback was that Sharon had spent more time than usual glaring at her, and somehow her glares had felt more intense. In fact, it seemed to Anna that the more she,

Carrie, and Theresa laughed, the angrier Sharon looked.

Anna had just pulled her pinny over her head when Ms. Gilbert blew her whistle and told the teams to set up. In another minute, she blew her whistle again, and the game began.

"Go, Anna, go! Go, Anna, go!" Zadie cheered from the sideline.

Matt had put Anna at center forward. It made Anna a little nervous, but he seemed to think she could handle it. Matt was playing the left wing, and Sharon had put herself in as the right.

"Now, Anna! Go through!" Matt yelled. Anna wasn't sure, but she assumed he meant for her to run toward the goal.

She did, watching as Matt took the ball down the side, dribbling the ball past one defender and then another. When he was about twenty yards out, he crossed the ball and yelled for Anna to shoot it.

Anna could hardly believe he had passed it to *her*. He really seemed to think she could handle it, and strangely, Anna was beginning to think so, too. She ran at the ball as fast as she could and kicked it. Whoosh! It went right into the net.

"I thought you said you couldn't play," Matt said, running over to slap her hand.

"I didn't think I could." Anna laughed.

"Nice one, Anna!" Carrie yelled, and she gave her a high five, too.

As Anna jogged back to the center of the field, she felt lighter than she had in days. Things were finally going her way, and it felt great.

"Lucky shot," Sharon sneered as she ran past Anna. "I'd like to see you try it again."

"Maybe I will," Anna said.

Sharon stopped and faced her. "What did you say?"

"I said . . . maybe I will," Anna repeated, but somehow it lacked the boldness it'd had the first time.

"Go for it," Sharon said, and she trotted back to her position. There was something about the way she had spoken the words that chilled Anna, but she tried to let it go. She'd just scored a goal, and Matt Dana believed in her. What could Sharon possibly do?

On the next play, Jeremy's team started with the ball. At one point, it looked like Jeremy might score, but Theresa managed to steal the ball away.

"Theresa—over here!" Sharon called, and Theresa passed her the ball. To Anna's surprise, Sharon was almost as impressive as Matt Dana.

She went through three opponents without much trouble and probably could have driven all the way to the goal. Instead, she called to Anna.

"Lee! This one's all yours!" she yelled, and she gave the ball a serious kick—straight into a huge puddle that splashed all over Anna, drenching her from head to toe.

"Yuck!" Anna shouted, wiping a huge glob of mud off her face. Laughter erupted all over the field, and Ms. Gilbert blew her whistle.

"All right, people—it's just mud. Play on!"

She blew her whistle again, and Sharon ran over to the ball. "Don't worry, I'll take it from here, Anna," she called, dribbling toward the goal. "Bad luck about that mud puddle, huh?"

Yeah, right. Bad luck, Anna thought. And something told her that she was going to keep right on having bad luck as long as Sharon Ross was around.

CHAPTER

Nine

"Girls," Mrs. Wessex called, interrupting Theresa midstory. She'd been telling Carrie and Anna about the time she'd knocked over an entire display of soda cans in the grocery store. "Back to work, please."

Carrie's face went red. She hunched over her drawing of King Tut's tomb and began coloring diligently. Theresa shrugged and started scanning the encyclopedia for more information about the process of mummification.

"Sheesh," Anna muttered. "I don't know why they call this class *social* studies if they're never going to let us talk." In spite of Mrs. Wessex's watchful eye, both Carrie and Theresa giggled. And thankfully, the bell rang before they could get into trouble for it.

"You're so funny, Anna," Theresa said as

they walked to their lockers. Anna grinned. In spite of Sharon's little stunt in gym class, this had been her best day yet.

"Hey—do you guys want to come over this afternoon?" she asked. "My house is still full of boxes and stuff, but my grandmother said she was going to make honey cakes today."

"Honey cakes?" Theresa asked.

"Yeah, they're sort of like pancakes, but sweeter and crispier. I guess she used to make them all the time when she lived in Korea. They're *really* good."

"Did your grandmother grow up in Korea?" Carrie asked.

"Mm-hmm." Anna nodded. "She moved to the United States right before my mom was born."

"Wow—that's cool," Carrie said. "And she lives with you?"

"Yep. So do you want to come over?" Anna asked again.

Carrie lowered her eyes. "Oh, um . . ." She stared down at her feet, then shot Theresa a nervous glance.

"The thing is—" Theresa started.

Suddenly—and without warning—Sharon burst into the conversation. "Are you guys ready?" she asked. "My mom said she'd be here right at three."

Anna tried to make eye contact with Theresa and Carrie, but neither one of them would look at her.

"Oh, hi, Anna," Sharon added as an after-thought. "Carrie, Theresa, Kimberly, and I are going to the movies. What are *you* doing this afternoon?"

"Uhhh—"

"Maybe you could come with us?" Theresa suggested, brightening.

"Yeah," Carrie said. She looked hopefully at Sharon.

"Sorry," Sharon said. "There's only room for four in my mom's van—the back is full of sports equipment."

"Oh," Theresa said, slouching. She and Carrie seemed genuinely disappointed. Sharon, on the other hand, was smirking—but only when Theresa and Carrie weren't watching.

"That's okay," Anna said. "I have a lot of stuff to do, anyway. I'm still unpacking and everything."

"Huh. That sounds like fun," Sharon said. Then she turned to Carrie and Theresa. "Come on, guys—let's go," she said.

"Okay," Carrie said. "I just have to grab my jacket."

"Me, too," Theresa added. "Bye, Anna. See you tomorrow."

"Yeah. See you tomorrow," Anna agreed. She went to her locker and packed up her things, trying not to pay attention as Sharon, Carrie, Theresa, and Kimberly walked out, laughing and talking about how good the movie was going to be.

"No room in her mom's van," Anna muttered to herself. "Yeah. I bet." There could have been seating for fifty and Sharon still would have found a way to exclude her. She was never going to have anyone to hang out with if Sharon had her way, and something told her that Sharon got her way most of the time.

Anna put on her backpack and started down the sidewalk toward home. Things had been going so well with Theresa and Carrie. Why did Sharon always have to come along and mess things up?

"And why does she have it in for me?" Anna wondered aloud.

"Because you're cool!" a tiny voice yelled. "Haven't you figured that out yet?" Anna glanced down to see Zadie cruising up on a miniature motor scooter.

"Where are you getting all this stuff?" Anna demanded. "Angels R Us?"

"Ha! Good one." Zadie laughed.

"And what do you mean, I'm cool?" Anna added. "I thought we went over that already. If I were cool, I wouldn't be spending the afternoon cleaning my room. If I were cool, I'd have friends to hang out with. I don't, and I'm not. Got it?"

Anna sped up her pace.

Zadie sped up her scooter. "*I* had it a long time ago," she yelled over the sound of her engine. It sounded like a buzzing mosquito. "*You're* the one who doesn't get it. Whoa! Cute guy, six o'clock! I'll see you at home!"

"Cute guy, what?" Anna asked.

"Hey, Anna—wait," a voice called. Anna turned to see Matt Dana approaching on his skateboard. "What's up?" he asked when he was a little closer.

Anna snorted. "I'm going home to clean my room," she said. "Doesn't that sound like fun?"

"About as fun as helping my dad clean the garage," Matt said with a laugh. He rode alongside as Anna walked, coasting ahead on his skateboard every once in a while and then looping back to stay even with her. A few times he hopped his board up onto the curb and back down again without falling.

"You're pretty good at that," Anna said.

"Lots of practice," Matt replied. He built up speed, then jumped off the curb, twirling the board beneath him, and just missed the landing. "Still need more, though," he added. "You want to try?"

"No way." Anna laughed. "I prefer water to pavement, remember? Fewer injuries."

Matt grinned. "You wouldn't get injured," he said. "You might bruise your shins or scrape your elbows or something, but nothing serious."

"Oh, is that all?" Anna joked. "Well, then—bring on the ramps."

"Actually, I have a few ramps in my backyard."

"No way," Anna said.

"Yeah. And my brother and I are building a half-pipe, too. I've been sketching out the plans for it in school."

"You draw?" Anna asked.

"Sort of," Matt said. "I like to sketch things. And I doodle a lot in class."

Anna chuckled. "That explains why you're always sharpening your pencils."

"Yeah, they wear out pretty quick. Plus, I hate to sit still for too long, and sharpening pencils is a good excuse to move around."

"And knock people over," Anna added.

"Oh, yeah. Sorry about that," Matt said. "I really didn't mean to, you know."

"I know. It's okay. Besides, you already apologized."

Matt nodded, then he rode up ahead on his skateboard and tried the twirling thing again. This time he landed it, and Anna clapped.

"All right! That was cool!" she said.

Matt glided back to her and stopped, kicking the board into the air and catching it. "Say the word and I'll give you your first lesson."

"I'll think about it," Anna said. "But I'm not sure I'm ready for the half-pipe."

Anna and Matt walked for a while without talking, and Anna began to realize that even though Carrie and Theresa had taken off with Sharon, she still wasn't alone. Matt was actually becoming a pretty good friend to her, and Sharon didn't seem to have nearly as much influence over him. Maybe he'd want to hang out sometime. They could go to the arcade and play Storm Ranger or something.

Just then, a minivan drove by, and someone yelled out, "Anna's got a boyfriend!" It was Kimberly Price, and as the van passed, Anna saw Sharon drawing a big heart on the fogged-up rear window. She didn't need binoculars to know whose initials were going inside.

Anna turned to Matt, who was scraping mud off the wheels of his skateboard.

"Wasn't that Sharon's car?" he asked. "Did someone yell something to you?"

Anna was relieved that he hadn't understood Kimberly's singsong voice, but it didn't stop her from blushing bright pink. "I—I don't know," she stammered.

"Huh. Weird," Matt said, hopping back on his skateboard.

"Yeah," Anna agreed, but all she could think was, *What if he* had *heard?* Would he think that she really did like him? That she wanted him to be her boyfriend? And if so, what would he think of her then?

He'd probably think I was a major loser, Anna thought. After all, he didn't seem to like the way Sharon fawned over him. If anything, he preferred the comfortable friendship he and Anna were developing. And she didn't want to lose that.

But if Kimberly and Sharon started teasing her about him on a regular basis—or worse yet, telling him that she liked him—he was bound to get uncomfortable. And then he'd stop hanging around her altogether, which would leave Anna alone, again—just the way Sharon wanted her.

CHAPTER
Ten

"It's like she doesn't want me to have any friends at all!" Anna said.

"Sharon wasn't the one who yelled," Zadie pointed out. "Kimberly was."

"Yeah, but Kimberly doesn't even breathe unless Sharon tells her to," Anna said. "And besides, Sharon was drawing the heart."

Anna flopped down on her bed next to the angel. "Why does she hate me so much? Why doesn't she want anyone to like me?"

Zadie lay back on a tiny pillow she had placed on top of Anna's pillow and put her arms behind her head. "I already gave you that answer."

"Oh, right. *Because I'm cool*," Anna scoffed. "Good one."

"It's true," Zadie said. She pulled a bag of

potato chips from out of nowhere and split open the top. "If you weren't a threat, she wouldn't care."

"What are you talking about?" Anna said. "How am *I* a threat to Sharon Ross?"

"Who won the last math contest?" Zadie asked, popping a chip into her mouth.

Anna scowled at her. "What does that have to do with it?"

"Sheesh. How can somebody so smart be so dumb?" Zadie muttered. "Just answer me. Who won the last math contest?"

"I did—with Carrie, Theresa, and Matt."

"Right," Zadie said. "And who won all of the math contests *before* you showed up?"

Anna shrugged. "Sharon and whatever team she was on, I guess."

"Right again," Zadie congratulated her. "Now, who won the mock spelling bee in English class last week?"

"*Zadie,*" Anna said, rolling her eyes.

"Just answer," the angel commanded, crunching another potato chip.

Anna sighed. "I did."

"Very good. And who do you think used to win all the mock spelling bees before you showed up?"

"How would I know?" Anna asked.

Zadie folded her arms and frowned. "Take a guess."

"Sharon?"

"Bingo! Question number three: Who are Sharon's best friends—besides Kimberly Price?"

Anna rolled her eyes. "Carrie and Theresa?" she guessed.

"Right again! And who do they really seem to be warming up to?"

"Warming up to?" Anna echoed. "You sound like my mother."

"I'm sorry—the answer is Anna Lee," Zadie announced. "Question four: What boy in the fifth grade does Sharon seem to have a little crush on?" Zadie continued.

"Zadie, what are you trying to—"

"Never mind," Zadie interrupted. "I'll answer that one for you: Matt Dana! And question number five: Who's been paying an awful lot of attention to you lately?"

Anna exhaled heavily. "Okay, I get the—"

"Matt Dana!" Zadie yelled, answering her own question again. "Jim, tell the lady what she's won."

"Cut it out, Zadie," Anna said. "I get the point. Okay. So maybe, in some small, strange way, Sharon might see me as a threat. But what am I supposed to do about it? Act dumb and stay friendless?"

"Well, you've already got half of it down."

"Zadie!"

"Sorry—bad joke," Zadie said.

Anna shook her head. "No, it's not," she said. "That's the problem. It's not a joke—it's the truth. I *am* friendless. And as long as Sharon keeps picking on me, I'm going to stay that way."

"So make her stop."

Anna hit her forehead. "What a great idea! Why didn't I think of that?"

"There's that attitude." Zadie frowned. She pointed her tiny index finger at Anna. "What you need to do is start using it for good—not evil."

"*Good, not evil?* Who am I, Wonder Woman?"

"No, but you're quick—and you know what I mean," Zadie said. "You have to start using your attitude to help yourself—not hurt yourself."

Anna groaned. "I don't have the slightest clue what you're talking about."

"Fine," Zadie said. She stood up and brushed the potato chip crumbs from her skirt. "I was hoping I wouldn't have to go this far, but it looks like I'm going to have to do the whole Ghost of Christmas Past thing."

"The whole what?"

"Ghost of Christmas Past," Zadie repeated. "You know—Charles Dickens? *A Christmas Carol*?" Anna gave her a blank stare. "Never mind. It's not important," Zadie said, jumping onto Anna's shoulder. "Just hang on."

"Why? Where are we—?"

Before Anna could finish her sentence, a gray mist formed in her room, and the next thing she knew, she was floating.

"Zadie—what's going on? Where are we?" Anna asked. Then suddenly, the mist began to dissolve and the scene became clear. They were in a large room filled with round tables and bright orange chairs.

"Jackson Intermediate!" Anna shouted. "And there's Mr. Metcalf! He was my homeroom teacher."

Just then, a bell rang, and five seconds later the cafeteria flooded with students. "Oh, wow!" Anna exclaimed. "There's Kristen . . . and Claire. And that's Hannah Galloway—she always had the best birthday parties. And there are Ian and Evan—they're twins, and they're so funny. And—oh, my gosh! Caitlin! Leah!" Anna yelled as her two best friends walked in.

She tried to run over to them, but Zadie stopped her. "They can't hear you or see you. We're just here to observe."

Anna sighed. "Still," she said, "it's so good to see them. I wish I could be back here for real. Then I wouldn't have to worry about people picking on me and making me look stupid."

"Shhh." Zadie put her finger to her lips. "Let's see what they're talking about."

In an instant, Anna found herself standing directly behind her friends in the lunch line. She was so close, she could have touched them, but they seemed to look right past her.

"That was so great when you told Jeff off at recess!" Leah gushed. "I still can't believe you did it."

"Neither can I," Caitlin said. "But I was just *so* mad. I mean, that was like the fifth time someone came up to me and asked me if I was his girlfriend. He must have been telling everyone that we were going out—just because my mom gives him a ride to school."

"What a creep," Leah said. "The best part was when you told him the only time you'd ever go out with him was in his dreams and your nightmares. What a great line!"

"Oh, that *is* good," Anna whispered to Zadie.

"Yeah, too bad I didn't make it up," Caitlin said.

Leah crinkled her nose. "You didn't?"

"No. I stole it from Anna, remember? She used it that time John Chase claimed she had given him that really mushy valentine."

"That's right!" Leah said. "Oh, my gosh, that was so perfect. I can almost hear her saying it: 'In your dreams and my nightmares, Chase,'" Leah mimicked.

"Huh. I'd almost forgotten about that," Anna told Zadie. "That was in fourth grade."

"Wow. She had some really great lines, didn't she?" Leah said.

Caitlin smiled. "Yeah. She was fast."

The two girls moved up to the front of the lunch line and grabbed their trays. Anna and Zadie moved with them.

"See?" Zadie said. "You *used* to use your attitude to put people in their place."

Anna shrugged. "I did it one time, Zadie. And it was over a year ago," she replied. "That doesn't prove anything."

Caitlin and Leah each grabbed a milk from the cooler and started along the buffet tables. When they got to the pizza, they each took a slice, and then Leah turned excitedly to Caitlin.

"Hey—do you remember that time we were at the mall and Allison Sanchez started making fun of Anna in front of everybody?" she asked.

"Uh-huh." Caitlin nodded. "She said Anna was so little, she looked like a second grader, and a strong wind would probably blow her away."

"Right," Leah said. "And do you remember what Anna said?"

Caitlin thought it over for a minute, then started to giggle. "She said, 'I'd rather be small and quick than big and dumb.'"

"Right, and Allison was ripped! She said, 'Hey—who are you calling dumb?'"

"And Anna said, 'Jeez, if you can't figure that out, it's worse than I thought.'"

"The look on Allison's face!" Leah exclaimed.

Both girls giggled, and Anna chuckled, too. "That *was* pretty good," she mused. "And Allison never teased me again." She glanced at Zadie, who was standing on her shoulder . . . *nibbling her own slice of pizza.* "Hey—where'd you get that?" Anna asked.

"Shhh! It's not important," Zadie told her. "Keep listening."

"But you know what my favorite Anna Lee line was?" Caitlin asked.

"What?" Anna and Leah said at the same time.

"It was that time Josh Hallett told Robin LaRue that she couldn't be on his kickball team at recess because they were having an all-guys' game," Caitlin said. "Remember that?"

"Oh, yeah," Leah said, "and Robin was really upset."

"Mm-hmm. So Anna marched right out to the middle of the field, where he was pitching, and she went up one side of him and down the other," Caitlin said. "She called him a—"

"Deleterious gynophobe," Leah put in.

"Yeah, that was it," Caitlin agreed. "And Josh said, 'What's that supposed to mean?' So Anna said, 'I'll tell you what—you go look it up. We're going to play kickball.'"

"Right." Leah giggled. "And then she yelled out, 'Girls against the guys!' and we all ran out to play."

"And we won!" Caitlin said.

"That was the best ever," Leah said. "I miss her."

"I miss you, too," Anna said. She tried to touch Leah's shoulder, but suddenly the gray mist was back. And before she knew it, she and Zadie were back in her bedroom at the new house. In Newcastle.

"Okay—so what'd you learn?" Zadie asked,

popping one last bite of pizza into her mouth.

"That I miss Doncaster," Anna said with a sigh. "And my old school, and my old friends."

"Anything else?" Zadie asked.

Anna shrugged. "I don't know. Not really."

"Not really?" Zadie screeched. "What's wrong with you?!" She started pacing up and down Anna's pillow, shaking her head and muttering. "Humans are *so* thick. The next time I have to come back here, I want to work with a different species. Do you hear me?" she yelled up at the ceiling.

"All right," Zadie went on, taking a deep breath. "Let's go over this one more time. Ready?" She gazed at Anna expectantly.

"Sure," Anna said.

"Okay. You grew up in Doncaster, right?"

"Right."

"And somehow you managed to make some pretty good friends there, right?"

Anna nodded. "Right."

"Phew—so far, so good," Zadie said. "Now— back in Doncaster, people also used to pick on you from time to time, right?"

"I guess," Anna said.

"But back in Doncaster, you used to stand up for yourself, didn't you?"

"I don't know," Anna said. "Kind of, I guess."

"No—not *kind of*," Zadie corrected. "You did. That's what your friends were just talking about—how good you were at putting people in their place."

"So?" Anna said.

"So . . . what happened?"

Anna flopped down on her bed. "We moved, that's what happened."

"Oh, I see," Zadie said. "And what—the airline lost your spine? You left it behind, in the corner of your old closet?"

"*Zadie,*" Anna moaned.

"No, really—I want to know," the angel insisted. "Where is it? You used to have one. Maybe it's in that box over there," she said, pointing her wand toward the box on top of Anna's bureau. "Maybe you just haven't unpacked it yet."

"Come on, Zadie—don't you get it? Things are different here. I had friends to back me up in Doncaster."

"You have people who want to be your friends here," Zadie countered.

"Yeah, but Sharon Ross is never going to let that happen," Anna said.

"Sharon Ross has nothing to do with it."

Anna clicked her tongue. "How can you say that? She picks on me all the time and makes me look like a great big doofus!"

"Only because you let her," Zadie said.

"I don't *let* her," Anna yelled. "She just does it."

Zadie shook her head. "John Chase tried to do it, but you didn't let him."

"That was different," Anna said.

"Allison Sanchez tried to do it, but you didn't let her, either. And Josh Hallett tried to do it to one of your friends, but you stopped him."

"Yeah." Anna sighed. "But here it's—"

"Different?" Zadie asked. "No, it's not. What's different is that you keep letting Sharon get away with it. You haven't even tried to stand up for yourself. Not once."

Anna propped herself up on her elbows and rested her chin on her hands. "I haven't, have I?" she said quietly. "Still . . . what's the point now? It's too late. Sharon's already made me look like a fool."

"Mm-hmm, and she's going to keep right on doing it if you keep making it so easy for her."

Anna closed her eyes. Zadie was right. Sharon had been bullying her since her first day of school, and she wasn't ever going to stop unless Anna made her.

"You're right," Anna said finally, looking at Zadie. "But . . . how am I supposed to stop her? Spill ice cream all over *her*? I couldn't do something like that."

"You don't need to," Zadie said. "All you have to do is be yourself. Use that attitude of yours to turn things around."

"I don't know, Zadie," Anna said. "It sounds so easy, but . . ."

"All right—one more thing. Remember this: No one can make you feel like a fool without your help. *So don't help her.* Got it?"

Anna sighed again. "Yeah. I think so," she said. Still, she couldn't help wishing that Zadie could just magically transport her back to Doncaster for good. Going back seemed like it would be so much easier than moving forward.

CHAPTER
Eleven

The next day in English, Anna tried to focus on her compound-verb work sheet, but she couldn't stop thinking about what Zadie had said. No one could make her feel like a fool without her help. It was really beginning to make sense.

After Matt Dana had knocked her over in this class, all Sharon had done was laugh—and make a rude comment later in the hallway. But really, what was the big deal? No one seemed to think any less of Matt, and he was the one who had caused the accident.

And in the mall, when Sharon had pulled Anna's seat away, Anna was the one who had turned it into a major scene. If she had just laughed at herself—or made a joke about Sharon "bumping" her chair—everything probably would have been fine. Sticky, but fine.

As for the soccer incident, Ms. Gilbert was right. It was just mud. *But I assumed everyone thought I was an idiot,* Anna realized. And she had continued to think it even after Carrie and Theresa had sat and worked with her in social studies and Matt Dana had kept her company on her way home.

None of them seemed to think any less of Anna because of all the things Sharon had said and done. *So why should I?* Anna asked herself. Zadie was right. The next time Sharon tried to make trouble for Anna, Anna wasn't going to let her. And that was that.

Anna looked down at her work sheet. *Write two sentences using compound verbs,* she read. She had started to write down the first sentence when she noticed a few people across the room giggling and staring at her. Then she saw Maria Mancini pass a folded-up piece of paper back to Lauren Graham.

Lauren unfolded the paper, read it, and smirked. Then she passed it back to Claudia Murray, who chuckled and continued it on to the next row.

Anna wasn't sure what was going on, but it obviously had something to do with her. Everybody who had read the note kept glancing in her direction and cracking up. She tried to concentrate on her work sheet, but she couldn't help feeling like everyone in the room was staring at her and laughing—probably because they were.

When the note finally made it to her side of the room, Anna couldn't wait to get her hands on it. She heard Matt Dana unfolding it behind her and waited. Any second now he would be passing it forward. Or so Anna thought.

Anna waited one minute. Then she waited two more. Finally, after five minutes had passed, she turned her head slightly and whispered, "Where is it?"

"What?" Matt asked.

"The note!" Anna hissed. "Where is it?"

"Anna," Mrs. Wessex called. "Please work on your own."

"Yes, Mrs. Wessex," Anna said. She picked up her pencil and tried to get back to work, but it was no use. On the corner of her paper, she wrote, *Give it to me!* Then she ripped it off and tossed it onto Matt's desk. For some reason, that made the whispers on the other side of the room grow louder.

"Okay, class, settle down," Mrs. Wessex said. "We only have a few minutes left."

Anna checked the clock. It was almost

lunchtime. Just then, a tiny slip of paper landed on her desk.

You don't want to see it, Matt had written. Anna flipped the scrap over. *YES, I DO!!!* she wrote in huge letters. Then she tossed the note back to Matt again. As she did, the bell rang to signal the end of class. Everyone was up immediately and rushing for the door.

"Ooh, Anna," Kimberly said as she walked by. "I had no idea."

"You might want to be a little more careful with your secret notes," Sharon added. Maria and Lauren giggled as they walked past, and a few other girls did, too.

"What are they talking about?" Anna demanded, turning to Matt.

"It's stupid," he said. "Just ignore them."

"Where's the note?" Anna growled.

"You really want to see it?" Matt asked.

"Yes!"

"All right," he said with a shrug, and he dropped it on her desk. "See you at lunch," he added on his way out the door.

Anna sat back down and unfolded the note so quickly, she almost tore it.

"Anna?" Mrs. Wessex said. "It's lunchtime. You should get to the cafeteria."

"I will," Anna assured her. "I just have to read something really quick." She looked down at the piece of paper in her hands and almost gasped. It said:

Dear Matt,
I'm so glad I met you. You're the best skateboarder ever and the cutest guy in the whole school. I miss you when we're not together. Will you be my boyfriend?
Love,
Anna

Zadie, who had been napping inside Anna's desk, stretched her arms above her head and yawned. "What's going on?" she asked. "Isn't it lunchtime yet?"

Anna didn't even bother to answer her. She just sat staring at the note with its loopy letters written in purple gel pen. *Sharon,* she thought. *How can she be so mean?*

"Hey—what's that?" Zadie asked. She jumped up onto the desk and then onto Anna's hand. "'Dear Matt,'" she started reading aloud. "Uh-oh. The Wicked Witch strikes again, huh?"

"Something like that," Anna muttered.

"So, what are you going to do about it?" Zadie asked.

"Die," Anna answered.

"What?!" Zadie screamed. "That's it? I thought we went over this yesterday! She can't make a fool out of you without your help! So what are you going to do? Help her? Or stop her?"

Anna looked at the note again. Everyone else seemed to think she had really written it. And if she didn't say anything, they were going to go right on thinking it—which was exactly what Sharon wanted. Well, for once, Sharon wasn't going to have things her way.

"I'm going to stop her," Anna said. And she stood up and headed for the cafeteria.

As she walked into the huge room, her knees felt just about ready to buckle. But Anna forced herself to keep going. Most of the fifth graders were already sitting down, so Anna walked straight through the lunch line and headed for where Sharon and her friends and Matt and his friends always sat.

"Excuse me," she said, standing at one end of the long table. Everyone kept talking. Anna cleared her throat. "Um, excuse me," she said again. A few people looked at her, but most of them were still gabbing.

She walked over to an empty seat next to Carrie. "Is anyone sitting here?" she asked.

"Actually, I was saving it for you," Carrie said.

"Good," Anna replied, but instead of sitting, she stood up on the chair so that she was towering above the rest of the table. Then she stuck her thumb and forefinger in her mouth and whistled the way her brother had taught her.

Like magic, everyone at the fifth-grade tables went silent. Anna swallowed hard. She wanted them to listen, but she hadn't realized just how weird it would feel to be addressing her whole class. Anna unfolded the note Sharon had written and cleared her throat.

"You can do it," Zadie whispered. "Here—take this." She placed a second piece of paper on top of the one Anna was holding. Then she jumped into Anna's jeans pocket and disappeared.

Anna looked at the paper Zadie had given her and smiled. *Perfect,* she thought. Then she cleared her throat again. "Um, for anyone who was just in Mrs. Wessex's room for English, I, um . . . wanted to talk about this." She held up the note that had been passed around the room.

A few people giggled, and Sharon smiled. "We've already seen it, Anna." She placed her hand over her heart dramatically. "Your feelings for Matt are no secret."

"Good," Anna said, eliciting a few more laughs. For a second she was worried that everyone was going to start talking again, but Theresa shushed everybody, and it was silent.

"Thanks," Anna whispered, glancing down at Theresa. Then she stood up straight. "What I mean is, I'm glad that most of you have seen it, because I just want to point a few things out."

Sharon squinted at her. It was a mini–death glare—a confused one—but Anna tried to ignore it.

"First of all," Anna said. "This is my notebook." She held up a dark blue binder and opened it. "As you can see, I use *white* lined paper. But this note is written on yellow."

"So?" Sharon said.

"Hold on—there's more," Anna said. "Second, it's written in purple gel pen, and I don't even have one of those." Some of the kids had started talking again, and Anna knew she had to get to the good stuff fast—before she lost them.

"Third, if you look at the handwriting in my notebook, you can see that I write really small. This note is written in big round letters."

"Maybe that's because you were so *in love* when you wrote it," Sharon suggested, drawing more giggles from the crowd.

"Actually, I thought maybe it was because *you* wrote it," Anna said. Immediately, the laughter stopped.

"You think *I* wrote it?" Sharon snapped.

"Well, you do use yellow notebook paper," Anna said. "Plus, you make big round letters, and you have a purple gel pen."

"No, I don't," Sharon sneered.

"Really?" Anna asked. "Then . . . how did you write this note to Kimberly?" She held up the paper Zadie had given her for everyone to see, then began passing it around. It was just a short one asking if Kimberly wanted to go to the mall after school, but the handwriting, the paper, and the pen all matched the note to Matt Dana perfectly.

"Where did you get that?" Sharon demanded.

Anna smirked. "Let's just say you should be more careful with your secret notes," she said. She stepped down and watched as the two notes Sharon had written made their way around the fifth-grade tables. Everyone was laughing—but for once, it wasn't at her.

Theresa and Carrie smiled over at her, and

they both gave her thumbs-up signals. Anna grinned and gave one back. "Go get your lunch," Carrie said. "We'll save your seat."

"Okay," Anna said, and she headed for the back of the line. "Hey, Zadie," she called, pretending to cough into her hand. "Did you hear that? I did it." Anna looked down at her pants pocket, half expecting the little angel to jump out with a tub of popcorn or some other kind of junk food clutched in her hand. But there was no sign of movement.

"Zadie?" she said again. Nothing.

Anna reached into her pocket carefully, but she didn't find Zadie. Instead she found one of the silver angel charms from her necklace. Anna felt the smooth metal between her thumb and forefinger, then flipped the charm over. On the back, the following words were engraved:

Stand up, be strong,
and every once in a while,
eat dessert first!

Anna clutched the charm in her hand and smiled. She was sad that Zadie was gone, but at the same time, she understood that she didn't need her anymore. She was going to be just fine on her own.

On her way through the lunch line, Anna grabbed an extra cookie—in honor of her tiny friend. When she got to the cashier, Matt Dana was in line behind her. He had come up for a second helping of apple crisp.

"Hey," he said, tapping Anna on the shoulder. "That took guts."

"Thanks," Anna replied.

"You'll be on the half-pipe in no time," he added with a grin.

Anna just laughed. But she thought, *Who knows? Maybe I will.* She walked back to the table where she'd just addressed the whole fifth grade and took her seat next to Carrie.

"That sounds fun," Theresa was saying to Sharon.

"Yeah, it should be cool," Sharon agreed. She glanced over at Anna with a bit of a scowl, but she didn't say anything.

"What should be cool?" Anna asked.

Sharon stared at her for a second, and Anna wasn't sure she was going to answer. "We're having a soccer game after school," she said finally. "Fifth graders against the sixth graders."

"You should play, Anna," Carrie said. She turned to Sharon. "Do we still need more people on our team?"

Sharon eyed Anna, then shrugged. "I guess," she said. "As long as you're not worried about getting dirty," she added.

"I can avoid the puddles if you can," Anna said, holding Sharon's gaze, and to her surprise, Sharon actually cracked a hint of a smile.

"No problem," she said. "Game's at three-thirty. Come on, Kimberly." Sharon and her number-one fan got up and headed back to the lunch line—probably to snag a Popsicle or something for dessert.

Anna unwrapped her first M&M cookie and took a bite. Sure, Sharon hadn't apologized to her—and Anna was pretty sure she never would—but somehow Anna felt like they had reached an agreement. It seemed obvious that they weren't going to be best friends or anything, but at the very least, it looked like they might be able to get along. And that was more than enough for Anna.

She took another bite of her cookie and thought about the charm in her pocket. Zadie was right. Eating dessert first was actually a pretty good idea.

UNICORN

CHAPTER

One

"Class, I have a special announcement to make," Mrs. Wessex said first thing Monday morning. The room went silent, and Carrie Weingarten glanced at her friends.

From her seat two rows over, Anna Lee just shrugged. She was too new to Elizabeth Cady Stanton Middle School to understand that Mrs. Wessex's special announcements were indeed *special.*

Theresa Allen, who sat right in front of Carrie, turned and grinned. *"Another tepee?"* she whispered, her brown eyes lighting up. Carrie smiled.

Last month, when they'd been studying Native Americans, Mrs. Wessex's "special announcement" had been that they were going to build a full-size tepee in the classroom. It had been awesome.

First they'd hiked through the woods behind the school to gather fallen birch limbs. Next they'd stripped off the bark, brought the branches inside, lashed them together, and covered them with pieces of leather donated by a local tannery. Then they'd painted the outside with Native American designs.

When it was finished, the tepee had taken up an entire corner of the room. It was large enough to fit about eight people inside at a time. Mrs. Wessex had divided the class into a bunch of different tribes that were native to New England, and each tribe had gotten their own day to "live" in the tepee.

Another one of those would be cool, Carrie thought. Or maybe some kind of pyramid, since they'd been studying ancient Egypt. *Or a model of the Sphinx or Cleopatra's barge . . .*

"It's time for us to start working on the annual fifth-grade production," Mrs. Wessex announced, interrupting Carrie's guessing game.

There were a few squeals of excitement around the room and a couple of "cools" tossed out, but all Carrie could do was blink.

"Already?" she murmured to Theresa. "I thought the fifth-grade musical was usually in the spring."

"Take a look outside," Theresa whispered back.

Carrie gazed out the window, surprised to see just one small mound of snow remaining at the edge of the parking lot. The rest of it was gone. Apparently, all the wet weather they'd had over the last few weeks—along with the milder temperatures—had melted the snow away.

It was still gray outside, but it didn't look cold anymore. There were even a few patches of grass on the front lawn that had started to turn from dead winter tan to vibrant spring green.

Okay, so maybe the *weather* was ready for the fifth-grade play, but Carrie still wasn't—even though she'd been waiting five years for it.

When Carrie was in kindergarten, her older sister, Lynn, had worked as a stagehand in *her* fifth-grade production of *Alice in Wonderland.* Mrs. Hendrickson, the music teacher, had allowed Carrie to sit backstage and help Lynn with props and costumes.

It had been love at first sight. Everything about the theater fascinated Carrie. Just standing *near* the stage made her giddy with excitement. But then after the final performance of *Alice in Wonderland*—the Sunday matinee—Carrie had walked out onstage to help take down the set and looked out at where the audience had been. And her heart leaped in her chest. It was then that she knew where she really belonged: not behind the stage but *on it*. Later that night she'd told her parents that she wanted to be an actress when she grew up. And now, in fifth grade, it was still true.

Carrie loved to sing and dance, and she could recite entire movie scenes from memory. But it wasn't just that she enjoyed all of those things: She was actually good at them.

At least, she was good at acting . . . *in front of the mirror*. And she was good at singing . . . *in the shower*. And dancing? She was the star of the family room . . . *when it was empty*. But give her an audience, and she fell apart.

Only a few days ago she'd nearly fainted giving a presentation on King Tut. She'd had it down pat the night before. But the minute she'd had to stand up in front of the class, her mind had gone blank, her knees had gone weak, and her mouth had gone stupid.

If I can't even do a stupid two-minute oral report, how am I ever going to perform onstage? Carrie wondered. She took a deep breath and tried to steady her nerves. After all, it wasn't like she had to do anything today. Mrs. Wessex had just made the announcement. They probably still had a week or so to read over parts and decide what they wanted to audition for.

Maybe if Carrie could practice in advance and really perfect one of the parts, she'd be able to work up the courage to do it in front of others. And really, she *had* to. It was the only way her dream of acting was ever going to come true.

Okay, she told herself, feeling a bit calmer. *It's all right. I've got time. I can do this.*

"What's the play, Mrs. Wessex?" Maria Mancini asked.

"We've chosen a modern version of *Cinderella,*" Mrs. Wessex said. "I think it should be a lot of fun."

"Cinderella," Sharon Ross repeated. "She has long blonde hair, right?" She flipped her own long blonde hair over her shoulder as she spoke.

Theresa mimicked her, throwing a few braids over her shoulder prima-donna style. Unfortunately, her hair was so long that it smacked Carrie in the face.

"Hey!" Carrie hissed, but Theresa just giggled.

"Not always," Anna said.

"What was that, Anna?" Mrs. Wessex asked.

"Oh, I just meant that Cinderella doesn't always have blonde hair," Anna said. "My grandmother has a book of old fairy tales from different cultures, and there's an Egyptian Cinderella with black hair and dark eyes."

Sharon scowled in Anna's direction, but Carrie and Theresa grinned.

"Love her," Theresa whispered, and Carrie nodded in agreement. Anna definitely had a talent for putting Sharon in her place.

"That's an excellent point, Anna," Mrs. Wessex said. "And you're right. Cinderella certainly doesn't have to have blonde hair."

"Hey—if it's a modern fairy tale, maybe she could have a shaved head," Jeremy Gray suggested.

"Or purple hair," Billy Rafuse added.

"Well, I'm not sure about that," Mrs. Wessex said, "but it's certainly open to interpretation. In any case, Mrs. Hendrickson and I will be holding the auditions tomorrow during your music period—right after lunch."

Tomorrow?! Carrie swallowed hard. Couldn't Mrs. Wessex have given them a little more notice? How on earth was she supposed to pick a part, get it right, and work up enough confidence to audition in just one day?

Forget it, Carrie thought. *I'm doomed.*

"Mrs. Wessex?"

It was Sharon again. She probably wanted to mention that she'd been thinking of shaving her head. Or dyeing her hair purple. Or black. Just in case. Carrie glanced over at Anna, who rolled her eyes.

"Yes, Sharon?"

"I was just wondering, do you have any music we should study overnight? Or maybe some lines we should memorize to prepare for the audition?"

Mrs. Wessex's eyes widened. "Well, that's quite industrious of you, Sharon, but no, you don't need to prepare anything," she said. "We'll read over the script this afternoon so everyone gets a feel for it. Tonight I'd just like everyone to think about what they might like to do for the play, whether it's acting, helping to design the set, working on costumes, lighting, sound, programs, tickets, advertising—there's a lot to be done. There should be something for everyone."

The class buzzed with excitement as everyone started talking about which jobs they wanted.

"Quiet, please," Mrs. Wessex said, raising one hand in the air and holding it there until the voices died down. "Now, anyone who wants to try out for a part can sign up tomorrow morning in class. I'll have sign-up sheets for all the other jobs, too, and we'll talk about the work involved in each one."

"I want a part," Carrie heard Maria whisper to Lauren Graham.

"Me too," Lauren replied.

Ugh. Carrie's stomach dropped. Everyone was going to be trying out for parts, and they were all bound to be better than she was. Not that it would be difficult. All they had to do was speak. It was more than Carrie could manage.

"Oh, and I almost forgot," Mrs. Wessex added. "I have another announcement to make." She retrieved a piece of paper from her desk and read it aloud. "Tomorrow we'll be welcoming a new student to our class. Ward Willis is transferring from Kennebunk Elementary School. I expect everyone to give him a warm welcome."

Anna gave a silent clap as she looked over at Theresa and Carrie. "I'm not the new kid anymore!" she mouthed.

Carrie smiled back at her. She'd stopped thinking of Anna as the new kid a while ago. It had only been a couple of weeks, but it already felt like they'd been friends for a long time.

In fact, the other day, when Carrie had botched her King Tut presentation, it had been Anna who'd tried to help her. She'd noticed that Carrie was feeling pretty down and loaned her a charm bracelet, saying it had brought her good luck once.

Carrie looked down at her wrist. She touched the silver angel charm and ran her fingers along the cool metal chain. Unfortunately, something told her it was going to take more than good luck to get her a role in the play. It was going to take a miracle.

CHAPTER
Two

"The play sounds pretty cool, huh?" Anna said as she joined Carrie and Theresa at their usual table in the cafeteria.

"Yeah," Theresa agreed. "I can't wait to sign up. What are you guys going to do?"

"I was thinking about helping with the ticket and program design," Anna said. "I kind of like fooling around on my computer with that stuff."

"Cool," Theresa said. "I was thinking costumes and props. And maybe set design, too—I'm not sure. I wonder how many committees we can sign up for."

"I don't know," Anna said. "What about you, Carrie? What are you going to do?"

"Huh? Oh, I—I'm not sure," Carrie stammered. She wasn't quite ready to admit that she wanted to audition for a part. It was as if she said it out loud, she'd have to go through with it. And no matter how much she wanted to, she wasn't sure she had the nerve. So instead she decided to focus on something less frightening—her lunch. Unfortunately, these days it was only *slightly* less frightening.

Her father had been on a major health kick lately, and more and more it was making its way into Carrie's reusable canvas lunch bag. She unrolled the top of it carefully and peered inside.

Hmmm. Not bad, Carrie thought, removing the contents—a veggie wrap, wheat crackers with hummus, and carob chip cookies for dessert.

"Whoa—your dad's slipping," Theresa commented. "That actually looks edible. And he packed cookies."

"Frookies," Carrie corrected her.

"*Frookies?*" Anna and Theresa repeated together.

"Yeah. They're sweetened with fruit juice instead of sugar," Carrie explained. "But you're right," she added, looking down at her spread. "This actually looks pretty good. Way better than yesterday's tofu-pineapple pie."

Anna shuddered. "No offense to your father, Carrie, but that was gross. Even my brother wouldn't have eaten it, and he eats everything."

"*No one* would eat it," Carrie said. "Not even

Dad. My mom made him throw it away last night and promise never to make it again."

"Whoa," Theresa said. "It must have been bad for your mom to say that. She's usually so mellow."

"It was the worst, Theresa," Anna said. "I had a bite, remember? It was *sooo* gross. I told Matt about it in the arcade yesterday, and he said it sounded like one of the rogues from Storm Ranger."

Theresa raised her eyebrows. "There's a tofu-pineapple monster in Storm Ranger?"

"No," Anna said, "but there *is* a warrior that started out as a leftover bowl of seafood stew and mutated."

Carrie and Theresa stared at Anna with narrowed eyes.

"Really," Anna insisted. "He's called Bouilla-beast." There was a moment's hesitation, and then all three girls burst out laughing.

"What's so funny?" someone asked.

Carrie turned to see Sharon approaching with Kimberly Price close behind. Sharon sat next to Carrie, and Kimberly took the seat next to her.

"We were just talking about Carrie's lunch," Theresa explained.

"Oh," Sharon said, glancing toward Carrie's food. "Whoa, Carrie—your dad packed cookies? What's up with that?"

"He's trying to make up for the fact that yesterday's lunch was an evil mutant bent on destroying the world," Anna said with a completely straight face. Again she, Theresa, and Carrie stared at one another for a moment . . . and then burst out laughing.

"I'm not even going to ask." Sharon shook her head. She took the small plastic cup of pasta sauce on her tray and poured it over her spaghetti. "So," she said, twirling some pasta around her fork, "have you guys thought about the play at all? Do you know what you're going to do?"

Carrie's smile disappeared. Why did everyone have to keep bringing up the stupid play?

"Costumes and props," Theresa answered right away. "And maybe set design. I'm hoping Mrs. Wessex will let me sign up for both."

"What about you, Lee?" Sharon asked. She always called Anna by her last name.

"I'm not sure," Anna said. "I *was* thinking ticket and program design, but set design sounds pretty cool, too. I think I might sign up for that."

"Really?" Theresa grinned. "That would be awesome." She glanced at Carrie and then back to Anna. "Then all three of us could work together."

Carrie narrowed her eyes. "All three of us?" she asked.

Anna smiled. "Yeah, that's what I was thinking, too. Wouldn't that be great?"

"Well . . . yeah, but . . ." Carrie wasn't sure what to say. "I, uh, haven't actually decided what I want to do yet."

"Really?" Theresa asked. "I just assumed you'd want to do set design because you're such a good artist."

"Yeah," Anna agreed. "That's what I figured, too. You draw so well."

"Oh," Carrie said. "Thanks. Well, I *might* do that, but—"

"At least we all know you're not trying out for a part," Kimberly said with a chortle.

Carrie's heart skipped. What was *that* supposed to mean? She looked to Theresa and Anna, surprised to see them both gazing back at her with . . . *pity*? Was that what it was? Carrie didn't know what to say, and apparently nobody else did, either. They'd all gone silent, and now everyone was staring at Kimberly.

"What?" Kimberly said. "I wasn't trying to be *mean*." She looked at Carrie. "I just meant . . .

well . . . you know . . . remember your Egypt presentation? *Ting Kut?*"

Carrie winced.

"It just seems obvious that you don't like standing up in front of people," Kimberly added. "That's all I meant. Not that you couldn't do it or anything."

"Right," Theresa jumped in. "I mean, I'm sure you *could* if you wanted to." She paused to glance at Anna. "Right?"

"Definitely," Anna said, nodding.

"We just didn't think you'd want to," Theresa went on. "And . . . you don't . . . *do you?*"

Carrie felt all of her friends' eyes on her while they waited for her reaction. She also felt her cheeks growing hot and knew they were turning a shade of red to match her hair. It didn't exactly seem like the right time to admit that she dreamed of being onstage—especially because clearly none of her friends thought she'd be good at it. They were obviously only saying that other stuff to avoid hurting her feelings.

"I don't know," she finally managed. "Probably not." Everyone seemed to relax at those two words. Everyone except Carrie. "Anyway, I know what you meant, Kimberly," Carrie went on.

"And you're right—I do get nervous talking in front of people."

"Who doesn't?" Kimberly said. "I hate oral reports."

"Me too," agreed Theresa.

"I don't," Sharon said. "I got over stage fright a long time ago."

"Stage fright?" Carrie repeated.

"Yeah, that's what it's called when you get scared about performing in front of other people."

"Oh," Carrie said. "Right." She picked up a wheat cracker and dipped it into the hummus. Maybe Sharon was trying to be helpful, but somehow having a name for her fear made it seem that much more real.

Sharon picked up a forkful of spaghetti but stopped just short of shoving it into her mouth. "Hey—you know what?" she said, gesturing at Carrie with her overloaded utensil.

"What?" Carrie asked.

"You *should* try out for a part."

Carrie nearly choked on her cracker. "I *what*?"

Sharon chewed her pasta, then dabbed at her mouth with her napkin. "You should try out for a part," she repeated. Everyone, including Carrie, stared at Sharon in surprise.

"I'm serious," Sharon insisted. "If you have

stage fright, the only way to get over it is to confront it. That's what my drama coach always says."

"Your *drama coach*?" Anna asked.

"Mm-hm," Sharon replied, twirling another strand of spaghetti onto her fork. "I take jazz, ballet, and acting classes, and my drama coach, Ms. Harkins, is always telling new students that if they want to get over stage fright, they just have to get up and perform. And it's true. After a while you get so used to being in front of people that it's not scary at all anymore."

"Really?" Carrie asked. She glanced at Anna and Theresa for their reactions. They both raised their eyebrows and shrugged. Obviously, they were just as puzzled as Carrie was. Not only was Sharon offering advice, she actually seemed to be offering *good* advice—without a selfish reason in sight.

"Sure," Sharon said. "Plus I already talked with Mrs. Wessex about the play. There's the lead role, Cindy Rellar, which I'll probably get, and then there are a bunch of supporting parts. If you tried for one of those, you wouldn't have to be onstage all that much, and when you are, I could help you out. I'd probably be out there, too—you know, because the lead gets the most stage time."

Okay. Now that sounded a little more like Sharon. But overall, the advice was good.

"Thanks," Carrie said. "I'll think about it."

"You should," Sharon said. "There are a lot of little parts to fill. Just about everybody who tries out is sure to get something. And who knows? If you get a small enough role, you might be able to work on set design, too."

"That would be perfect," Theresa said.

"Yeah," Anna agreed. "Then you'd get a chance to get over your stage fright and the three of us could still work together. Wouldn't that be great?"

"Yeah. Great," Carrie said, forcing a smile. A *little part* would be okay, but it wasn't exactly what she'd had in mind. She wanted a lead role—like the one Sharon was trying out for—but no one else seemed to think that she could handle it.

And, unfortunately, Carrie had a feeling they were right.

CHAPTER
Three

"Can we do Sound Factory next?" Carrie asked as she and Theresa passed through the food court at the mall. "The new Strawberries and Cream CD came out this weekend, and I really want to get it."

"Okay," Theresa said, "but Sara's is on the way, so let's stop in there first."

Carrie groaned. Sara's was the accessory store, and—in Carrie's mind—one of the most boring stores in the entire mall. She squinted at Theresa. "Do you really need another hair clip?" she asked.

"Do you really need another CD?" Theresa shot back.

Carrie rolled her eyes. "All right," she said with a sigh, "but just for a minute, okay? I don't want to spend the whole afternoon looking at barrettes and bracelets."

"I'll be quick," Theresa said with a big grin. When they reached Sara's, she bounced into the store and headed straight for the hair accessories. Carrie shuffled in behind her, stopping to browse through a spinning rack of sunglasses. She pulled out the ugliest pair she could find— bright purple rims with neon green lenses—and tried them on.

"What do you think, Resa?" she asked.

Theresa glanced up and grimaced. "Definitely a fashion *don't*," she answered, shaking her head. Then, without so much as a smirk, she went back to rummaging through the clips, combs, and barrettes.

Carrie frowned. It was too bad Anna hadn't been able to come. She wasn't into accessorizing any more than Carrie was. Theresa, on the other hand, was always trying to get the two of them to put their hair up and wear a little lip gloss. "It's fun," she was constantly telling them and "It'll make you feel older," to which Anna had once replied, "So will wearing my grandmother's false teeth, but I'm not trying those on, either."

Carrie smiled. If Anna had been there, she would have laughed at the ugly purple-and-green glasses and then tried to find something even worse. Unfortunately, she'd had to go to the dentist, and her mother hadn't been considerate enough to make the appointment during school hours.

"Hey—how about this?" Theresa asked, holding up a green hair clip shaped like a big butterfly.

Carrie shrugged. "It's okay," she said, "but it doesn't really look like you."

"It's not *for* me," Theresa said. "It's for you." Carrie rolled her eyes. "Oh, come on, Car—it would be perfect. This bright green clip in your dark red hair? It would be so sweet. Plus it would help you to keep some of that hair out of your face."

"Thanks, but no thanks," Carrie said, even though her bangs were hanging down over her eyes and she had to keep brushing them away. A clip actually would be a big help while she was growing them out, but she kind of liked the way the curls hid her face. Besides, she didn't want to encourage Theresa by giving in.

Theresa sighed and put the clip back in its bin, then moved on to jewelry.

Carrie walked over to join her. "Are you almost ready?" she asked.

"Just about. Ooh—look at that." Theresa reached for a necklace at the top of the jewelry stand, stretching her hand up. "Oh, no—oops!"

There was a loud crash as Theresa knocked over a whole rack of earrings. They clattered across the floor and under tables, and everyone turned to stare. Blushing, Theresa quickly knelt down to start picking up the earrings. In a flash, one of the store clerks was beside her.

"You can just leave them there," the clerk said, glaring at Theresa. "I'll take care of it."

"I—I'm sorry," Theresa said, still trying to scoop up all the earrings.

The clerk placed her hand on top of Theresa's. "Miss, really—just leave them there," she said. Her tone was short and clipped.

"Okay, but . . . I'm *really* sorry," Theresa repeated, stepping away.

"Mm-hm," the clerk mumbled, without looking up. As Carrie and Theresa left, she muttered something about irresponsible kids and needing to get a new job.

"Jeez. She didn't have to be so mean about it," Theresa said when they were safely out of earshot. "It was just an accident."

"I know," Carrie said. "Don't worry about it." She felt bad for Theresa. Stuff like that was always happening to her—spilling food, knocking over huge displays, tripping over things. It had to be embarrassing. *Kind of like standing up to give a report on King Tut and freezing.* Carrie snorted at the thought.

"What?" Theresa asked.

"Oh, nothing. I was just thinking about my King Tut presentation."

"Kimberly really wasn't trying to be mean at lunch today, you know," Theresa said.

"I know," Carrie said. And she did—but that didn't mean it hadn't hurt.

The two girls walked silently past a nutrition store and a pet store, two shoe stores, and a gift shop, and before Carrie knew it, they were just outside Sound Factory. Theresa started in, but Carrie caught her by the elbow. "Hey," she said, pulling Theresa aside. "Do you think Sharon was right?"

"About what?"

"About stage fright. You know, today at lunch when she said all that stuff about just getting up and performing?"

Theresa shrugged. "I don't know. I guess so. I mean, that's kind of like what my dad always tells me. *'You have to face your fears, Theresa,'*" she said in a deep, fatherly voice. "Of course, he's usually talking about trying whatever strange vegetable is on my dinner plate, but I guess it could work for other stuff. Why?"

Carrie bit her lip. "Well . . . *because.*"

"Because *why*?"

"Because . . ." Carrie took a deep breath. She had to tell someone, and Theresa was her closest friend. "Because . . . I think I want to try out," she blurted. "For the play."

Theresa blinked. "Really?"

Carrie winced. *Oh, no.* It was true. Theresa didn't think she could do it. Her best friend, who knew her better than anyone else in the world, didn't think she could—

"That would be awesome," Theresa said, breaking into a big grin. "It would be so cool to see you onstage."

Carrie's jaw dropped. "Really?" she asked.

"Absolutely." Theresa nodded. "And you know what? You'd be great—I can totally see you up there."

"You can?"

"Yeah."

"Am I talking? Or am I just staring out at the audience like an idiot?"

Theresa clucked her tongue. *"Carrie,"* she said. "Of course you're talking. And you're singing and dancing, too. And the audience is clapping like crazy."

Carrie smiled. It was a nice image. She'd pictured herself onstage thousands of times, and she'd never frozen in her imagination, either. "Wow," she murmured. "That would be so great." She squinted at Theresa, trying to determine whether her friend was being honest or just nice. "So . . . you *really* think I should audition?" she asked.

"Definitely," Theresa said.

Hmmm. No hesitation, direct eye contact, Carrie assessed. Theresa seemed to mean it. And Sharon had seemed sincere when she'd suggested Carrie try out at lunch. *So maybe,* Carrie thought, *just maybe I should.* It was simply a matter of working up the nerve.

"Hey," Theresa said, glancing over Carrie's shoulder. "There's your sister."

Carrie turned and saw her older sister, Lynn, and Lynn's best friend, Stephanie Lane, walking out of Maxine's. Each of them was carrying a large double-handled shopping bag.

Maybe they won't notice us, Carrie thought. She'd had enough of her sister during the car ride to the mall.

It wasn't that she and Lynn didn't get along, exactly. It was just that they rarely agreed. On anything. And Carrie didn't feel like arguing with her sister in the middle of the mall.

Unfortunately, Theresa didn't notice that

Carrie was more or less hiding behind a potted palm. Theresa cupped her hands around her mouth and called, "Hey, Lynn!" Lynn looked up, waved, and headed their way.

"Check out this skirt," Lynn said, pulling a multicolored miniwrap out of her bag. "And I got this top to match. Maxine's is having such a great sale. You two should really check it out."

"Nice," Theresa said. "Maybe we will." She glanced at Carrie, but Carrie only shrugged.

"I just want to hit Sound Factory," she said. "After that, I don't care."

"That's my sister," Lynn said. "Always blowing all of her money on CDs."

"What's wrong with that?" Carrie said.

"Nothing," Lynn admitted. "Except that you never have any cool clothes to wear and you're always begging to borrow mine."

"I don't beg to borrow—"

"Hey—guess what?" Theresa cut in.

Carrie frowned. She knew Theresa hated to watch her and her sister fight, but did she always have to interrupt just when Carrie was about to put her sister in her place?

"What?" Lynn asked.

"Mrs. Wessex told us today that the class play is going to be a modern version of *Cinderella*,"

Theresa blathered, "and Carrie's going to try out for a part."

Carrie's eyebrows shot up. "Theresa!" she hissed. She hadn't meant for it to become headline news.

"You are?" Lynn asked, taking a step back. "Really?" She looked stunned.

"Well . . . I'm thinking about it," Carrie said.

"Huh. I know you wanted to be an actress back when you were like, *six*, but ever since that whole karaoke thing I thought you kind of gave that up. Remember that? You said you were never going to sing in public again."

Carrie cringed. Actually, she'd pretty much forgotten about it. Until now. Leave it to her sister to make matters worse.

"Lynn," Stephanie said, "that was like, your twelfth birthday, wasn't it? Carrie was only eight—she probably doesn't even remember it."

Seven, Carrie thought, *and yes, I do.* It had been one of the most embarrassing moments of her life—one that she had managed to block out . . . up until this very moment.

"What happened?" Theresa asked.

"Oh, my gosh, she never *told you*?" Lynn said. She gaped at Carrie, who scowled back. "Theresa, you *have* to hear this. It's such a funny story."

"It's not funny, Lynn—it's stupid," Carrie said. "And boring. And I'm sure Theresa doesn't want to hear about it."

"Oh yes, I—" Theresa started, then she paused, craning her neck to look over Lynn's shoulder. "Hey, wait—isn't that . . . ? Matt!" she called. "Over here!"

Carrie turned to see Matt Dana walking out of Sound Factory with another boy who she didn't recognize. Oh, great. Just what she needed. A larger audience for her sister's humiliating story.

Gee, Theresa, maybe that old couple on the bench would like to hear it, too. Why don't you call them over? Carrie thought bitterly.

"Hey—Theresa, Carrie, what's up?" Matt said as he approached. Then he nodded to his friend. "This is Ward."

"*MC Spence,*" the boy cut in.

"Oh, right," Matt said. "I forgot. Sorry."

"No worries, man," Matt's friend said. "It's just a name for the rhyming game—I may achieve fame, but I'll remain the same."

Carrie and Theresa—and Lynn and Stephanie—all stared at Matt and . . . *MC Spence.*

"Do people actually *call* you that?" Theresa asked.

"Not yet," Ward said. "I just made it up."

"What does *Spence* mean?" Stephanie asked.

"Nothing. Spencer's my middle name," Ward said.

"Oh," Lynn said, nodding. "So you're . . . *MC Spence*. That's . . . cute."

There was a moment of silence that Carrie noticed seemed to make everyone in the group feel awkward—everyone except Ward, that is. He was rifling through the pockets of his baggy cargo jeans for something. "Cool," he said when he finally pulled out what looked like a piece of lint.

"Anyway, Ward," Matt went on, "I mean, *MC Spence*—is the new kid Mrs. Wessex was talking about. I know him from the skate park."

"Oh, hi," Theresa and Carrie said at just about the same time.

"This is Theresa," Matt continued, "and that's Carrie."

"And this is my sister, Lynn," Carrie said, practically sneering her sister's name, "and her friend, Stephanie."

As everyone said their hellos, Carrie checked out MC Spence. Too bad Anna wasn't here— she'd be psyched to know that not only was she no longer the newest student at ECS, but she was no longer the shortest, either. Or if she was, it wasn't by much. Ward was only about four-six, which would place him right around Anna's height—maybe even an inch below.

He was wearing a black T-shirt that said RAP THIS across the chest, and he had headphones hanging around his neck. Carrie followed the wires to see a Discman clipped onto his side pocket, where she could also see the corner of a Sound Factory bag poking out.

"So," Spence said with a nod, "you guys hang at Elizabeth Cady with Matt?"

"We go there, yeah," Theresa said. "You're starting tomorrow?"

"Yeah, the 'rents got a new place, so I had to switch schools." He shrugged. "It's cool, though, you know? I'll get to chill with my buddy Matt." He pulled the Sound Factory bag from his pocket and took out a CD.

Carrie gasped. "You got the new Strawberries and Cream! Can I see it?"

Spence grinned. "You into them?" he said, handing her the CD.

"I was just on my way to buy it," Carrie answered.

"Cool," Spence said with a nod. "Check it out—there's a new version of 'Pretty Girl' on there."

Carrie flipped the disk over to see all the tracks. "Awesome—it has 'Automatic Focus,' too—I love that song. And it looks like there's a bunch of new stuff." Carrie was just about to ask Spence if he knew anything about the track called "On the Corner of Milk and Market" when she heard her sister sigh.

"Well, Steph and I have to get going," Lynn said. She always made a big show of being bored by Carrie and her "little friends," as Lynn referred to them. "We only have about an hour left, Carrie. Don't forget to meet us at the big clock at four—"

"Forty-five. I know," Carrie said, rolling her eyes. Lynn had reminded her approximately twenty-three times now—as if Carrie was the one who was perpetually late. *Oh, well,* Carrie thought. *At least she's leaving.*

"Wait," Theresa said. "What about the karaoke party? You haven't told me the story yet."

Carrie gave her sister a panicked glance. *Not in front of Matt and his friend,* she thought, hoping that for once her and Lynn's shared genes would aid their communication. But Lynn was clueless. As usual.

"Oh, right," she said. "I almost forgot." It didn't even seem to cross her mind that the story might be embarrassing for Carrie. Or maybe it did, and she just didn't care.

"Okay, so I asked for a karaoke party for my twelfth birthday," Lynn started. Carrie felt her face beginning to grow warm. It wasn't fair that redheads blushed so much more easily than everyone else. "So my parents took me and some friends and Carrie to the Silver Dollar— you know, that diner where they have karaoke in the back room?" Theresa nodded. "Well, when we got there, we all told Carrie she had to sing because she has a great voice. Plus we thought it would be cute since she was only eight."

"Seven," Carrie corrected her. "I was seven."

"Okay, *seven*," Lynn said. "So anyway, she got up to do 'It's a Hard Knock Life.'"

Carrie felt the blush spread to her neck. She knew what was coming.

"She did a great job," Lynn continued. "She was like one of those kids on a TV talent show or something. She was dancing around the stage, singing her heart out. It was adorable. We used to have pictures, but Carrie made us throw most of them out. Because—" Lynn stopped, her green eyes sparkling.

Here it comes, Carrie thought, wishing she could disappear.

"Because, see, Carrie got *so* into the song that she didn't realize her skirt had gotten hitched up in the back. Every time she turned, the whole place could see her underwear!"

"Oh, my gosh!" Theresa said, grinning at Carrie.

"Tell them what kind of underwear it was," Stephanie reminded Lynn.

"Oh, that's right!" Lynn said. "I almost forgot. Carrie, you should tell them."

Carrie let out a sigh. Why not? She was already humiliated. "Scooby-Doo," she said. "It was Scooby-Doo underwear. And for *months* all my sister's friends called me Scooby."

Matt and Spence chuckled, and Theresa burst out laughing. "That is *such* a great story," she said between giggles. Then she slapped Carrie on the shoulder. "I can't believe you never told me that!"

"Must've slipped my mind," Carrie said sarcastically. She glared at her sister. "Thanks, Lynn."

"Oh, stop it," Lynn said, rolling her eyes. "You were only eight."

"*Seven,*" Carrie insisted.

"All right—*seven.* It's not like it happened yesterday or anything."

"Yeah, don't be embarrassed, Carrie. It's

cute—really," Theresa said. "But," she added with a smirk, "just in case, maybe you should stay away from the Scooby underwear tomorrow—you know, for your audition?"

"You're trying out for the play?" Matt said.

"Well, I—"

"That's cool. Spence says he's gonna try out, too."

"Oh. Great," Carrie said, forcing a smile. She looked over at Theresa, who was still giggling about the whole Scooby story.

Wonderful, Carrie thought. Why had she thought that confiding in Theresa was a good idea? Thanks to her so-called *friend,* everyone was going to be expecting her to audition tomorrow. And with everyone expecting it, just how was she supposed to back out?

CHAPTER
Four

Carrie gave a nervous tug on the angel charm Anna had given her as she walked into Mrs. Wessex's classroom Tuesday morning. She looked around for Theresa and Anna, but they weren't there yet. Sharon was standing next to Matt's desk, though, so Carrie headed over there. "I'll have to talk to whoever's in charge of costumes," Sharon was saying to Matt, "to make sure they get mine right. I think Cindy should wear pants instead of a dress because, you know, it *is* supposed to be all modern or whatever. But they have to be the right kind of pants."

Carrie shook her head. The way Sharon was talking, it sounded like she'd already been given the lead role. Obviously, she just didn't consider any of the other fifth-grade girls serious competition—least of all Carrie.

"Hey, Carrie," Sharon said when she saw her. "We were just talking about the play. Do you think you'll end up working on costumes? Because I need to—"

"Yo, Matt, Scoob, what's up?"

Carrie turned and saw Spence coming over to them. Along with the backpack slung over one shoulder, he was carrying a skateboard covered with stickers from different bands.

"Scoob? What's that mean?" Sharon asked.

Carrie flushed. "It's nothing," she said.

Sharon frowned, then stood up straighter and grinned at Spence. "I'm Sharon Ross," she said. She gave her head a little shake so her blonde hair flipped behind her shoulder. "You must be the new guy."

Spence laughed. "Yeah, that's me," he said. "The true-blue newbie, kickin' it with Scooby." He dropped his backpack onto the chair next to Matt's and slid his skateboard under the desk. "But you can call me MC Spence."

"*O-kay,*" Sharon said. She glanced at Matt, clearly uncertain what to make of his new friend. "MC Spence, huh?"

Spence nodded. "You got it."

"Are you . . . a *rapper*?"

"I'm working on it," Spence said. "I'm a fan

of the free verse, unrehearsed. It's like a rhymin' curse, for better or worse."

"Wow," Sharon gushed. "That is *so* cool. Did you just make that up—like, off the top of your head?"

Carrie tried not to laugh. So Spence read a lot of Dr. Seuss—what was the big deal? Sure, he seemed pretty good at the whole rhyming thing, but come on—Sharon looked like she was ready to ask for his autograph.

"Spence freestyles at the skate park sometimes," Matt said. "He's good."

"I bet," Sharon said. "I'll have to stop by and check it out sometime."

"You know it," Spence said. "The more the merrier. Hey—" he went on, turning to Carrie. "Did you end up getting that disk last night?"

Carrie nodded. "I've already listened to the whole thing twice," she said. "My favorite track is—"

"'Press Play'?"

"Yes! How did you know?"

"It's the best track on there," Spence said.

"We just got a new stereo system at home," Sharon announced. "You guys should come over so we can try it out."

"Nice," Spence said. "Carrie and I could bring the grooves—right, Scoob?"

Carrie winced. She'd thought she'd escaped that nickname four years ago, but now it looked like she was stuck with it all over again.

Just then Anna and Theresa came into the room, followed by Mrs. Wessex. Carrie walked over to them.

"Hey, is that Matt's friend?" Anna asked, pointing at Spence. "Theresa said you met him at the mall yesterday."

"Yeah, that's him," Carrie said. "MC Spence."

Anna raised her eyebrows. "Do people actually call him that?" she asked.

As if on cue, Sharon giggled and said, "Wow, MC Spence—you're *so* funny."

"Sharon does," Carrie replied. "How was the dentist?"

"No cavities," Anna said, baring her teeth.

"All right, class—let's get started," Mrs. Wessex said. Reluctantly, everyone shuffled to their seats. When they were finally settled, Mrs. Wessex held up a clipboard.

"I'm going to pass around this sign-up sheet for the class play. Now, this one is only for people who want to try out for a role. While it's going around, we'll talk about the other jobs that are available, and then I'll pass around a second clipboard so you can sign up for any committees that interest you. Maria, could you get this one going?" Mrs. Wessex asked.

Carrie watched as Maria took the clipboard and immediately scribbled her name at the top of the page. She passed it to Lauren Graham, who did the same. From there the clipboard continued down the row, and Carrie's eyes remained glued to it as it passed from one person to the next. It seemed like a lot of people were signing up.

"So, are you gonna do it?" Theresa whispered as she handed Carrie the clipboard.

Carrie lifted her shoulder in a half shrug, pretending not to care even though her heart was pounding like crazy. She stared down at the paper, gripping her pencil tightly. All she had to do was write two words—*Carrie Weingarten.*

She looked at the angel charm on her wrist and glanced toward Anna, hoping for encouragement. But Anna was writing in her notebook. Spence, on the other hand, who was just behind Anna and to the left, caught Carrie's eye. He nodded toward the clipboard and cocked his head.

Carrie pressed her lips together. *Come on, Carrie, just sign up!* she urged herself. If she didn't do something soon, other people were going to start noticing that she was just sitting there with the clipboard, too. But every time she told herself to just sign her name, it was like her hand didn't get the message.

She peeked over at Spence again to see if he was still watching, and he gave her an encouraging nod. *He thinks I should do it,* Carrie realized. And for a moment her spirits lifted. But then she realized that Spence didn't know her at all. He had no idea exactly what he was encouraging.

He hadn't witnessed her pathetic King Tut presentation. He didn't know that she blushed eighteen shades of red every time she walked into math class a little late. And he had no clue just how flustered she got speaking in front of people.

Of course, once he saw her audition, he'd know all of that. And he'd understand perfectly why she couldn't just sign her name and pass the clipboard on like everyone else. The problem was that this audition meant way too much to Carrie. The play wasn't just a fun school project for her. It was a chance to realize her dream. Or fail at it.

Carrie gazed down at the list one last time and clenched her pencil so hard, the tip of her index finger went white. Then, feeling her stomach turn, she handed the clipboard to Billy Rafuse. Without signing her name.

★   ★   ★

When lunchtime finally came, Carrie just wanted to be alone. She couldn't face having everyone ask why she hadn't signed up for the tryouts. So instead she retreated to her favorite spot—a beanbag chair in the back corner of the library.

There was only one thing that was going to make Carrie feel better right now, and that was writing. Thankfully, she always kept her journal nearby. She pulled her backpack onto her lap and began feeling around for the familiar spiral-bound book with its rough, glitter-encrusted cover.

That's strange, Carrie thought when she didn't find it immediately. It was usually right on top. She shifted the contents of her backpack around and even checked the front zippered pocket. No journal. Frustrated, Carrie fumbled through everything again but still had no luck.

Finally, she unzipped the backpack all the way and began removing items one at a time. Before long the backpack was empty and the floor in front of her was cluttered, but her journal was still nowhere in sight.

Carrie took a deep breath and retraced her steps. She knew she'd packed it that morning. She'd put it in just as her father had handed her a container of soy yogurt to go with the fried tempeh flat-bread sandwich he'd made her.

In fact, her journal had been the reason she'd double bagged the yogurt—to make sure it didn't leak and get the pages all sticky. Carrie looked at the stuff in front of her. Her notebook, her science book, a bunch of miscellaneous work sheets, her math book, three pens, a ruler, her lunch sack, and the yogurt, still double bagged. Where. Was. Her. Journal?

Could it have fallen out in one of the classrooms? Carrie shuddered at the idea, and her heart started pounding. If someone picked it up and read her private thoughts—especially all the stuff she'd written last night about how much she wanted to try out for the play but how scared she was to do it—she'd be mortified. Anyone who saw it would think she was a total baby. She could feel her face getting red just thinking about it.

Carrie peeked inside her empty backpack one last time, feeling around with her hand just to make sure. No luck—just bits of glitter. *Shoot,* Carrie thought. Now she was going to have to go back to all the classrooms she'd been in that morning and hope she could find the diary before someone else did.

CHAPTER
Five

Carrie let out a sigh as she jogged down a flight of stairs. So far she'd checked four of the five classrooms she'd been in that morning, two bathrooms, and most of the hallways. She'd asked every one of her teachers if they'd seen a journal with a blue sparkly cover, but none of them had.

Yet everywhere Carrie went, there seemed to be traces of blue glitter—on the floor here, under a chair there. It was like the journal had gotten up and run away all by itself. Or like Hansel and Gretel had stolen it and were leaving themselves a trail so they could find their way home.

Carrie shook her head, feeling like she was going crazy. She hated misplacing things.

She headed down the hall toward Mrs. Wessex's room. English had been her last class before lunch, and it was the only one she hadn't checked. She was almost there when she spotted something sparkling near the water fountain. She knelt down next to the fountain, shocked to see the corner of her journal peeking out.

"Thank goodness," she breathed. She grabbed the book and hugged it closely. The journal—and all of her private thoughts—were safe and sound, finally.

Carrie held the journal out in front of her, inspecting it. A lot of the glitter had come off, but that was okay. Everything else seemed to be in place. The blue satin bookmark was still hanging down the side, and—

"Oh, no. Where's Bob?" Carrie whispered. The end of the bookmark was frayed, and the silver unicorn charm that usually dangled from it was gone.

"Psst—over here," a voice called out.

Carrie blinked, then glanced around. She was the only one in the hallway.

"Who . . . who said that?" she whispered.

"Down here!" the squeaky voice called again. It seemed to be coming from . . . *under the fountain.*

Carrie bent down and stared at the carpet. There was a red pen cap lying there, but she didn't see anything else. She picked up the cap and examined it closely, wondering if maybe there was a tiny speaker hidden inside and someone was playing a joke on her.

"Ahem," the voice said. Carrie jumped. "Don't tell me you honestly think that piece of plastic is talking to you."

"I . . . uh . . ." Carrie swallowed nervously. She still couldn't tell where the voice was coming from.

"Then again, what would I expect from someone who would name a beautiful unicorn *'Bob'?*"

Carrie crouched down and peered under the fountain. *"Oh . . . my . . . gosh,"* she breathed.

There, backed against the wall, was a tiny, one-inch-tall white unicorn with a long, flowing mane, big brown eyes, and an iridescent horn.

"B-b-b-b-b-b-b?" was all Carrie could manage.

The unicorn nodded. "Bob," it said. "Nice name for a female unicorn. Remind me not to ask for your creative input when it comes to naming my children."

"B-b-b-b-b-b-b," Carrie stammered again.

"Yeah, I have a hard time saying it, too. Honestly. *Bob?* What were you thinking? Why couldn't you have given me a pretty name, like Francesca . . . or Cordelia—something with a little more personality? Or at the very least, something *slightly fem-i-nine.*"

"B-but . . . I—I didn't know you were a g-girl," Carrie whispered. She glanced left and right to make sure no one was witnessing her talking to what was probably just a figment of her imagination. "I—I named you after my uncle Bob. H-he was the one who gave me the bookmark. H-how did you—?"

"Come to life? Break free? Drag your journal under here?" Bob asked.

"Uh . . . yeah," Carrie murmured. She still couldn't believe what she was seeing—*and hearing*.

"Magic, a sharp horn, and determination," Bob said. "Now—do you think you could get me off this floor? Dust bunnies give me the willies. I swear I saw one over there with teeth."

Carrie put her journal down, looked around one more time, and held out her hand. The unicorn climbed on, her hooves softly padding against Carrie's palm. Carrie felt each hoof step. She saw the tiny creature right there in her hand. She had even heard it speak. But she still couldn't believe what was happening.

"I . . . I don't get it. I mean . . . what . . . how . . . *why* . . . ?"

"Long story," Bob replied, shaking her mane. "Let's just say some people on my side of the uni-verse knew you needed a little encouragement, so they gave me permission to appear to you."

"Wait. *Your* side of the universe. Where's that? And *who* gave you permission? And how did they—?"

"Look, Carrie," Bob said, tapping her tiny hoof. "We could go back and forth about this forever and you still probably wouldn't understand it. Besides, like the cream in the middle of an Oreo and that gross stuff that you find in the corners of your eyes when you wake up in the morning, some things are best left unexamined. They just are what they are."

Carrie nodded uncertainly. "Okay . . . I guess." She reached down and gently petted the unicorn with the index finger of her free hand. Somehow the feeling of Bob's soft mane under her fingertip cemented things in Carrie's mind. "Wow, you actually *are* real."

"One hundred percent," Bob said. "No additives, no preservatives. Your dad would like that—not that he'd be able to talk to me. You're the only one who can see or hear me."

"Oh," Carrie said, taking a quick look down the hall. "So anyone who saw me right now—"

"Would think you were talking to your hand," Bob finished.

"Right," Carrie said. "Okay." She stood up

carefully, balancing Bob in her hand, and scanned the hallway again. Still alone. Thankfully. "Hey—what were you doing with my journal, anyway? Did you have to drag it around in order to get yourself loose?"

Bob cocked her head to one side. "Sure. We'll go with that."

"What do you mean?"

"I mean that's as good an explanation as any, so let's believe it."

Carrie scowled. "You can't just choose what to believe," she said. "It's either true or it isn't."

Bob shook her head. "Humans," she muttered, rolling her eyes. "I'd almost forgotten what an unenlightened species you are."

"Huh?"

"Forget it. We can talk about that later. Right now I need a comb and a mirror."

"Why?"

"So I can fix my hair," Bob said.

"Your *hair*?"

"Yes—my hair," Bob repeated. "You know—my mane and my tail? I like to keep myself looking presentable." Bob studied Carrie for a minute, then gave her a disappointed frown. "Not that I'd expect you to understand," she muttered.

"What did you say?"

"Nothing," Bob replied. "But you know, Lynn and Theresa are right—you really should put a little more effort into your appearance."

"What? How do you know Lynn and Theresa? And how do you know what they think of my appearance?"

"Well, I've been attached to your journal for the last year," Bob said, "and I'm a very good reader."

"You read my journal?!"

"Just skimmed it, really," Bob replied. "Unless there was something really juicy. But anyway, about that mirror—let's get going. I'm having a bad mane day."

"A bad mane day?"

Again Bob cocked her head at Carrie. "Of all people, I'd think *you'd* be able to relate," she said, eyeing Carrie's mass of red curls.

Carrie gasped. "That wasn't very nice."

"Hey—all I'm saying is that I think your hair and a barrette could be good friends."

"I thought you said you were sent here to encourage me," Carrie said. "Why are you being so insulting?"

"It's just friendly advice," Bob said. "Take it or leave it."

"I'll leave it, thanks."

"Fine," said Bob.

"Fine," echoed Carrie.

They were standing in the middle of the empty hallway, silent for a moment, until Bob said, *"About that mirror . . ."*

Carrie groaned. "Oh, all right. I suppose I could use a bathroom break before music class, anyway. Just let me put my journal in—hey!" Carrie picked up the journal and ran her hand along its glittery cover, fingering the spot where the silver clasp had been. "Bob—what happened to the lock? Did you break it off?"

Bob looked innocently at the ceiling. A little too innocently.

Carrie narrowed her eyes at the unicorn and noticed for the first time that the end of her horn was a bit bent—like she'd used it to pry something up.

"Bob," Carrie said suspiciously. She opened the journal and began flipping through it. As she did, a few small bits of paper fell loose from the spiral binding.

Carrie eyed the unicorn. "What did you do?" she asked, holding the little white animal close to her face. "Did you tear out some of the pages?"

Bob looked back at Carrie with twinkling eyes. *"May-be,"* she said.

"What did you do with them?"

Bob shook her head. "Sorry—can't say. But don't worry, I put them someplace where they'll do some good."

"Do some good? What are you—?"

Just then the bell rang, and Carrie jumped. Shoot. She had to get to class.

Carrie gazed at the unicorn. "I want those pages back, Bob—wherever you put them. But we'll have to talk about that later." Carrie stuffed her journal into her backpack, then looked from Bob to her bag and back again. "What should I do with you?" she asked.

"I suppose I can ride in the front pocket," Bob said, "but it's going to make these knots in my mane even worse. I'm going to need some detangler when we get home—and some moisturizer, too. The air in there is so dry."

"Fine," Carrie said. "Detangler and moisturizer. I'm sure my sister has plenty of both. Just get in. And get me those journal pages."

"You'll have them soon enough," Bob said with a smirk. Then she jumped into the backpack.

Carrie wanted to ask the unicorn what she

meant by "soon enough," but she had to get going if she didn't want to be late. Music class was on the other side of the school.

Thankfully she made it into Mrs. Hendrickson's room just as the final bell was ringing. There was only one seat left—the chair closest to the door—so Carrie sank into it, panting, and pulled her backpack onto her lap. When she'd recovered from her hundred-yard dash across the school, she glanced across the room and saw Anna and Theresa. They were both looking at her, concerned.

"Where were you during lunch?" Theresa mouthed, but Carrie just shook her head. She'd have to explain later—once she'd come up with a good explanation. Something other than, *I was just hanging out with my friend Bob the Unicorn.* That didn't seem like it would go over very well.

"Okay, it's time to get started," Mrs. Wessex said from the front of the room. "First we're going to hold the tryouts for the roles, and then we'll talk about what the rest of you will be doing for the play. For everyone who's auditioning, I'm going to give you a script and have you read in groups. Then Mrs. Hendrickson will have each of you sing for her."

Carrie looked down at her desk. Great. Now

she had to sit and watch her classmates try out for roles that she could have had a shot at if she hadn't been such a wimp. Oh, well. It wouldn't be so bad working on set design. She did like to draw. And at least she, Theresa, and Anna would be working together.

Mrs. Wessex slipped on her reading glasses and grabbed the audition sign-up sheet from the piano. She paused before reading the first name and cast a quick glance at some papers on the table behind her. When she turned back around, she stared right at Carrie.

"The first group will be . . . *Carrie Weingarten*— along with Sharon Ross and Kimberly Price." Mrs. Wessex smiled at Carrie as though they were sharing a secret joke, but all Carrie could do was stare.

She couldn't have heard that right. Had Mrs. Wessex really said her name? No way. Carrie hadn't written her name on that sign-up sheet. What was Mrs. Wessex thinking?

Sharon and Kimberly both walked up to the front of the room and took copies of scripts from their teacher, but Carrie was frozen in her seat.

"Carrie? Are you ready?" Mrs. Wessex prodded gently.

Carrie clutched her backpack closer, still not moving. "Ow!" she heard from inside the zippered pocket. Then there was a muffled, "Get up there!" Carrie glanced down to see the zipper coming undone and a tiny horn poking through the opening.

"Uh—" She gulped.

"Carrie?" Mrs. Wessex said again. "Why don't you come on up? I know you're really excited about this play."

You do? Carrie thought. *But how?* Then she saw it. The telltale blue glitter, sparkling in the light.

Bob had put the pages *someplace where they'd do some good,* she had said. So that's what she'd meant. Somehow she'd managed to get them to Mrs. Wessex. Carrie glared down at the unicorn.

"No need to thank me," Bob said. "Just go."

"Carrie?" Mrs. Wessex called.

Carrie looked at Anna and Theresa, who were both smiling and nodding at her.

"Bust a move, Scoob," Spence said, causing a few girls to giggle. His unique way of speaking—and the fact that he was Matt Dana's friend—had already earned him his share of admirers.

Carrie felt like dying, but what could she do? It was either sit there like an idiot while Mrs.

Wessex called her name again and again or get up and do the audition. Neither option appealed to her, but bowing out at this point seemed like an even worse idea.

So, with a deep breath, Carrie stood and walked up to the front of the room. Like it or not, she was about to try out for the class play.

CHAPTER
Six

Carrie could barely hold the script, her hands were shaking so badly. "I—I'm going to the prom, and you can't stop me," she read aloud. Her voice was trembling, too.

"Cindy, you know you're grounded this weekend," Sharon read as Cindy's stepmom. Sharon hadn't looked too happy when Mrs. Wessex had said Carrie would be reading the Cindy Rellar part, but then Mrs. Wessex had explained that she was simply listening to the way everyone read. She'd decide who should play which parts later.

"But I'm grounded *every* weekend," Carrie argued as Cindy. She looked at Sharon and tried to imagine her as a cruel stepmom who would never let Carrie do anything. It wasn't much of a stretch. "You always let *her* go anywhere she wants," Carrie continued, pointing at Kimberly, who was reading the part of Cindy's stepsister, Staci. "I did all my chores, just like you asked. You can't keep me from going to the dance!"

"Get real, Cindy," Kimberly read, sticking her nose in the air. She, too, seemed pretty well suited for the role she was reading. "If Mom let you go to the dance, what would you wear, anyway? Those *jeans* you have on every day? And that ratty old sweatshirt?"

"I could borrow one of your dresses," Carrie shot back. "You have plenty." Her voice had more of an edge to it now—probably because she was beginning to feel a little angry on her character's behalf. Cindy's stepsister and stepmother were so nasty.

As they went on, Carrie continued to feel less like she was reading a part and more like she, Sharon, and Kimberly were having an actual fight. By the end of the scene she'd all but forgotten that the entire class was watching—until Mrs. Wessex cut in.

"Nice job," Mrs. Wessex said after Sharon had read the last line. "Great work, all of you."

Carrie blinked. She'd been so focused on the scene, she'd almost forgotten where she was.

"Now let's hear each of you sing something,"

Mrs. Wessex continued, "and then we'll move on to the next group. Carrie, why don't you go first?"

"Oh. Uh, okay," Carrie said.

"We're simply going to have everyone sing two verses of 'The Happy Wanderer,' which Mrs. Hendrickson tells me you've been working on in class. Mrs. Hendrickson will do a brief introduction on the piano so you can get the key, and then you can come in. Ready, Carrie?"

Carrie nodded, but she felt her stomach tossing and turning all over again. Reading was one thing—singing was on a completely different level. There was much more potential for embarrassment.

As Mrs. Hendrickson began, Carrie's mouth suddenly went dry. She licked her lips, but it didn't seem to do the trick. When the music came around to the spot where Carrie was supposed to come in, she opened her mouth, but no words came out—just a little squeak.

A few students chuckled, and Carrie coughed and cleared her throat.

"Would you like me to start again?" Mrs. Hendrickson asked, giving her a warm smile.

"Yes, please," Carrie said, her voice barely a whisper. She cleared her throat again and moistened her lips.

Sharon let out a sigh. "I guess we'll be here for a while," she muttered.

Carrie tried to ignore her. She knew Sharon was just mad that she hadn't gotten to read Cindy's lines.

But as Mrs. Hendrickson started playing the song a second time, Carrie felt her mouth going dry again, and she worried that Sharon might be right. Then, just before Mrs. Hendrickson reached Carrie's cue, Carrie felt a prick right above her ankle. She glanced down and saw Bob perched on her shoe. She was so shocked, she gasped slightly. It wasn't much of a noise, but it was enough that when Mrs. Hendrickson finished the intro, this time Carrie was able to find her voice.

She blurted out the first few words, realizing the notes were a little off, but at least she'd managed to get started. And by the second line Carrie had the melody under control. Eventually, she was able to concentrate on the music and shut out everything else—even Bob.

"My backpack on my baaaaack," she finished. Then she waited with her eyes closed as Mrs. Hendrickson played the last notes on the piano.

The room was absolutely silent, and Carrie

swallowed a few times, afraid to make eye contact with anyone. Then, to her surprise, people began clapping. Carrie opened her eyes to see Anna and Theresa with their thumbs up, grinning wildly. Then she saw Maria Mancini mouth, "Wow," to Lauren Graham, and Lauren nodded. Amazingly, no one seemed to be laughing.

"Carrie, that was beautiful," Mrs. Hendrickson said.

Carrie slowly met her gaze. "Really?" she asked, her heart thumping in her chest.

"Yes," Mrs. Wessex agreed. "What a wonderful voice you have! I'm so glad you decided to audition," she added, her eyes twinkling. She reached for the journal pages on the table and passed them to Carrie with a smile.

Carrie felt a few light pokes at her ankle and looked down to see Bob prancing back and forth between her shoes, doing some kind of weird unicorn victory dance.

Okay, so maybe Bob had done her a favor after all. Now that the audition was over, Carrie was glad she'd gone through with it. It hadn't been nearly as bad as she'd expected. And Mrs. Wessex and Mrs. Hendrickson—and even some of the other kids—seemed to think she'd actually done okay.

Maybe she had a shot at making her dream come true after all.

"Fifty-one, fifty-two, sixty-three, sixty-four—"

"Hey! You skipped ahead," Bob interrupted.

Carrie paused, holding the toothbrush in midair. "Okay. You know that whole *one hundred strokes a day* thing is just a myth, right?" she said. "It's not really going to make your hair any shinier."

"Interesting theory," Bob said. "I'll think about it while you do the last forty-six strokes."

Carrie rolled her eyes, but she went on brushing. It was easier than listening to the demanding little unicorn whine about how matted her mane was getting from traveling by backpack.

To pacify her, Carrie had gotten a spare toothbrush from the school nurse after lunch and promised to comb out Bob's hair during social studies. Mrs. Wessex was always good about giving out bathroom passes.

"Ninety-nine, one hundred," Carrie finished. "There—are you satisfied?"

Bob pranced back and forth on the countertop, tossing her freshly brushed mane like a show horse. "Ahhh," she sighed. "Much better, don't you think?"

Carrie rolled her eyes. "Whatever you say, Bob."

"*Bob!*" the unicorn scoffed. "Ugh. You have got to stop calling me that."

"What do you want me to call you?"

"Anything," Bob said. "Anything. But. Bob."

"Jim?" Carrie ventured with a smirk.

"Oh, you're a riot," Bob said.

"Sorry," Carrie replied with a chuckle. "How about . . ." She racked her brain for a name the unicorn would like. "Sabrina?"

Bob shook her mane. "Sounds like a cat," she said.

"All right. What about . . . Ella?"

"As in *Ella-phant*?" Bob snorted. "No thanks."

"Wow, you're picky," Carrie said.

"No, I'm not," Bob replied. "You just haven't mentioned any good names yet."

"*O-kay* . . . Mary?"

"Too plain."

"Angelica?"

"Sounds snobby."

"Margaret?"

"Too stiff."

"Polly?"

"As in *'wants a cracker'*?"

"Bob!" Carrie snapped. "Those are all perfectly good names."

"This from the girl who named me *Bob*," Bob muttered.

Carrie shook her head. "Forget it. We'll have to come up with something later. Right now we have to get back to class."

"Okay," Bob said, checking herself out in the mirror one more time. "But first let's go look at that cast list."

"The cast list?"

"Yeah. Didn't Mrs. Hendrickson say she'd have it posted by the end of the day?"

"Well, yeah, but—"

"It's the end of the day. So let's go look," Bob said.

Carrie groaned. "I don't know."

"What do you mean, you don't know? Don't you want to see what part you got?"

"But what if I didn't get one?"

"Are you kidding? Of course you got one. Your audition was great. Didn't you hear your teachers and your friends? They were all gushing about your voice."

"Yeah," Carrie said, "but they're my teachers and my friends. What else are they going to say?"

Bob stamped her hooves impatiently on the sink. "You're a piece of work, you know it? You have to believe in yourself, Carrie."

"I do," Carrie insisted. "Most of the time."

"Yeah, well . . . no time like the present," Bob said.

"What's that supposed to—wait! Bob!" Carrie called, but it was too late. Bob had speared Carrie's bathroom pass with her crooked horn and scooted under the door. By the time Carrie had thrown the toothbrush into her backpack and gotten out of the bathroom, Bob was rounding the corner at the end of the hall.

"Bob!" Carrie hissed, but the little unicorn continued at a gallop, and Carrie had no choice but to chase her. She raced after Bob down one hall and around the corner, then down another hall and up a flight of stairs.

She finally caught up to Bob just outside Mrs. Hendrickson's classroom, arriving there out of breath for the second time that day. Bob slowed to a trot and then pranced around the group of kids who were crowded around the music room door. Carrie stood back, noticing that most of her class was out there.

"What's going on?" Carrie said to no one in particular.

"Mrs. Wessex let us out early to look at the cast list," Maria replied. "You should check it out," she added with a grin.

Carrie looked at the group of people clustered there. They were all scanning a piece of paper that was taped to the outside. The cast list.

I can't do it, Carrie thought. *I can't look.*

Just then Anna, who was near the front of the group with Theresa, caught sight of her. "Hey, Carrie! Come see where your name is!" she called.

"I—I got a part?" Carrie murmured.

"You've got to be joking, girl," Spence said, clapping her on the back. "With that voice you really think there's a chance you *didn't* get one?"

"Well . . ."

"Carrie! Come look!" Theresa called.

Oh, boy, Carrie thought. *Here goes.* Slowly, she walked forward. Her friends seemed excited—that was a good sign, right? Then again, they hadn't expected Carrie to try out for the play in the first place. They'd probably be psyched to see her name next to *Prom Guest #1.* Carrie, on the other hand, was hoping for more, and she was afraid she was about to be disappointed.

"Believe in yourself!" she heard a little voice call. Then she heard the sound of tiny hooves prancing away down the hall.

All right, Carrie thought. *Here goes.*

She walked to the front of the crowd and

scanned the names on the list. Kimberly had gotten the part of Cindy's stepmom, and Lauren Graham was Staci, Cindy's stepsister. Maria was playing the other stepsister, Drew, and Jeremy and Billy were part of the prom band.

Carrie continued to run through the list, all the way down to the tiniest parts—but she didn't see her name anywhere. Her stomach tightened as a wave of disappointment rushed over her. It didn't seem fair. She'd actually had the guts to try out—well, with a little push from Bob, but still. And look what had happened.

She hadn't even managed to get Princess Charming, who only had a couple of lines and then sang one song with the chorus. And forget about Prom Guest #1—that had gone to Sally Betze.

"So—what do you think it means?" Theresa asked.

That I suck, Carrie thought. Why were her friends being so mean, anyway? Were they trying to make a point by showing her that she hadn't made the list?

"You should go in now," Anna said. "Mrs. Hendrickson is in there."

Carrie squinted. "What are you talking about?" she asked.

Theresa rolled her eyes. "Didn't you see?" she

said, tapping the top of the paper. There were a few sentences there, but Carrie had skipped over them and gone straight to the list of names. Now, however, she took a minute to read them.

The lead role of Cindy Rellar is being adapted. Sharon Ross and Carrie Weingarten, please come see me ASAP.
—Mrs. Hendrickson

Carrie's eyes widened. *Adapted?* What did that mean?

"Excuse me, I need to see the list," Sharon said, pushing her way through the crowd.

"Hey, Sharon, there's a—" Theresa began.

"Hold on," Sharon said, waving her hand impatiently. "I have to find my name." She scanned the list, just as Carrie had, and then blinked.

"I don't get it," she said. "Why isn't my name up there? Hey, wait a second . . . I don't even see Cindy Rellar listed. What's going on?"

"That's what I was trying to tell you," Theresa said. She pointed at the note.

Sharon read it, and her expression settled into a deep frown. "*Adapted?* What does that mean? And why would she want to talk to both of us?" she added, scowling at Carrie.

"I don't know," Carrie said.

"Well, let's go find out," Sharon replied. Without hesitation, she pushed open the music room door and marched in.

"You wanted to see us?" Sharon said as she and Carrie approached the piano, where Mrs. Hendrickson was looking over some music.

"Yes," Mrs. Hendrickson said, standing. "I wanted to talk to you about the lead role—Cindy Rellar. You see, Mrs. Wessex and I were troubled over what to do. We had two extremely talented young ladies and only one lead role. It just didn't seem right to choose either one of you when you were both so good."

Carrie's jaw dropped. Mrs. Hendrickson was talking about her. *She* was one of the extremely talented young ladies.

"So . . . what are you saying?" Sharon asked. Her whole face had gone white. "Neither one of us gets to be in the play?"

Mrs. Hendrickson laughed. "No, of course not," she said. "What we decided to do is split the lead role into *two* lead roles, which would have been hard to explain on the cast list. Carrie will be Cindy, and you, Sharon, will be Cindy's best friend—Rae Punzille, who's staying with Cindy and Cindy's family while her mother is away on business."

"I'm playing . . . ?" Carrie couldn't even say it.

"Cindy Rellar—yes," Mrs. Hendrickson said. "Is that all right?"

"Oh—*yeah*. I mean—yes—definitely," Carrie stammered.

The lead. Carrie had actually won *the lead* in the class play! Sure, she was splitting it with Sharon, but that didn't matter. It was still the lead role—exactly what she had wanted but had been too scared to really hope for. She couldn't wait to tell Anna and Theresa.

"We're going to divide up the lines that were originally Cindy's between the two of you," Mrs. Hendrickson explained, "and Mrs. Wessex will add a little more dialogue for both of you so you'll still have plenty to do. Then we'll have you sing a duet with two solo parts. You have such nice voices—I can't wait to hear how beautiful you sound together!"

The lead role. A duet. Two solo parts. Two. Solo. Parts. *Wait a second* . . . solo? The word bounced around in Carrie's brain like a Super Ball let loose in a gymnasium. Suddenly everything began to sink in. Carrie was going to be acting in front of a whole audience. And singing. Solo. *Alone*. She gulped.

"Mrs. Wessex will have the new scripts for you tomorrow," Mrs. Hendrickson said. "We worked on them a bit this afternoon, and she's making the finishing touches at home tonight so they'll be all ready for our first rehearsal. Congratulations, both of you."

"Thanks, Mrs. Hendrickson," Sharon said.

"Yeah, thanks," Carrie echoed, but her mouth had gone dry again and her voice was a bit raspy.

"So—what did she say?" Theresa asked as Carrie and Sharon exited the music room.

"They're splitting the lead," Sharon said. "Carrie's playing Cindy, and they're writing an entirely new role for me."

"Way to go, Scoob!" Spence said.

"That's awesome!" Theresa added.

"Wow, Carrie," Anna said. "You got the lead!"

"Actually," Sharon cut in, "*I* got the lead. I'm playing Rae Punzille. Mrs. Wessex is creating the role just for me."

"If Rae Punzille is the lead, how come the play is called *Cindy Rellar: A Modern Fairy Tale*?" Anna asked.

"I don't know," Sharon replied, tossing her hair over her shoulder. "All I know is that Mrs.

Hendrickson and Mrs. Wessex thought I deserved a bigger part, so they're making one for me. I'd call that the lead. And I wouldn't be surprised if they changed the name of the play, either."

"*O-kay*," Theresa said. She raised her eyebrows at Carrie and Anna.

"Hey—keep it chill, ladies," Spence cut in. "It's all good. The important thing is that you both got parts. And even more important is the fact that I'm going to be the emcee."

"The *emcee?*" Theresa questioned.

"Spence is the narrator," Matt said, stepping forward. He'd been so quiet, Carrie hadn't even noticed him standing there before.

"You say narrator, I say emcee," said Spence. "It's all the same. But what about you, dude? You're the man—you're Charlie Prinze."

Carrie glanced back at the list. Matt was playing the male lead? How had she missed that?

"That's awesome, Matt," Theresa said.

"Yeah," said Matt, but he didn't exactly look thrilled.

"Mrs. Wessex *made* Matt audition," Anna explained. "She said there weren't enough boys on the list and that he was a really good reader, so . . ."

Matt scowled. "So I'm Charlie Prinze—Cindy's prom date."

"Cheer up, buddy," Spence said, clapping him on the shoulder. "Maybe you can pick Carrie up for the prom on your skateboard."

Matt's frown dissolved, and he raised his eyebrows. "Do you think Mrs. W. would go for that?" he asked.

"Why not?" said Spence. "It's supposed to be a modern fairy tale. Tell you what—we'll start working on getting your skateboard in the play just as soon as I convince her to change *narrator* to *emcee* in the program."

Matt chuckled. "Cool," he said.

"Well," Sharon said, folding her arms across her chest, "for all we know, you might be taking Rae to the prom now—not Cindy. We'll just have to wait and see when Mrs. Wessex hands out the new scripts tomorrow."

Carrie swallowed hard. Sharon seemed pretty upset about the way things had turned out.

"Hey, um . . . congratulations, Sharon," she said, trying to smooth things over. "I'm really glad we're going to be in the play together. And I know I'll feel a lot more comfortable being onstage with you. It's just like you said at lunch yesterday, remember? You'll be up there to help me out if I get nervous." She gave Sharon a weak smile, hoping she would agree that things really had turned out for the best.

Sharon held Carrie's gaze, but she didn't return the smile. "Yeah, I guess so," she said. "But you know, even I'm not going to be able to help you if you just freeze up the way you did in your audition today. If you don't kick that stage fright before opening night, you're going to ruin the whole play. Come on, Kimberly. Let's go," she added, and the two of them headed off down the hallway.

Carrie stared after Sharon, realizing that even though she'd gotten through the audition okay, her troubles weren't over. Now she had an entirely new problem to confront: her costar.

CHAPTER
Seven

"Can you even *see* with all that hair in your eyes?" Bob asked.

It was Wednesday afternoon, and Carrie had stopped at the bathroom before play rehearsal to give Bob her daily brushing.

"Of course I can," Carrie said. Although she did have to kind of squint to look past her bangs sometimes. "Ninety-eight, ninety-nine, one hundred," she counted. "There." She stuffed the toothbrush into her backpack and watched as Bob pranced back and forth on the counter, admiring her mane.

"You know what I don't get?" Carrie asked.

"What?"

"Why you care so much about how you look when I'm the only one who can see you," Carrie said. "Are all unicorns this vain?"

Bob stopped and faced Carrie. "It's not vanity,"

she insisted, stamping her hooves. "I just take good care of myself, and I happen to take a certain pride in my appearance. Unlike you, I'm not scared to stand out."

Carrie scrunched her eyebrows together. "*What* are you talking about?"

"You," Bob said, "and the way you hide behind that wall of hair. It's like you're afraid to be noticed."

Carrie clicked her tongue. "I am not," she said. "I just don't care all that much about my appearance."

"You *say* that," Bob said. "But I'm not so sure it's true."

"Of course it's true," Carrie said. "If I cared about my appearance, I'd let Theresa find me some hair clips and get some lip gloss and try to look like the cover of every teen magazine in the grocery store."

"*Maybe,*" Bob admitted. "But if what you say is true and you really *don't* care about your appearance, why did you get so worked up about trying out for the play?"

"Because I was afraid I'd make a fool of myself," Carrie said.

"You mean by messing up lines or singing off-key or something and then having people laugh at you or think you're stupid because of the way you would *appear* to them?"

"Well . . . *yeah*, but—"

"See, I think it's pretty much the same. It all comes down to worrying about the way other people see you," Bob said. "Which is why you don't even want to let anybody look."

"What do you mean?"

"I mean," Bob said slowly, "that you let your hair hang in your face so you can hide. When you don't want people to know what you're thinking or how you feel, you just look down, and that mass of curls covers everything—your eyes, your expression—everything."

"You're crazy," Carrie said.

"You're the one talking to a unicorn," Bob reminded her.

"True," Carrie replied, "and if I don't stop, I'm going to be late for rehearsal." She hefted her backpack onto the counter and unzipped the front pocket. "Hop in."

"Fine," Bob said. "But when you're reading your lines today, get that hair out of your face and speak up. Don't be afraid to really try."

Carrie pushed open the bathroom door and stepped into the hallway. "You sound like my mother," she told the unicorn.

"Who does?" Sharon asked.

Carrie started, surprised to see Sharon just one step behind her. "Oh, um . . . no one. I was just practicing. For the play. Trying to, you know, figure out how I would feel if I were Cindy."

Sharon rolled her eyes. "It's called *getting into character*," she said. "We've worked on that a lot in my drama class."

"Oh," Carrie replied. She was already sick of hearing about Sharon's drama class. Fortunately, Sharon was silent as they walked down the hall. Unfortunately, it was the kind of silence that made Carrie feel like Sharon wanted to bite her head off, chew it up, and spit it out.

When they were almost to the music room, Sharon stopped and turned to Carrie. "Look," she said, "I'm not exactly thrilled about the whole double-lead thing."

"Really?" Carrie said. "Gee—I never would have guessed."

"Funny," Sharon sneered. "Anyway, the thing is, I want this play to be good."

"So do I," Carrie said.

"Well, that means *you* need to be good. You're going to be onstage for most of the play, so you can't freeze or forget your lines or stutter through them."

Carrie swallowed hard. Those were all things she was afraid she might do. They were all things she *had* done when she was giving her King Tut presentation, and that had only had to be two minutes long. The play would probably last at least an hour, and like Sharon said—Carrie was going to be onstage for most of it. "I—I know," she told Sharon.

"Good," Sharon said. "So here's what you need to do. Today is just a read through."

"A read through?"

"Yeah. That's when the cast just sits in a circle and reads straight through the script so that everyone gets to do all their lines."

"Oh," Carrie said. That didn't sound too bad.

"But even though it's just a read through, there are two things you should start working on now: your voice and your movements."

Carrie tilted her head. Why was Sharon telling her all of this? She actually seemed to be helping.

"When you're onstage," Sharon continued, "you have to realize that it's not like TV."

"Thank goodness," Carrie muttered. She was scared enough about performing in front of an auditorium full of people. She certainly didn't need the added pressure of being broadcast to millions more.

"On TV, actors have microphones and sound people to make their voices loud enough. Plus they have cameras to do close-ups so you can always see if they're smiling or upset or whatever. But onstage, it's just *you*."

Again Carrie swallowed hard. If this was supposed to be a pep talk, it wasn't working.

"So when you're reading your lines, remember these two things: you need to talk really loud and make your movements really big. Got it?"

Carrie squinted, then nodded. "I guess," she said.

"And you need to start doing both of those today," Sharon went on.

"But I thought you said it's just a . . . *read through*?" Carrie asked.

"It is," Sharon said. "But if you start out reading in your regular voice and not moving around at all, you're going to get used to it. Then when we start practicing for real, you'll have to break those habits. And considering the fact that you already have stage fright to worry about . . ."

Carrie sucked in her breath and rubbed her sweaty palms together. The butterflies in her stomach made her wonder if it was possible to have stage fright when she wasn't even onstage.

And if she got it right now, would it be called *hall fright*? Or just *Sharon fright*?

"I could give you a few other tips," Sharon offered.

"You have . . . *more*?" Carrie asked, her eyes widening.

Sharon must have noticed the concern in Carrie's eyes because she backed off. "Actually, why don't you just work on those for today: talking loud—it's called projecting," she added, "and making your movements big. Use your hands, your arms, your head—you could even stand up, although Mrs. Wessex will probably want us all to just sit at the table today."

Carrie nodded. "All right," she said, taking a deep breath. "Talk loud, use big movements. I can do that."

"That's it," Sharon said. "And if you do it from the beginning, it'll be easy when you're finally onstage."

"Right," Carrie said.

Sharon started toward the music room again, but Carrie stopped her.

"Um, Sharon?" she said. "Thanks."

Sharon just shrugged. "Like I said—I want this play to be good."

Carrie nodded and followed her into their first

rehearsal, feeling a little guilty for having assumed that Sharon would be hard to work with.

When they got inside, Carrie noticed that the room was set up exactly as Sharon had predicted. There was a big table in the center of the room, with chairs around it, and there was a script at each seat. Matt and Spence were already there, along with Maria, Lauren, Kimberly, Sally, Jeremy, Billy, and the rest of the cast. It looked like Sharon and Carrie were the last to arrive.

"Okay, everyone—we're all here now," Mrs. Wessex said. "Let's get started." Everyone filed over to the table and took a seat. Carrie ended up between Maria and Lauren with Sharon, Matt, and Spence directly across from her.

"We're just doing a read through today," Mrs. Wessex said. Carrie caught Sharon's eye and smiled. She'd been right about everything so far. Again Sharon just shrugged like it was old news to her—like she'd been going to play rehearsals every day of her life.

"If everyone will flip to page one, we'll jump right in," Mrs. Wessex said. The noise of rustling paper filled the room as everyone opened their scripts. "As you can see, the play now starts with a solo by Cindy."

Carrie's shoulders tensed. She had to start the whole play? *Alone?*

"But we'll be skipping the songs for today and focusing on the straight speaking parts."

Phew, Carrie thought. She needed more time to work up to the whole solo idea. "So that means we'll be starting with you, Ward," Mrs. Wessex said, nodding to Spence. He'd already given her his whole MC Spence spiel, but Mrs. Wessex was a stickler for using people's real names.

"That's cool," Spence said. He cleared his throat and began to read. "Good evening, ladies and gentlemen. Welcome to the fifth-grade production of *Cindy Rellar: A Modern Fairy Tale.* Our story unfolds—" Spence set down his script and looked up. "Hey, Mrs. W.—I thought this was supposed to be modern."

"It is, Ward."

"So then why am I saying stuff like, 'our story unfolds'? Shouldn't it be more, I don't know . . . hip?"

Mrs. Wessex furrowed her brow. "What did you have in mind?"

Spence shrugged. "I don't know, something like . . . *Yo! This is the story of Cindy Rellar / Wants to go to the prom, but they keep her in the cellar. / She's got a harsh stepmom and some stepsisters, too; /*

They're in her face, they're on her case, they want her glass shoe. / She—"

"Uh, thank you, Ward," Mrs. Wessex interrupted amidst the giggles and squeals of everyone around the table. Matt was nearly doubled over with laughter, and Sharon was staring at Spence with awe. Even Carrie, who was trying so hard to focus on the tips Sharon had given her, had to smile.

"I'll definitely take that into consideration," Mrs. Wessex said. "But for now, why don't we just read what's in the script?"

"Whatever you say, Mrs. W.," Spence said. And he went back to reading his regular lines, which, admittedly, sounded kind of boring after the little rap he'd just done.

When Spence was finished with the introduction, Mrs. Wessex spoke up again. "Well, maybe we *could* spice that up a bit," she said, giving Spence a little smile. "But let's keep going for now. Carrie?"

Carrie checked the script. The next lines were hers. She cleared her throat and took a deep breath, then glanced across the table at Sharon.

"Big," Sharon mouthed. *"And loud."* Carrie nodded, and Sharon gave her a thumbs-up. Then Carrie cleared her throat one more time and got ready.

According to the stage directions in the script, Cindy was supposed to be cleaning the floor as the play started. *Big movements,* Carrie thought as she set her script on the table. *And talk loud.* She sat up straight and gripped an imaginary sponge in one hand and pretended to be carrying a bucket in the other. "Work, work, work!" she bellowed. "That's all I ever do around here! If only my stepsisters—"

"Uh, Carrie?" Mrs. Wessex cut in. "I'm glad you've found your voice, but it probably doesn't need to be quite that loud."

Carrie blinked at Sharon, who seemed to be smirking. "I was just trying to, um . . . *project,*" Carrie said, hoping she'd used the right word.

"Oh, yes." Mrs. Wessex nodded. "I understand. And that's very important. But this is just a read through, and there will be microphones hanging above the stage."

"There will?" Carrie shot a fierce look at Sharon, who just shrugged innocently.

"Of course," Mrs. Wessex said. "So I'm sure your voice will carry beautifully."

"Oh," Carrie said. "Right."

"So, why don't we start that scene again, and just use your normal speaking voice. That should be fine."

Carrie looked back to the script, trying to focus on her lines, but she couldn't help feeling a little stupid. Of course, it didn't help that Maria and Lauren both had their hands over their mouths like they were trying hard not to laugh.

Forget them, Carrie told herself. *Just read.* She cleared her throat a third time and pretended to be holding her sponge and bucket again. "Work, work, work," she repeated, this time in her regular voice. "That's all I ever do around here. If only my stepsisters would help out. Then maybe I'd have time to go to the mall and find a dress for the prom."

At that point the stage directions called for Cindy to continue cleaning the floor while the narrator said a few more lines. So Carrie dipped her imaginary sponge in her imaginary bucket and pretended to scrub the table.

Big movements, she told herself, moving her hand in a large circle. Unfortunately, her big movement knocked over Lauren's big water bottle and made a big puddle in the middle of the table.

"Carrie!" Lauren yelled.

"I didn't mean to," Carrie said. "I was just . . . pretending to scrub the floor."

Mrs. Wessex took a deep breath. "Matt, could

you go get us some paper towels, please? Charlie Prinze doesn't come in until the next scene."

"Sure," Matt said, standing and sprinting toward the door.

"Walk, please!" Mrs. Wessex called after him. Matt slowed down until he got to the door, but everyone heard his footsteps speed up again as soon as he was in the hall.

Mrs. Wessex sighed and shook her head. "All right, let's keep going," she said. "But why don't we just focus on *reading* today," she added, looking straight at Carrie. "This is a small space, and we don't want to have any more accidents. There will be plenty of time to work out all of our movements and gestures when we begin practicing on the stage."

"Yeah, no more scrubbing the table, Carrie," Sharon joked. "At least not till Matt gets back with the paper towels."

Everyone else laughed, but Carrie just bit her lip. She felt like such an idiot. Partly for yelling her lines and knocking over Lauren's water, but mostly for having believed that Sharon would actually try to help her.

"All right, calm down, everyone," Mrs. Wessex said, looking a bit weary. "Ward, let's take it from your next line. Ready?"

"No worries, Mrs. W.—I've got it all under control," Spence said. "Check this out." Spence stood up, holding a piece of paper on which he'd scribbled some words instead of his script. Then he started rapping again.

"The big dance was only a week away,
But Cindy Rellar didn't have no time to play.
She had to cook, she had to clean, she had to scrub the floor,
And whenever she finished, they just gave her more—
More work to do, more jobs, more stress,
When all Cindy wanted was to score a dress."

Spence finished his rap and glanced up. "What do you think?" he asked. Everyone around the table started clapping and whistling, but Mrs. Wessex was holding her head in her hands.

"It was . . . *very imaginative*, Ward," she said when the applause had died down. "But we can't just have everyone changing their lines around anytime they wish. I think it's important at this point that we stick to the script."

Spence frowned. "But—"

Just then Matt returned . . . riding his skateboard. He rolled across the music room floor, tossed a bundle of paper towels to Spence, and then came to a dramatic stop right in front of

Mrs. Wessex, kicking his board into the air and catching it.

"Matthew Dana!" Mrs. Wessex exclaimed. "What do you think you're doing? You know you can't ride that thing in here!"

"It's for the play," Matt said.

Mrs. Wessex's eyebrows shot into the air. "It's . . . *what*?"

"For the play," Matt repeated. "See, Spence and I figured Charlie Prinze would be a skater. Hey—do you think Mrs. Hendrickson would let me use the risers as rails?"

Mrs. Wessex glanced around the table, then pressed her eyes closed. "Let's take five, everybody," she said. "Use the bathroom, get a drink of water. I'll wipe off the table, and we'll meet right back here."

Nobody needed to hear that announcement twice. In no time they were all on their feet and headed out of the room. But just as Carrie was about to go, Mrs. Wessex stopped her.

"Carrie," she said, "as one of the leads in the play, I think you could help to set a more serious tone for these rehearsals. Now, I know you're nervous, but when you come back from the break, I'd like you to try to focus on simply reading your lines. No shouting, no actions, no gestures—just straightforward reading. Do you think you can do that?"

"Um, sure," Carrie said. "I'll try."

"Thank you," Mrs. Wessex said. "I think that will make a big difference."

Carrie's heart sank as she walked out the door. So far, the rehearsal wasn't going very well, and it seemed like Mrs. Wessex thought Carrie was to blame. She'd been so stupid to trust Sharon.

Almost as stupid as Mrs. Wessex was to trust me with a lead role, Carrie thought.

CHAPTER
Eight

"I hate that store, you know," Carrie whispered as she walked out of Sara's with Bob perched on her shoulder. "And I don't see how you're going to make that big green butterfly clip work in your mane."

"Trust me," the tiny unicorn said. "It'll be perfect. You'll see."

"Whatever," Carrie muttered. She was just glad to be out of there and on her way to Sound Factory. According to Spence, they had some new V-3 disks that were "kickin'," as Spence said. Carrie wanted to grab a copy before they sold out.

That was where she'd been headed when Bob had spotted Sara's and thrown a uni-tantrum, demanding that Carrie stop and buy her a few things at the accessory store—a ring she could wear as an anklet, a pair of hoop earrings to use as chokers, a temporary rose tattoo for her left flank, and the green butterfly hair clip, which Carrie thought would look even more ridiculous on Bob than it would on her.

"Okay," Bob said as Carrie headed for the music store. "We have fifteen minutes before we have to meet your friends, right?"

"Right," Carrie replied. She had agreed to meet up with Anna and Theresa after rehearsal to help them scout out prop and costume ideas for the play.

"So . . . whaddya say we make a quick stop in the bathroom so I can try on some of my new stuff?"

"No way," Carrie said. "I'm going to Sound Factory."

"*Pleeeeease,*" said Bob.

"Look—you're lucky I even bought you that stuff after what you got me into," Carrie snapped. An older couple walking past stared at Carrie with concern, and Carrie realized she needed to be more careful about talking to Bob in public.

"You should be excited about the play," Bob said from her perch on Carrie's shoulder. "You got a lead role. That's what you wanted, right?"

"Yeah, back when I was stupid enough to think I could actually pull it off. Weren't you listening at rehearsal today?"

Bob was quiet for a second. "Actually, I took a nap," she admitted. "I need to get my—"

"Beauty sleep?" Carrie guessed. Bob nodded. "Oh, but you're not vain at all," Carrie said sarcastically.

"All right, so I'm a little vain," Bob said. "At least I dare to be myself."

Carrie groaned. "Not this again."

"Sorry," said Bob, "but you're going to keep hearing it till you get it. You need to stop worrying so much about what everyone else thinks and just do your best. And get that hair out of your eyes," she added.

Carrie shook her head. "Vain," she said.

"Stubborn," Bob shot back.

"Sound Factory," Carrie said, "finally." And she headed into the store.

"Ugh," Bob said. "I'm going to take another nap. Wake me up if you see a mirror." And with that, she leaped off Carrie's shoulder and dove straight into the Sara's bag.

"Good riddance," Carrie muttered. She walked over to the hip-hop section and went straight to the *V*s. There wasn't much in there, and it didn't take her long to reach the end. "Shoot," she said. "They're sold out."

"I could burn you a copy," a voice said.

Carrie glanced up to see Spence flipping through the new releases. "Really?" she asked.

"Sure." Spence picked up a CD and passed it to her. "Have you heard this?"

Carrie read the label. *Fuzzy Squash*. "Yeah, but just a couple of songs," she said. "They had it in one of the listening stations last week. It's not that good."

"Too bad," Spence said. "Their first album really rocked."

"Yeah, I heard the second one was pretty good, too," Carrie said, "but I haven't been able to find it here."

Spence leaned closer. "Mall stores never have the best selection," he confided. "There's this place down on Fifth Street, though—near the skate park? It's called Beat of a Different Drummer, and they have tons of stuff. Fewer of the mainstream hits and more bands like Medusa and Safe Zone."

Carrie's eyes widened. "I've been looking for the Safe Zone CD for so long," she said.

"They've got it," Spence told her. "If you ever pick it up, stop by the skate park afterward. Matt and I are there all the time, and I usually have a portable stereo. We could pop it in."

"Cool," Carrie said.

"Carrie!" Theresa and Anna called, running up to her at the same time.

"I told you she'd be here," Theresa said to Anna, and Anna handed her a quarter.

"I guessed food court," Anna said with a shrug. "But anyway . . . how was your first rehearsal?"

"Yeah—tell us all about it," Theresa said.

Carrie grimaced. "It started out bad and got worse," she said.

"Really? What happened?" Theresa asked. Carrie didn't feel much like talking about it, so she looked to Spence for help.

"It's like this," Spence said. "We gave the lines a try, but my rhyming didn't fly, we had Scooby standing by, splashin' water in my eye; we wiped the table dry, Mrs. W. wanted to cry, and when Matt came boarding in, I thought she was gonna die."

Carrie laughed. It was a pretty accurate description, although Anna and Theresa looked totally confused.

"Someone want to explain that again?" Theresa asked. "In English?"

Carrie shook her head. "Not really," she said.

"Oh, come on—it couldn't have been that bad," Anna prodded.

"It was," Carrie said. Her friends looked at her with disbelief. "I'm serious," Carrie insisted. "First I yelled all my lines and spilled water all over the table. Then I was so upset about messing up that I couldn't get any of my lines out. I stuttered through everything in a really quiet voice, and it was so bad that Mrs. Wessex dismissed us early. We didn't even finish the read through."

"Yikes," Anna said.

"Double yikes," Carrie agreed. "It was so bad, I don't even think I should go back tomorrow." She looked at Spence. "You guys would probably be better off without me."

"No way, Scoob—you're the only one that laughs at my rhymes."

Carrie cocked her head. "That's not true," she said. "Everyone laughs at your rhymes."

"Not Mrs. W.," Spence said.

Carrie winced. "Yeah, she doesn't really seem to like it all that much," she told Theresa and Anna.

"Too bad," Theresa said. "I liked the idea of having an emcee instead of a narrator."

"Yeah, I think it works," Anna agreed.

"Me too," said Spence. "I'm going to go home and write up more new lines for tomorrow."

Carrie raised her eyebrows. "You're going to keep doing it?" she asked.

"Yeah, why not?" Spence said. "I gotta be me, and Mrs. W. will come around."

Carrie wasn't so sure about that. "You really think so?"

"Sure," Spence said. "And if she doesn't, what's the worst that can happen? I'll have to do the lines straight up and be boring for a few nights. I can cope."

Wow, Carrie thought. Spence seemed so cool about it all—like it was no big deal. If only she could be that relaxed about the play. Then maybe she'd be able to say her lines without sounding like such a fool. And get up onstage without freezing. And make her dream of becoming an actress come true.

Right, Carrie thought. *And maybe Sharon will apologize for giving me all that bad advice.*

Nope. After today's rehearsal it seemed pretty clear. She wasn't the natural actress that she'd thought she was, and the sooner she gave up on that dream, the better it would be—for everyone.

CHAPTER

Nine

"Carrie—you'd better get up! You're going to be late for school!"

Carrie lay in bed, staring at the glow-in-the-dark moon and stars stickers on her ceiling. She'd gotten them for her seventh birthday and still remembered how cool she'd thought they were.

Just then the door to Carrie's bedroom swung open, and her mom stood there, her arms crossed over her chest. "Your father made you soy pancakes and they're getting cold," she said.

Great—more soy products. Luckily, Lynn had been sneaking her cherry Pop-Tarts on the car ride to school. But not today. Lynn had left early for some kind of college fair. Not that it mattered. Carrie wasn't planning on going to school anyway.

"I don't feel well," she moaned. "I think I'm coming down with something."

Ms. Weingarten rushed over and put her hand on Carrie's forehead. She frowned. "You do feel a little warm," she said. "Let me get the thermometer."

She was back in two seconds and popped the thermometer into Carrie's mouth. Carrie tried to think warm thoughts while they waited for the thermometer to beep. *Summer,* she told herself. *Barbecues, blackflies, mosquitoes.* Finally, the thermometer sounded, and Carrie's mom took it out.

"Hmmm, ninety-eight point eight," Ms. Weingarten said. "That's not much of a fever."

"Yeah, but my stomach really hurts," Carrie said quickly. "Maybe there was something wrong with that casserole Dad made last night." With her father's cooking, food poisoning was always a possibility.

"He *did* use a lot of high-fiber grains," Carrie's mom muttered. "Really, I wouldn't mind if your father calmed down a bit from this *healthy* diet." She shook her head. "I have to admit, lately my stomach's been feeling a little uneasy, too."

"So can I stay home, then?" Carrie asked hopefully. If she could get out of play practice for just one day, she was sure it would run more smoothly without her. Then maybe Mrs. Wessex would be more inclined to let her quit when she asked.

"Well, if your stomach's *really* bothering you—"

A loud crash interrupted her mom, and Carrie looked over to see her backpack on the floor, papers spilled everywhere. Right on top was the bright pink sheet with the rehearsal schedule for the play. A glance at the desk chair where her backpack had been confirmed what Carrie had already suspected. Bob stood on the edge of the chair, looking down at her work with pride.

"How did that happen?" Ms. Weingarten said, walking over to pick up the papers. Without thinking, Carrie jumped out of bed and dashed over to grab the rehearsal schedule before her mom could see it.

"Carrie, you're—what are you doing?" her mom asked. She looked at Carrie with confusion, and then slowly her features transformed into her mom face. Her eyes got all scrunched together and her lips formed a tight line. "Carrie, what's on that piece of paper?" she asked, her voice firm.

Slowly, Carrie handed it over.

"Aha," Ms. Weingarten said, scanning the schedule. "Today is your second rehearsal for the play. Well, you sure got out of bed fast for someone with a horrible stomachache."

Carrie looked down at the floor, feeling bad for lying to her mom. "You don't understand, Mom. I really messed up yesterday. I can't go back. They're better off without me there. Really."

"Carrie, I know you're nervous," her mom said. "But you made a commitment to take this role, and you have to follow through."

Carrie glared at Bob. Stupid unicorn. Now she'd never be able to quit. Even if Mrs. Wessex was willing to let her, her mother never would.

"Don't you need a nap?" Carrie asked as she headed toward Mrs. Hendrickson's room that afternoon.

"Nope," Bob said. She had demanded that Carrie let her ride on her shoulder again, like she had at the mall, because riding in the backpack made her sleepy, and she wanted to stay awake through this rehearsal.

"Are you sure?" Carrie asked. "Because I think you might be getting bags under your eyes."

"Really?" the little unicorn gasped. Then she looked up at Carrie and grinned. "Nice try," she said, "but I'm coming with you. And I'm staying awake. You're going to go in there today and knock 'em dead. Trust me."

Carrie snorted. "Why should I? So far you've stolen my journal, shown pages of it to my teacher, whined until I bought you all kinds of stupid jewelry and hair stuff, and ratted me out to my mom."

"All for your own good," Bob said.

Carrie groaned. "Yeah, well, do me a favor and don't do me any more favors, okay?"

"Believe in yourself and I'll leave you alone," Bob said. Then she jumped off Carrie's shoulder and pranced into Mrs. Hendrickson's room.

"Where are you—?" Carrie started, but Lauren and Maria were coming, so she had to just let Bob go.

"Hey, Carrie, did you practice your lines?" Sharon asked when she saw Carrie walk in.

Carrie nodded. She'd wolfed down her lunch so that she could spend the rest of the period, along with study hall, reading over her lines and song lyrics.

"Well, you better take a look at this," Sharon said, passing her a piece of paper.

"What is it?"

"An e-mail Mrs. Wessex sent me last night.

She asked me to forward it to you, too, but I don't have your e-mail address."

"What do you mean, you don't have my address?" Carrie asked. "You e-mail me all the time."

"I know, but I loaded some new software the other day, and I guess it erased part of my address book. Anyway, take a look at the note."

Carrie squinted at Sharon, not quite sure what to make of her whole e-mail excuse. It certainly didn't sound legitimate. The e-mail itself, however, looked real.

```
Dear Sharon and Carrie—
    After yesterday's rehearsal, I
decided to make a few changes. Sharon, I
would like you to play the part of Cindy
Rellar, and Carrie, I would like you to
take over as Rae Punzille. I believe
that Mrs. Hendrickson and I miscast the
two of you to begin with and that every-
one will benefit from this simple
change. Please study your new lines and
be ready to practice your duet—with
Sharon as Cindy and Carrie as Rae—first
thing at practice tomorrow afternoon.
                    Sincerely,
                    Mrs. Wessex
```

P.S. Sharon, could you please forward this
e-mail to Carrie? I don't have her address.

Carrie blinked and read the note over again. "I—I don't get it," she said. "Why would Mrs. Wessex do this? And why would she just tell you and not me?"

"She has my home e-mail because my mom is part of the Booster Club, but she doesn't have yours. And like I said," Sharon continued, "I would have forwarded it to you, but I couldn't find your address."

Carrie frowned. "But . . . why would she send an e-mail? Why didn't she just tell us in class today or something?"

"You're kidding, right?" Sharon asked. She glanced around, then lowered her voice. "You were practically in tears when you left rehearsal yesterday. She probably didn't dare to tell you in person. You get embarrassed so easily, she probably just thought e-mail would be safer."

"I don't know, Sharon," Carrie said. She skimmed the note again. It did sound like Mrs. Wessex's writing, but Carrie didn't dare to believe what Sharon was saying. What if it was just another trick? *Or worse,* Carrie thought, *what if it isn't?*

What if Mrs. Wessex really had switched their parts? But that didn't sound like something Mrs. Wessex would do—at least not through an e-mail.

Carrie held the note out to Sharon. "I don't buy it," she said. "You're just trying to make me—"

"Carrie? Sharon? Could you come over here, please?" Mrs. Wessex called.

Sharon glowered at Carrie and snatched the paper out of her hand. "Coming," she called, and she headed over to the piano. Carrie followed her cautiously, still wondering about the e-mail and whether it could possibly be true.

"Since we have Mrs. Hendrickson here, I'd like to start out with your duet today," Mrs. Wessex said. "Carrie—did Sharon tell you about the changes I made?"

"The—? You—?" Carrie stared at Sharon in disbelief. Sharon grinned. "She . . . um . . ." It was true. The e-mail had been real. Mrs. Wessex really had switched their roles. And after only one rehearsal.

"Carrie?" Mrs. Wessex asked, furrowing her brow.

"I, uh . . ." Suddenly, Carrie felt like the whole room was spinning. Her face was hot, her arms were tingling, and she felt like she was going to throw up. "I don't feel well," she managed finally. Then she turned and sprinted for the door.

"Carrie?" she heard Mrs. Wessex call, but she wasn't stopping for anything. Carrie kept running until she was outside where she could take deep breaths of the fresh cool air.

"Hey, Scoob—what's up?" Spence called as he rushed out the door.

"Nothing," Carrie said. She wasn't about to explain the situation to Spence or to anyone else. It was too humiliating. Let them hear it from Mrs. Wessex. Or Sharon. "I just—I feel really sick all of a sudden. Can you tell Mrs. Wessex I had to leave?"

"Sure thing," Spence said. "See you tomorrow."

Yeah, Carrie thought, *but probably not at play rehearsal.* After all, it had only taken Mrs. Wessex one play rehearsal to cut Carrie's lines back. After today, she'd probably eliminate Carrie altogether.

CHAPTER
Ten

"Why did you run off like that?" Bob demanded back in Carrie's room.

"Glad to see you were so on top of things today," Carrie said sarcastically. "Thanks for looking out for me."

Bob jumped up onto Carrie's pillow and stared her in the eyes. "Would you cut it out already? I said I was sorry—I just got side-tracked in the prop room. There were all these mirrors. . . ."

Carrie exhaled sharply and rolled over to face the other way. But Bob wouldn't give up. She jumped onto Carrie's head and ran down her cheek onto the pillow so that they were face-to-face again.

"What happened?" she repeated.

"Mrs. Wessex switched me and Sharon. Now

I'm supposed to play Rae, and Sharon's playing Cindy."

Bob snorted and shook her mane. "That doesn't make sense. Why would she do that?"

"Because she doesn't want me to wreck the play."

"Did she say that?" Bob asked.

"No."

"Well, what did she say?"

"Nothing," Carrie said.

"So then . . . how do you know she switched your parts?"

Carrie sighed. "Sharon told me. Mrs. Wessex sent her an e-mail last night, and Sharon showed it to me right before rehearsal."

"That sounds kind of sketchy to me," Bob said.

"I thought so, too," Carrie said, "but then Mrs. Wessex asked me if Sharon had told me about the changes, so I figured it was true."

"Hmmm," Bob grunted. "I don't like the sound of this." She pranced back and forth a few times, tossing her mane, then came to a stop. "Here's what you're going to do. Get—"

"Aaagh!" Carrie groaned. "There's nothing for me to do. I'm a bad actress, and I'm never going to get any better. Would you stop trying to help me?"

Bob stared at her for a moment. "Yes," she said. "But only on one condition. You get Anna and Theresa on the phone and tell them what happened this afternoon. You do that, and I'll leave you alone. Okay?"

Carrie narrowed her eyes at the little unicorn. "Okay," she said. And she grabbed the phone.

One hour later Carrie, Theresa, and Anna were on their way into Access Café on Main Street in Newcastle.

"There's an open computer over there," Anna pointed out. Carrie and Theresa followed her, and they pulled up three chairs in front of the monitor.

"Thanks for the ride," Bob whispered into Carrie's ear. "Don't leave without me."

Carrie felt Bob hopping off her shoulder and watched the unicorn trot off to another free computer in the back corner of the café. True to her word, Bob had left Carrie alone ever since she'd gotten off the phone with Theresa and Anna. Now her friends were the ones who wouldn't let the whole Sharon role-switching thing go.

"I still don't believe Mrs. Wessex sent Sharon that e-mail," Anna said. "I wish you'd stayed for the duet. Then we'd know exactly what changes

Mrs. Wessex was talking about. I'm sure it wasn't anything like what Sharon told you."

Carrie sighed. "I don't know. It makes sense," she said. "I did okay in the audition, but I was terrible at the rehearsal yesterday, and I *was* practically in tears. Mrs. Wessex probably figured I'd be happy to switch parts with Sharon. Rae does have fewer lines. And Cindy is supposed to start the whole play off with a solo. Mrs. Wessex probably just realized there was no way I could pull that off."

"Carrie, cut it out," Theresa said. "You're being way too hard on yourself. For one thing, you were better than okay at the audition—you were *great*."

"And you could definitely pull off the solo," Anna added. "You have an amazing voice—way better than Sharon's."

"Thanks," Carrie said, but she was sure her friends were just being nice. "So . . . why are we here, anyway?"

"To check out Sharon's story," Anna said. "It'll be easier to do here because there's a faster Internet connection. See, first we need to find out Mrs. Wessex's e-mail address. I'm sure she's listed as one of the contacts on the ECS home page, so we can get it from there. Then—"

"Hey, Anna," Theresa interrupted. "Isn't that Mrs. Wessex over there?"

Carrie looked over at the entrance to the café and groaned. "Oh, no. I can't let her see me," she said. "I asked Spence to tell her I was sick!"

"Okay, just try to sit a little lower," Theresa said, "and she won't see you over the monitor."

"What if I go talk to her?" Anna suggested. "I can make sure she sits with her back to us." Without waiting for an answer, Anna jumped up and hurried over to their teacher, who was just starting to look around the café for a spot.

Carrie hunkered down in her chair but tried to peek out enough to watch what happened. She saw Anna talking to Mrs. Wessex, carefully steering her to the other side of the café.

"Isn't she awesome?" Theresa asked Carrie.

"Yeah, she's brave," Carrie agreed.

In a minute Anna was back, and her brown eyes were lit up with excitement. "You guys won't believe this," she said as she sat down next to Carrie. "I knew it! I knew I was right."

"About what?" Theresa asked.

"Listen to this." Anna focused her gaze on Carrie. "Mrs. Wessex just told me that she doesn't usually come here, but she had to because her computer at home isn't working, and she hasn't been able to check her e-mail in three days."

Anna sat back and folded her arms across her chest.

"Oh, my gosh," Theresa began. "That means . . ."

"There's no way she could have sent that e-mail to Sharon!" Anna said. "See? I *knew* Sharon was lying."

"Well, then what did Mrs. Wessex mean when she asked me if Sharon had told me about the *changes*?" Carrie asked.

"I don't know," Anna said. "But it was probably just something small that Sharon blew way out of proportion to upset you."

Carrie shook her head. She'd done it again. She'd fallen for one of Sharon's tricks and let it ruin another whole day of rehearsal.

"Don't worry, Carrie," Anna said. "We'll find a way to get her back."

"Yeah," Theresa said. "You just go home and relax. Work on memorizing your lines or something. Anna and I will come up with a plan to put Sharon in her place."

"Ooh, I can't wait for school tomorrow," Bob said when she and Carrie were back in Carrie's room. They were on Carrie's bed, in the middle of Bob's one hundred brush strokes, since Carrie hadn't gotten a chance to do them at school that day. "What do you think Theresa and Anna are going to do?" Bob asked.

"I don't know," Carrie said. "I'm trying not to think about it too much. Every time I realize that I fell for another one of Sharon's stupid tricks, it makes me want to—"

"Hey, easy on the mane," Bob yelled out.

"Sorry," Carrie said, realizing she'd been brushing kind of hard. She loosened her grip on the toothbrush and finished the last five strokes. "It just makes me so mad."

"Then you're right—you shouldn't think about it," Bob said, admiring her mane. "Besides, we've got other business tonight."

"We do?" Carrie asked.

"Yep," Bob told her with twinkling eyes. "Take a look in your backpack," she said.

Carrie laid down the toothbrush and went to open up her bag. A bunch of computer paper spilled out with the Access Café logo on top.

"What's all this?" Carrie asked. She read the heading at the top of the page. " 'Tips on getting over stage fright'?"

"It took me a while," Bob said. "I had to type one key at a time with my horn! But I finally managed to spell out *stage fright* at Google, and it came up with all this cool stuff."

"Wow," Carrie said, looking at the little unicorn with newfound appreciation. "That was actually a really good idea, Bob."

"Don't look so surprised," Bob said indignantly.

Carrie chuckled, scooping up the unicorn as she walked back to her desk and sat down to read through the papers.

"'Tips for getting over stage fright,'" she read aloud. "'Number one: Picture the audience in their underwear.'"

"*Ew!*" she and Bob both screeched at the same time.

"What's the next one?" Bob asked.

"'Number two: When memorizing your lines, practice them out loud—not just in your head.'"

"Sounds good," Bob said. "Keep going."

"'Number three: Read through your lines outside of rehearsals with a friend who is not in the play. Your friend will be more focused on you than the other characters' lines and therefore more able to offer you feedback.'"

"Not bad," Bob said. "What else is there?"

Carrie flipped through the pages, soaking in all of the advice. She especially liked the tip about pretending that she was just having a real conversation with someone, as her character, and no one else was watching. That was kind of how it had felt in the audition when she was arguing with Sharon and Kimberly about Cindy going to the prom.

"Hey, what's this?" Carrie asked when she got to the last page. She scrunched up her nose. The stuff on that page didn't have anything to do with stage fright—it was some article out of a parenting magazine.

"Oh, that . . . How'd that get in there?" Bob asked, tilting her head.

"'Unique names for girls'?" Carrie read. *"Bob—"*

"Huh. That one must have got mixed in with my stuff by accident," the little unicorn said, shifting from one side to the other. "But you know, since we have it . . . maybe we should take a look at it. It might be interesting."

"Mm-hm," Carrie said. "Mixed in by accident, huh?"

"I swear," Bob said, her eyes twinkling.

"I bet," Carrie muttered. But she scanned the article anyway. "All right. How about Katherina?"

"I'd have to wear a tutu."

"Esther?"

"Sounds like a hen."

"Nanette?"

"Too prissy."

"Molly?"

"That's a lapdog."

"Regina?"

"Vacuum cleaner."

"Clementine?"

"You want to name me after a fruit?"

"Bob!" Carrie yelled.

The unicorn snorted and stamped her feet. "Yeah, I guess you're right," she said finally. "That's the only name that seems to fit. Fine. Forget the list. Bob it is. Now go get your script—you've got some lines to learn!"

CHAPTER
Eleven

Carrie nibbled at her egg-free egg-salad sandwich, watching the cafeteria line for Sharon. She and Anna and Theresa had been at the lunch table for a few minutes already, and Carrie was so anxious, she could barely eat. They'd told Carrie that morning that they were going to spring their "trap" for Sharon at lunchtime—but they'd been totally mysterious about what they were going to do.

"Hey, there she is," Theresa said.

Sharon and Kimberly walked out of the line together, then headed straight for their table and sat down.

"Hey, Carrie, do you think you'll make it through rehearsal today?" Kimberly asked. She smirked at Sharon.

"Yep, I'll be there," Carrie said. "Actually, I

even learned most of my lines last night. And the lyrics to the songs, too."

Bob, who was resting on Carrie's shoulder, gave her a proud little poke.

"That reminds me, Sharon," Anna said, sounding supercasual. "Did Mrs. Wessex send you any more e-mails?"

Sharon looked at Carrie, narrowing her eyes. "No," she said. "Why?"

Anna shrugged. "Well, I got one from her last night. She needed me to know some stuff about the set design. She said we didn't need as many chairs at the prom because she's decided Rae isn't going to be there."

"What? Why not?" Sharon demanded. "That's the biggest scene in the whole play. Rae has to be there."

"That's what I thought at first, too," Theresa said. "But then I thought about it and realized that the play's really about Cindy, you know? I mean, Rae's just a supporting character. No one's really going to miss her if she doesn't go to the dance."

"Rae is not a supporting character!" Sharon hissed. "She's just as big a role as Cindy. Of course people are going to notice if she's not there."

Anna shrugged again. "Well, that's the way Mrs. Wessex wants it."

"That doesn't make sense," Sharon said. Her face was so red, it rivaled Carrie's hair. "She can't cut Rae out of the last scene."

"Sure, she can," Theresa said. "It's her play—she wrote it."

Carrie had to bite her lip to keep a straight face. She watched her friends with amazement. Sharon was totally losing it, but Theresa and Anna were perfectly calm.

"And just when was she going to tell me about it?" Sharon asked.

"I don't know," Anna said. "Probably today at rehearsal. After all, it's not like it really affects you."

"Of course it affects me!" Sharon yelled. "She's cutting me out of the last scene—she's taking away my solo."

"Oh, no," Theresa said. She touched Sharon's arm as if she were trying to comfort her. "She's not cutting *your* part—she's cutting *Carrie's*. The two of you switched roles, right?"

"Yeah, Carrie told us all about it," Anna said. "She's playing Rae now, and you're Cindy."

"We—" Sharon started. "I—" she tried again. But she couldn't go any further. Theresa and

Anna had executed their plan perfectly, and now she was trapped. She grabbed hold of her lunch tray and stood up. "I'm going to go talk to Mrs. Wessex," she said. "Come on, Kimberly." Like the loyal lackey that she was, Kimberly stood and followed Sharon out of the cafeteria.

"All right!" Theresa, Anna, and Carrie all shouted when she was gone, slapping each other high fives.

"That was beautiful, you two," Carrie said.

"Thanks," Theresa said. "It was mostly Anna's idea. She can be really sneaky when she needs to be. I'm glad she's on our side."

"There's no other side I'd rather be on," Anna said.

"So . . . what do we do now?" Carrie asked.

"Nothing," Anna said. "We just let Sharon figure out that we tricked her and that will be that."

"Do you think she'll try to trick me again?" Carrie asked.

"Uh-uh." Anna shook her head. "From what I've seen, Sharon only bites until someone bites back."

"And she definitely just got bitten," Carrie said.

★　　　★　　　★

"I can't believe it's almost midnight."

"Me neither. But I think we have time for one last dance before you have to go."

Carrie smiled at Matt, feeling like she really was Cindy Rellar at the prom with the boy of her dreams.

"Beautiful!" Mrs. Wessex declared. "Wonderful job, all of you. And now we'll work on the final song."

Rehearsal that afternoon had been amazing. Carrie had followed the tips Bob had gotten online—except for the one about picturing people in their underwear—and she'd barely messed up at all. It really helped that she had most of her lines memorized now. And Sharon hadn't been acting up, either—though *Rae* hadn't looked too happy when Cindy and Charlie Prinze had their dance.

"Matthew, you can leave your skateboard over there," Mrs. Wessex instructed as everyone moved over to the piano. She'd finally caved and allowed him to use the board—but only when he arrived at the prom, and only if he promised not to try any "fancy stunts." She'd even decided that Spence could rap his lines since he really was showing a lot of "initiative" and "creativity."

Now came the final test—would Carrie sound okay during her duet with Sharon?

Mrs. Hendrickson played the opening notes, and everyone sang along to the group verse. Then they got to the part where it was just Carrie and Sharon.

Closing her eyes, Carrie continued to sing, trying not to think about anything but the music. She'd gone over the lyrics so many times with Bob that she could picture them in her head. And every time she started to feel nervous, she just pretended she was singing along with the car radio. Tip number twenty-two.

When it was Sharon's turn to sing by herself, Carrie opened her eyes and waited, twisting her hands together. And when her part came around, she was ready.

"Everything must end," Carrie sang, all by herself. *"But even so, at least now I know, I have what I need—a real, true friend."*

The rest of the cast joined in for the final verse of the song, and then they were done.

Carrie felt a burst of pride—she'd done it! She'd made it through the entire rehearsal without getting freaked out. She could feel Bob jumping around on her shoulder, and she knew the unicorn was just as excited.

"Nice work, everyone," Mrs. Hendrickson said.

"Yes, I'm very pleased with how hard you've all been working," Mrs. Wessex added. "And just think—in a week you'll get to perform for a real audience. Imagine how exciting that will be!"

Carrie gulped. She'd been so focused on doing okay in rehearsal that somehow she'd forgotten that she still had to do this in front of other people. Bob and her friends had helped her make it this far, but what if she fell apart when it really mattered?

CHAPTER
Twelve

"I still don't get it," Carrie said as she carefully put Bob's earring chokers around the little unicorn's neck. "Why do *you* need to get dressed up for *my* play?"

Bob sighed. "Just put on my anklet, would you?"

Carrie took the open-ended rhinestone ring and slid it over Bob's hoof, tightening it so it would stay in place. "There—you look beautiful," she said.

"Really?"

"Yes, really," Carrie said. "But what about this?" She picked up the green butterfly hair clip.

"That," Bob said, "is for you."

Carrie started to protest, then tilted her head and stared at her reflection in the mirror. This *was* a special occasion, and her bangs were still hanging in her face, even though her mother had tried to curl them out of the way.

"Go for it!" Bob said with a grin.

Before she could change her mind, Carrie pulled her hair back and cinched the clip in place. It actually looked okay. And it did feel nice to have her hair off her forehead. Not to mention the fact that she could see a lot more clearly.

"Awesome—you're going to knock 'em dead," Bob said. "Just remember everything we talked about. And if you have to, use that 'picture the crowd in their underwear' trick. But only as a last resort."

Carrie laughed in spite of her nerves. "Okay," she said. "Only as a last resort."

She carried Bob out of the bathroom and walked down to the auditorium. Somehow tonight, with all the lights and the people milling around, it looked bigger than it had during rehearsals. But Carrie tried not to think about it too much. Instead she walked over to the piano and set Bob in a flower arrangement there. The little unicorn had insisted it would be the perfect place to watch from. Then Carrie went backstage and joined the rest of the cast.

"Carrie, you look great!" Kimberly said when she saw her. Theresa had picked out matching boot-cut black pants and V-necked shirts for Cindy and Rae to wear. All they had to do was change into dresses for the prom scene.

"Thanks," Carrie said. "You, um . . . you look good, too."

Kimberly's stepmom costume wasn't really as cool as what Carrie and Sharon got to wear. She was stuck in a loose dress with big tacky flowers all over it. But at least she did look like she could be somebody's mother.

"Hey, Carrie, can I talk to you for a sec?" Sharon asked.

Carrie frowned. "I guess so," she said.

They hadn't really talked much since the scene in the cafeteria the week before—just enough to get through rehearsals. And that had been fine with Carrie. The less time she spent thinking about Sharon, the better.

Carrie followed Sharon back to the prop room.

"So, I just wanted to say—um, break a leg," Sharon said.

Carrie scowled at her. "I can't believe you. Here I thought you were going to apologize, and you go and say something mean." She turned to leave.

"No, wait!" Sharon said, grabbing her arm. "You don't understand—'break a leg' is what actors say before a performance. It's just an expression. It means 'good luck.'"

Carrie eyed Sharon suspiciously. "Oh. Well . . . is that all you wanted to say? *Good luck?*"

Sharon nodded. "That and . . . well, that I'm sorry I was . . . I mean, I'm sorry I didn't . . . I know you'll do a good job tonight, Carrie," she said finally. For once she actually looked sincere. It wasn't an apology, exactly, but Carrie knew it was probably the best Sharon could do.

"Thanks," Carrie said. "You too."

"All right, then," Sharon said, tossing her long hair behind her shoulder. "Are you ready to show everyone just how good we are?"

"Ready."

They rejoined the rest of the group, and Mrs. Wessex went out onstage to let the audience know they were ready to begin.

Theresa and Anna had already been backstage getting some of the props ready, and as soon as they saw Carrie, they rushed over to her.

"Hey, how do you feel?" Theresa asked.

"The truth?" Carrie winced. "I'm *so* nervous."

"You'll be fine," Anna reassured her.

"Better than fine," Theresa added, squeezing Carrie's hand. "You'll be great!"

"Thanks, guys."

Hearing her friends' encouragement helped, but right then Carrie couldn't imagine how she was going to hear anyone's lines over her heart pounding its way straight out of her chest.

"Five minutes until curtain call," Mrs. Wessex sang out.

"Hey, Scoob!"

Carrie turned around and saw Spence standing there. His costume looked pretty much like what he wore to school every day, which was fitting since he seemed to be playing himself. Mrs. Wessex had even let him call his character MC Spence.

"Are you ready?" Carrie asked.

"Sure," Spence said with a shrug.

Carrie squinted at him. "Are you nervous?" she asked.

Spence mulled the question over for a minute. "Well," he said, "my heart's beating double time, my head's filling up with rhyme, my pulse continues to climb, but this feeling—it is sublime."

"So . . . a little bit?" Carrie said with a grin.

"Yeah, a little bit," Spence said. "But it's all good. The adrenaline just means you're ready, right?"

Carrie shook her head. He was too much. "Yeah. Ready," she said, "but not steady . . . Freddie."

Spence winced. "We'll work on that," he said, and Carrie laughed.

"Places, everyone!" Mrs. Wessex called. "We're ready for the curtain."

Mrs. Wessex began ushering everyone to their spots, and before she knew it, Carrie was out there onstage, ready to begin her solo. She heard Mrs. Hendrickson start in on the piano, and as the curtain parted, Carrie came in right on cue.

"*I dream of a day all my own,*" she sang. "*With no work to be done.*" From the wings she saw Spence, Anna, and Theresa all giving her thumbs-up. In the flower arrangement she could see Bob shaking her mane from side to side.

And before she knew it, her song was over and the audience was clapping. It was an amazing feeling, knowing that the applause was for her, and suddenly she understood what Spence had said about the adrenaline.

Her heart was pounding and her arms were tingling, but she didn't feel scared anymore. She just felt excited . . . and ready.

"I want everyone to know how proud we are of you," Mrs. Wessex said later that night.

The cast was assembled in Mrs.

Hendrickson's room, where they'd met up after changing out of their costumes. In a few minutes Carrie would be heading out to Ed's Soda Shop at the mall with her friends to celebrate, but right now she was just basking in the moment.

The final curtain call had been amazing. The cast had come on in groups, and the audience had applauded all of them. But when Carrie, Sharon, Matt, and Spence had come out for their final bow, the applause had picked up even more, until it sounded like thunder. And then the audience had actually stood up and given them a standing ovation.

Now that it was over, Carrie couldn't help noticing that the whole night had felt like a dream. A really good dream. *A flying dream.* And as nervous as she'd been at the beginning of the night, she was ten times more excited to come out and do it again tomorrow night.

"Yes, you all did a wonderful job," Mrs. Hendrickson added. "Great work!"

"And don't forget," Mrs. Wessex said, "we're meeting here tomorrow at 6 P.M. to get ready for the next show. Tonight was wonderful, but I have a feeling tomorrow night is going to be even better. Thank you, everyone."

Everybody clapped and cheered, still buzzing

with excitement from having pulled off their first performance without a hitch. Eventually, though, people drifted off to go find their families and friends.

Carrie headed back to the auditorium and went straight to the floral arrangement. "Did you see, Bob?" she whispered as she got close. "I did it! I starred in the school play and I didn't even mess up. It was so much fun! I can hardly wait for—" Carrie looked at the flowers. "Bob?" she called out softly.

There was no response.

Frowning, Carrie spread a few of the stems apart so she could see the edge of the basket better. Then she stuck her hand straight into the green flora foam and felt around. After a few moments of searching, she brought her hand back out and examined the things she'd found. A hoop earring, a rhinestone ring, and a small, silver unicorn.

"Bob," Carrie whispered, staring at the charm in her hand. All at once a lump formed in her throat. It was funny. As annoying as the little unicorn had been at times, Carrie had really gotten used to having her around. It was hard to believe that it had been less than two weeks since she'd first found her under the water fountain.

Carrie thought about their first meeting and

tried to remember exactly what it was the little unicorn had told her. Something about a few people on her side of the universe thinking that Carrie needed encouragement. And she definitely had. But now it seemed Bob's job was over, and it was time for her to go back to . . . her side of the universe, wherever that was.

Carrie looked up to the lights and smiled. "Thanks, Bob," she said softly. Then she looked down at the charm and laughed. The second hoop earring—one of Bob's chokers—had remained around her neck when she'd turned back into a charm. *She'd like that,* Carrie thought. *Permanent jewelry.*

But what was even neater about the earring was the way it had twisted around at the top, forming a perfect loop. Carrie took one look at it and knew exactly what it was meant for.

She unclasped the charm bracelet that Anna had given her and slid the unicorn charm on next to the angel one that had been on it originally.

"You make a nice pair," Carrie said to the two charms, and just for a second she could have sworn she saw Bob's eyes twinkle—just a little.

FAIRY

For Ward, who speaks a language all his own
—B.R.

CHAPTER

One

"Resa! Do you have my silver hoops?" Amy Allen called, leaning through her sister's bedroom door. "You know, the ones I loaned you last week?"

Theresa winced. "Um, I don't think so," she replied, squinting her big brown eyes. "Are you sure I didn't give them back?"

Amy shook her head. "I just checked my jewelry box, and they're not in there. And I loaned them to you over a week ago."

"Maybe you put them somewhere else," Theresa suggested. Her sister groaned.

"Unlike you," Amy said, "I put my things back where they belong. If my earrings aren't in my jewelry box, then I don't have them, which means *you do.* So cough 'em up."

Theresa glanced around her room, her eyes

darting to every spot where it would have made sense to set earrings—her nightstand, her bureau, her desk. *"Well,"* she said slowly. She tugged on one of her long brown braids and twisted it around her finger nervously. She willed herself to remember where she'd put them, but the memory wouldn't come.

Amy folded her arms across her chest. "You lost my earrings, didn't you?"

"No-o."

"Then where are they?"

Theresa sighed. "I'm not sure."

"Resa! Those were my favorite—"

"I'll find them, Amy. I just—"

"Theresa! Amy! Breakfast!" Mr. Allen called from downstairs.

Amy gave her sister one last glare. "You better," she said. Then she turned and headed downstairs.

Phew, Theresa thought. *Saved by the bacon.*

She took one last look around her room and shook her head. Where had she put those stupid earrings? Oh, well. She'd have to solve that mystery later. Theresa snagged her backpack from the chair at her desk and headed for the kitchen, where her mother, father, and eight-year-old brother, Nicky, were already seated around the table.

"So," Mr. Allen began, once Theresa had taken her seat, "do you kids have anything interesting going on in school this week?"

"We're starting our clay sculptures in art class today," Nicky said. He chomped on a muffin, and crumbs spilled all over the table. "I'm not sure what I'm going to make yet."

"Well, I'm sure you'll think of something really inventive, Nicky," Mrs. Allen said. "What about you girls? Anything fun happening at school?"

"Not really," Amy said, rolling her eyes. "I'm probably going to go shopping after school today with Stephanie. You know, because I guess I *need some new earrings.*"

"Oh," said Mrs. Allen. "You girls enjoy that. What about you, Theresa?"

Theresa brightened up a little despite Amy's earring comment. "We're going to start planning the spring carnival."

Mrs. Allen knit her brow. "Is it time for that already?" she asked.

"Duh," Amy said, rolling her eyes. "It *is* spring."

"Amy, don't talk to me that way," Mrs. Allen said.

"Sorry," Amy said sheepishly. "I just meant

that it's April, and Resa's class did their play about two weeks ago, which means it's time for spring carnival. Middle school is *so* predictable."

"So are sophomores with crushes," Theresa muttered under her breath. Then, when her sister glared at her, she mouthed the name *Chip*. Theresa had overheard Amy on the phone last night, telling one of her friends all about her huge crush on some guy named Chip.

"Excuse me?" Mrs. Allen asked.

Amy reached over and pinched Theresa hard on the thigh. "*Ow*—nothing," Theresa said. "I was just saying that I'm really excited. I hope my class wins the ice cream party."

Amy raised her juice glass and looked Theresa in the eye. "You won't," she said. Then she took a long sip of orange juice.

"Amy, that's not very supportive," Mrs. Allen said.

Amy half shrugged. "Maybe not, but it's true," she replied. "The fifth grade *never* wins. It's practically tradition."

"Just because your fifth grade didn't win doesn't mean mine can't," Theresa said.

"It wasn't just *my* fifth grade that didn't win," Amy replied. "*No* fifth grade has ever won. *Ever.*"

"Really?" Theresa asked.

"If you don't believe me, check the trophy cases by the office. There's a list of every class that's ever won, and there's not a single fifth grade on it."

Theresa narrowed her eyes. That didn't seem right, but why would Amy lie? Especially when she knew Theresa could check.

"Well, then, perhaps Theresa's class will be the first," Mr. Allen said. "More muffins, anyone?" He held up the plate. Theresa, Amy, and Mrs. Allen all shook their heads.

"Yeah, right," Amy said. "If Theresa has anything to do with it, they'll misplace their theme."

"What?!" Theresa exclaimed.

"It's true—you'd lose your feet if they weren't attached to your ankles."

"Amy—that was uncalled for," Mrs. Allen chided her. "Apologize to your sister, please."

"*Sor-ry,*" Amy whined in a singsong voice.

Theresa waited until her mother wasn't looking and then stuck out her tongue.

"Real mature," Amy murmured. She folded her napkin and set it on the table, then stood to take her plate to the sink. At the same time, Mr. and Mrs. Allen stood to clear the table. Theresa gulped down the last bite of her muffin and took her plate up, too.

"We're going to win, you know," Theresa said while she waited for her sister to finish rinsing her plate.

"Mm-hm," Amy replied without turning around. "And winged monkeys are going to come live under my bed."

Theresa clicked her tongue. "Why do you have to be so rude?"

"I'm not rude. I'm just honest," Amy said. "There's no way your class is going to win. I already told you—the fifth grade never wins. Get over it already." She opened the dishwasher, placed her plate on the bottom rack, and walked away, leaving Theresa standing there fuming.

So the fifth grade had never won spring carnival before. So what? That didn't mean Theresa's class couldn't do it. And if it meant proving Amy wrong, Theresa was going to make sure that they did!

CHAPTER

TWO

"I brought 'The Lion and the Mouse,'" said Anna Lee, removing a sheet of paper from her notebook. For English class Mrs. Wessex was having the fifth graders research Aesop's fables. They were working in groups of three, and each student was responsible for finding one fable to share.

"Which one is that?" Theresa asked.

Anna pushed her straight, jet-black hair back behind her ears as she glanced up from her work. "It's the one where the lion catches a mouse but lets him go," she said. "Then the mouse helps him later by chewing a hole in the net the lion is caught in."

"Oh—I know that one," Carrie Weingarten replied. "The moral is something like 'Small creatures can do big things,' right?"

"That's the one," Anna said. "So what did you guys bring?"

"I have 'The Fox and the Grapes,'" Carrie said, removing her own sheet of notebook paper on which she'd copied down her fable. "It's about a fox that wants some grapes that are growing up high, but he can't reach them. He tries and tries to get them, but he can't. So finally he just walks away and says that he could tell they were sour anyway."

"I've heard that one before," Theresa said, twirling several of her tiny braids around her finger, "but I don't really get it. What's the moral supposed to be?"

Anna grinned and leaned in close, her dark, almond-shaped eyes sparkling. "It's about being a sore loser," she whispered. "You know, like when Sharon doesn't get her way and then pretends she's better off anyway?"

Carrie giggled. "Right. Like the time we beat her in the math contest and she said it didn't matter because she was getting tired of winning free ice cream."

Theresa smiled, remembering how thrilled she and her friends had been to win—and how upset Sharon had been to lose. Sharon Ross preferred to come in first. At everything.

"That must be where the expression 'sour grapes' comes from," she said. "My dad's always saying that to my brother when he says Monopoly or whatever is a stupid game . . . *right after he loses.*"

"I've heard him do that before," Carrie said. "Nicky is cute and I love him and all that, but he can be so whiny."

"Tell me about it," Theresa said. "You guys are lucky you don't have little brothers. They can be such a pain."

"Trust me," Anna said, "big brothers can be just as bad."

"And so can big sisters," Carrie added. "But then, I guess you know that."

Theresa nodded. Amy was definitely as big a pain as Nicky—sometimes bigger.

"So what fable did you bring, Theresa?" Anna asked.

"Oh, yeah," Theresa said. "Hold on a second, it's right here." She began to fumble through her backpack, searching for the page she'd printed out last night. "It's a really good one," she said. "'The Fox and the . . . Sheep'? No, that wasn't it. It's—" She tried to remember the other animal from the fable while she rifled through all of the loose papers inside her backpack.

"Was it 'The Fox and the Crow'?" Anna suggested.

"No," Theresa said without looking up. "It wasn't a bird. Wait a minute—I think it's in my notebook." Theresa removed a blue, spiral-bound notebook that was overflowing with various work sheets and printouts.

"Whoa," Carrie said. "I hope it's not in there."

Theresa glanced up. "Why not?" she asked.

"Because if it is, you'll never find it," Anna answered. Both she and Carrie were staring wide-eyed at the mess Theresa was making as she piled more and more papers onto her desk.

Theresa rolled her eyes. "Don't worry—I'll clean it all up once I find my fable," she said. "I know it's in here somewhere." She held the notebook by its front and back covers and shook it over her desk. A ton of papers fell out, and Theresa examined every one, but her fable was nowhere to be found.

Anna grimaced. "Theresa, maybe you should just—"

"Let me check one more place," Theresa said, holding up an index finger to her friends.

"Was it 'The Fox and the Stork'?" Carrie suggested. "I saw that one online at Aesop.com."

"*No-o,*" Theresa said. "I told you it wasn't a bird."

"What about 'The Fox and the Monkey'?" Anna asked. "I almost did that one."

Theresa groaned. "No, it wasn't a monkey, either. Just wait and I'll find it." She began unzipping all of the pockets on her backpack.

The first one was empty. The second one held her calculator. "Hey, I've been looking for that," Theresa mumbled, setting it on the desk. The third pocket contained a note that she, Carrie, and Anna had been writing back and forth during math class yesterday, and the last pocket, which was really too small to hold much of anything, had a quarter and three pennies.

"Shoot!" Theresa said, slouching forward. Amy was right. She couldn't keep track of anything. Theresa shook her head. "I swear I printed it out and stuck it in here last night so that I wouldn't forget it."

"Maybe it fell out," Carrie offered, shrugging.

"Or maybe you *meant* to put it in your backpack, but you forgot," Anna added.

"Hmmm," Theresa said. "Maybe." She frowned. "Man, I hate forgetting things. It was a really good fable, too—one I'd never heard before. That's why I chose it."

"Well," Carrie said, her hazel eyes full of hope, "maybe we can help you remember it."

"I'm sure we can," Anna agreed. Again she tucked a few stray strands of shiny black hair behind her ears. It was her getting-down-to-business move. "We already know it has a fox and one other animal, right?" she asked. Theresa nodded. "Do you remember anything else about it?"

Theresa closed her eyes and pursed her lips. "Let's see . . . The fox was stuck in a well." She opened her eyes and smiled. Slowly the details of the fable were coming back to her.

"What else?" Anna asked.

"Well, the other animal—whatever it was— came along and asked the fox what he was doing at the bottom of the well. Really he'd fallen in and gotten trapped, but he told the other animal that he was down there drinking the water because it was the best water ever. So the other animal, who was really thirsty, jumped in, too. Then the fox climbed on its back to get out and left it stuck in the well."

"Is that it?" Anna asked.

Theresa shrugged. "I think so."

"Well, that's good," Carrie said. "It sounds like you remember the whole thing. So all you need to do is write down what you just told us and hand it in to Mrs. Wessex as your fable."

"I guess," Theresa said. "Except that I don't remember the other animal or what the moral was."

"Maybe we can figure it out," suggested Anna.

"Figure what out?" someone asked.

Theresa turned around to see her friend Spence looking over her shoulder. He was in the group right next to her, Carrie, and Anna, with his friends Matt Dana and Kevin Hathaway.

"Are you guys done?" Matt asked, nodding in their direction.

"Almost," Anna said. "We're just trying to figure out Theresa's fable."

Kevin scrunched up his eyebrows, which were barely visible through the curly dark hair that was perpetually in his eyes. "Figure it out? Which one is it?" he asked.

"That's the problem," Theresa said, sighing. "I can't remember. I printed it out last night, but I left it at home, and now I can't remember. It's about a fox stuck in a well and some other animal that he tricks into helping him out."

"Hey—I know that one," Matt said. "It's 'The Fox and the Goat.'"

Theresa sat up suddenly. She felt like a light had gone on inside her head. "The goat! That's it!" she said. "Now I remember. Matt's right—it's 'The Fox and the Goat,' and when the fox gets out of the well, he refuses to help the goat, even though he promised he would. Then when the goat complains, the fox says something like, 'Well, you shouldn't have gotten in without knowing how to get out.' And *that's* the moral."

"The sly fox said to the goat down deep / next time fella, better look before you leap," Spence rapped.

Carrie smiled and shook her head, sending her red curls bouncing.

"Right," Theresa said, grinning. "Look before you leap. That's it exactly. Thanks, Spence. Thanks, Matt."

"No problem," the two boys replied at the same time.

"Then we're done," Carrie said. "Resa just needs to write that one down, and then we can start on the next part of the assignment."

"The next part?" Theresa asked.

"It's right here on the work sheet Mrs. Wessex gave us," Anna said.

Theresa combed through all the papers littering her desk, but the work sheet wasn't among them. "I must have left that at home, too," she said with a sigh.

"You can share mine," Anna said. She slid a piece of paper halfway between her and Theresa and read from it. "'Part two: When you've finished discussing your fables, choose one to present to the rest of the class in a creative manner.'"

"*In a creative manner?*" Carrie repeated, squinting.

"There are some suggestions here," Anna said. "We could turn it into a poem, draw pictures to illustrate it—"

"Or you could turn it into a rap," Spence cut in. "Hit it, Kev."

Right on cue, Kevin started beat boxing, making all sorts of drumlike noises with his mouth and hands. After a few beats Spence jumped in.

"The hare and the tortoise, they started to race / and that hare was laughing at the turtle's slow pace. / He ran up one hill and down the next, / then decided to chill and have a rest. / But the turtle kept chugging and passed right by / that crazy hare who thought he was so fly / and when Hare woke up, he was in disgrace / 'cause slow and steady Tortoise had won the race."

Spence ended his rap with his hands crossed and tucked into his armpits, his thumbs pointing upward.

Carrie laughed and clapped. "That's awesome, Spence!"

"Carrie Weingarten and Ward Willis," Mrs. Wessex called from her desk. She always used Spence's real first name, even though he'd told her over and over to call him Spence, which was short for his middle name, Spencer. "Are the two of you working?"

"Just practicing our presentations, Mrs. W.," Spence said with a grin. At the same time, Carrie gave Mrs. Wessex her best wide-eyed, innocent look.

Sure enough, Mrs. Wessex's features softened into a smile, as they always did when she was dealing with Spence. "All right," she said. "Just keep the noise down, please."

Carrie nodded at her teacher, then turned back to Spence. "She loves you, you know," she whispered.

"What's not to love?" Spence said with a shrug.

Anna sighed. *"Please,"* she said. "Anyway, your rap was really good," she added. "Is that what you guys are going to do?"

"Something like that," Spence said. "We

gotta get Matt in on the beat boxing, though."

"Or not," Matt said.

"Come on, Matt—you have to do *something*," Anna told him.

"Oh, I'll do something," Matt said. "Just not that. These two can handle the music," he said, gesturing at Spence and Kevin. "I'll take care of the visuals."

"That's right—you draw really well, don't you?" Anna said.

Matt shrugged. "I don't know about *really well*," he said, running one hand through his shaggy blond hair, "but I definitely draw better than I beat box."

Anna giggled, then turned back to Carrie and Theresa. "Speaking of visuals, we need to come up with some for *our* presentation. Which fable do you guys want to do, anyway?"

"I like Resa's," Carrie said. "Are you just about finished with it?"

"Yep," Theresa said, scribbling down the last few words. She'd been writing so fast, her hand was beginning to cramp.

"So then let's do that one," Anna said. " 'The Fox and the Goat.' How do you guys want to present it?"

"I know," Theresa said. "I'll be the goat. Carrie

can be the fox—because of her red hair—and Anna, you can be the narrator. We'll set up some chairs in a circle to be the well, and then we'll act it out. It will only take me a minute to rewrite it as a play."

Without hesitation, Theresa ripped a blank sheet of paper from her notebook and began writing again. She stopped when she realized her friends were both staring at her. *"What?"*

"It's just . . ." Carrie started.

"That was so quick," Anna said. "I mean, you got the idea like—"

"Lightning fast," Spence jumped in. "Yo—Tee leaves stuff home and gets all fretful / but she's so creative, no one minds that she's forgetful."

Anna and Carrie laughed, but Theresa felt her face getting hot. Being disorganized and absentminded weren't exactly the things she wanted to be known for. Unfortunately, they seemed to be two of the things people noticed most about her.

Her sister was always on her case for forgetting to relay phone messages, among other things—*like losing earrings,* Theresa thought. And her mom was constantly reminding her that she needed to be more organized so she wouldn't misplace things so often. Even Nicky had started bragging that his room was neater than Theresa's, and he was only eight.

Theresa sighed. It seemed like she was constantly being told how mixed up and forgetful she was. Of course, this was the first time anyone had rapped about it.

"Well?" she asked, looking to her friends. "Is it okay?"

"Is what okay?" Anna and Carrie said together.

"My idea—presenting the fable as a mini-play."

"Oh—yeah, it's great," Anna said. "I was just surprised by how fast you came up with it."

"Me too," Carrie said. "Spence is right. You *are* really creative."

"Thanks," Theresa said, although she couldn't help wondering why Carrie and Anna seemed so surprised. She'd always been creative, hadn't she? Why did it seem like her friends were just realizing it?

Probably because all they see when they look at me is how disorganized and absentminded I am, Theresa thought. Just like everybody else. She fingered the charm bracelet Carrie had given to her a couple of weeks ago when she'd been having a particularly bad day. She'd managed to lose her sneakers, break a picture frame, and mess up the flowers for the school play, all in the space of ten minutes.

According to Carrie and Anna, the bracelet had brought each of them good luck. They'd passed it on to Theresa, saying that it looked like she could use a little good luck, too, but so far it didn't seem to be working. In fact, Theresa was beginning to think she should give the bracelet back to Carrie before it ended up with Amy's earrings—lost.

"Resa—are you okay?" Carrie asked.

"Yeah," Theresa lied. "I just—"

"All right, class," Mrs. Wessex called out. She stood up from her desk and walked to the front of the room. "We're just about out of time. You can finish up with your fables at the beginning of class tomorrow, and then we'll start the presentations. Oh, and don't forget—after lunch, the whole fifth grade is meeting back here for a class discussion of spring carnival."

Whispers of excitement shot around the room. Spring carnival was one of the most anticipated events of the year at Elizabeth Cady Stanton Middle School.

"Settle down, everybody," Mrs. Wessex said. "We don't have time to discuss the details right now. Just remember to come back here after lunch and be ready to be creative—we're going to try to come up with an idea for our class theme."

Just as Mrs. Wessex finished speaking, the bell rang, and everyone was on their feet.

"Did you hear that, Tee?" Spence said, nudging her as they walked out of the room. "We need your creativity."

Theresa smiled. True, Spence had rapped about her forgetfulness just a few minutes ago, but at least he was focusing on the creative part now.

"We sure do," Kevin added. Then he turned to Carrie and Anna. "Just make sure she doesn't forget to come to the meeting, okay?"

Too bad Spence was the only one.

CHAPTER
Three

"I can't believe the fifth grade has never won," Anna said as she set her tray of pizza down on the lunch table.

"I know," Carrie replied. "Not once in *ten years*."

"Twelve," Theresa said, peeling the foil top off her yogurt. "ECS has been holding spring carnival for twelve years; this will be the thirteenth. So far the eighth grade has won six times, the seventh grade four, and the sixth grade twice. But the fifth grade—*never*."

Theresa's friends stared at her. She dipped her spoon in and stirred.

"Thank you, Encyclopedia Allen," Anna said.

"Seriously," Carrie added with a giggle. "When did you become such an expert on spring carnival?" Carrie unwrapped her turkey sandwich and took a giant bite.

"Five minutes ago," Theresa said. "I stopped and checked the trophy cases next to the office on my way down here."

Anna squinted. "There are *trophies* for spring carnival?"

"Plaques, actually," Theresa said. "The class that comes up with the best theme and has the best booths gets a plaque with their class picture and year on it. And they get their picture in the paper, too. It's a pretty big deal."

"Not to me," Carrie said. "I mean, winning the plaque is cool and everything, but what I really want is the ice cream party."

"There's an ice cream party?" Anna asked. She opened her eyes so wide that both Carrie and Theresa had to laugh.

"I keep forgetting you're new here," Theresa said. She and Anna and Carrie had become so close that it was hard to believe Anna had only lived in Newcastle for six weeks. It seemed like the three of them had always been best friends.

"Yeah—there's an ice cream party," Theresa continued, "but it's not just *any* ice cream party. It's the *biggest* ice cream party *ever*."

Carrie nodded. "Ed's Soda Shop brings in something like thirty-two flavors along with tons of toppings—sprinkles, dips, candies, those little crunchy cookie things, hot fudge, caramel, whipped cream, cherries—just about everything you can think of."

"And you don't get tiny scoops, either," Theresa said. "Everyone fills huge bowls, and you can go back as many times as you want."

"Wow," Anna said. "That sounds awesome."

"My sister won when she was in seventh grade," Carrie added. "Lynn said it was like going into an ice cream parlor and taking whatever you wanted without having to pay."

The three girls sighed. Ed's Soda Shop had become their favorite after-school hangout, and the thought of having tons of ice cream—with all the trimmings—delivered to them for free was like a dream.

"We *have* to win," Carrie said.

"Definitely," Anna agreed.

"Double definitely," Theresa said. "We have to win that ice cream *and* end the fifth-grade losing streak." *And prove to my sister—and everyone else—that I can be involved in something without messing it up,* Theresa thought.

"Yeah," Carrie agreed. "But first we need to come up with a really good theme."

A slow smile crept onto Theresa's face. "I have an idea."

"You do?" Carrie and Anna asked at the same time.

Theresa nodded. "Mm-hm. I've been thinking about it all morning," she said, and she *had* been—ever since Amy had told her the fifth grade had no shot at winning. *We'll see who's laughing when I'm demolishing my second banana split,* Theresa thought.

"So?" Anna asked. "What's your theme?" She pulled an olive off the top of her pizza and popped it in her mouth.

"Okay," Theresa said. "I was thinking the theme should be—"

"Hollywood," Sharon Ross said, taking the seat next to Carrie's. "It's going to be Hollywood." She unwrapped a pat of butter and began mashing it into her potatoes while Theresa, Anna, and Carrie exchanged a bewildered look.

"Hollywood?" Anna asked.

"Yeah. You were talking about spring carnival, weren't you?"

"Well . . . yes," Theresa started, "but—"

"Then if you want to win, you should listen to me. My aunt is an interior decorator, and I have all kinds of ideas that will make the fifth-grade section the best."

Theresa rolled her eyes. Sharon was always

butting into things and taking over. And usually, because she was sort of a class leader, people just let her. Or at least they always had, until Anna had arrived.

"I'm sure your ideas are great, Sharon," Anna said with a twinge of condescension that made Theresa smirk. "But first we all have to agree on a theme."

"A theme? You mean for spring carnival?" Matt asked. He and Spence had arrived at the lunch table together, along with a few other fifth-grade boys, and plunked their trays down right in the middle opposite one another.

"Yo, ladies," Spence said. "Tell me you're going to win us that ice cream party."

"Hey—how did you know about the ice cream party?" Anna demanded. "You're newer here than I am."

"My man Matt filled me in," Spence said, grinning. "And when there's ice cream to be eaten, M. C. Spence will not be beaten. So . . . do we have a theme yet?"

Theresa perked up. This was her chance to show *everyone* just how creative she could be. Then maybe they'd all stop thinking of her as the forgetful, disorderly one. "Well, I was thinking we could do—"

"Hollywood," Sharon cut in for the second time. "I said it's going to be Hollywood." She gave Theresa a smug smile, then shoved a fork-ful of mashed potatoes into her mouth.

"That sounds cool," Kimberly Price said as she took the seat across from Sharon. Of course, Kimberly thought everything Sharon said was cool. If Sharon had suggested that they all go drink from a mud puddle, Kimberly would have been the first one outside with a straw.

"Hollywood, huh? What would we do for booths?" Matt asked.

"Tons of things," Sharon said. She set down her fork and leaned forward. "We could have dress-up booths and glamour photos. We could give out Oscars and Emmys. People could make their hand- or footprints in clay, just like they do when they give people stars outside Grauman's Chinese Theatre. We could have a karaoke machine and we could film people singing to make music videos. There could be celebrity look-alike contests, people could have their pictures printed out to look like they were on magazine covers . . . lots of stuff."

Theresa glanced around the table. Kimberly was nodding enthusiastically—of course—and Spence and Matt were kind of squinting, like they were trying to picture it all. Carrie and Anna just kind of shrugged when Theresa looked their way, and the other kids who had sat down while Sharon was talking seemed to be only half listening. No one seemed to think Hollywood was a bad idea, but no one seemed to be super-impressed by it, either.

Theresa ran her thumb and forefinger along the slender silver chain of her charm bracelet. She touched the angel and the unicorn that had supposedly brought Anna and Carrie good luck and wished for a little good luck of her own.

Then she took a deep breath and cleared her throat. "That sounds really interesting and everything," Theresa said, "and you have a lot of great ideas, Sharon, like Anna said, but . . . I have another suggestion."

"What's wrong with Hollywood?" Sharon demanded.

"Nothing," Theresa replied. "Except, well— didn't the eighth grade do something like that last year?"

"So?" Sharon said, cocking her head.

"*Soooo* . . . I just thought maybe we should try to do something original. Something that hasn't been done before," Theresa replied.

Carrie nodded. "Now that I think about it,

I'm pretty sure my sister's class did some kind of Hollywood theme one time, too. And it wasn't the year that they won."

"Sounds like that theme's been played out," Spence said.

Sharon sat up straight and narrowed her eyes. "Just because other classes have done it doesn't mean that we can't. We just have to do it better than they did."

"True enough," Spence said, and for a moment Sharon beamed triumphantly. "But," Spence continued, "we should cheer. / The original idea / is nothing to fear."

Sharon's smile turned into a scowl. "Do you always have to rhyme?"

"Only part-time," Spence replied with a grin. Matt chuckled, and the others did as well, but Sharon didn't look amused.

"So what's your idea, Theresa?" Matt asked, ignoring the glare Sharon was giving him.

"Oh—uh . . ." Theresa looked around. Suddenly everyone at the table was listening to her.

"Yeah, what is it?" Sharon snapped.

"Well, it's . . ." Theresa rubbed her lucky bracelet and cleared her throat. It was now or never. "I was thinking we could do . . . *three thousand four*."

There was silence at the table. Everyone stopped eating and stared blankly at Theresa.

"Three thousand and four *what*?" Sharon asked finally, tilting her head down and raising her eyebrows.

"No." Theresa shook her head. "Not three thousand and four *of* something. Three thousand four—*the year*," she explained. "You know, like a thousand years from now?"

"Ohhh," Carrie said. "I get it. So all our booths would have to be kind of . . . *futuristic*, right?"

"Right," Theresa said, feeling a bit more relaxed now that she'd gotten the words out. "We could call it 'Welcome to 3004' or '3004: A Space Odyssey' or something like that."

It was quiet for another minute, and Theresa chewed on the inside of her cheek as she waited for reactions. Then finally Spence nodded. "That's cool," he said. "I like it."

"Yeah," Matt agreed. "Me too."

Theresa's stomach fluttered with excitement. "Really?"

"Definitely," Anna said. "That's a neat idea."

Sharon clicked her tongue. "But what would we do for booths?" she demanded.

"There are lots of things we could do," Theresa said. "We could have a booth that showed what kind of clothes people will wear in the future. It could be a dress-up booth, like you were saying, or maybe just one of those wooden cutout things that you stand behind and have your picture taken. You know—so it looks like your head is on whatever body is in the picture?"

"I love those," Carrie said. "My dad and I had our picture taken like that once. I was a fisherman and he was a mermaid—it looked really funny. And I might even have a Polaroid camera we can use. I'm pretty sure my uncle has one."

"Great," Theresa said.

"Hey, since it's supposed to be the future, we could serve fortune cookies with funny predictions, like . . ." Anna squinted as she thought it over. Then suddenly her eyes lit up. "Like— 'In 3004 your great-great-great-great-great-great-great-granddaughter will be president of the earth.'"

"Or, 'In 3004 McDonald's will serve thirty million people . . . *on Mars*,'" Kimberly added with a smile. Sharon shot her a glare.

"Yo, we could do something about music in the future, too," Spence said.

"We could call it 'moon rock,'" Kimberly suggested, and again everyone laughed—except Sharon.

"I still think Hollywood would be better," she said. "Matt—you could do something on famous athletes."

Matt nodded thoughtfully, and then his face lit up. "I wonder what kind of extreme sports you could do in zero gravity," he said.

Sharon groaned.

"Hey—we could do something on food, too," Carrie added. "I'm sure people in 3004 would eat way differently than we do now."

"Right." Anna nodded. "And we can—"

"Okay—wait a second," Sharon jumped in. "You guys are all talking like we've already chosen this as our theme. Don't forget, we're having a class meeting next period to vote on ideas, and people might choose Hollywood."

As she looked around the table, Theresa noticed that just about everyone was avoiding eye contact with Sharon. It seemed pretty clear that none of them were considering voting for her idea. Then again, there were something like seventy-five fifth graders altogether, and Theresa was only sitting with six of them.

"That's true," Theresa said. "We don't really know what the theme is going to be yet."

Spence shrugged. "I like the future thing, man. There's so much we could do with it." He picked a french fry off his tray and started waving it around for emphasis. "Crazy space vehicles, life on other planets, intergalactic hip-hop . . ."

"Bungee jumping off space stations," Matt added. "I like the future thing, too—it's awesome."

"And no one's ever done it before," Theresa added.

Sharon frowned. "You don't know that," she scoffed.

"Yes, I do," Theresa replied. "The plaques in the trophy cases name all of the themes people have done, and no one's ever done anything about the future."

"So we could be the first," Anna said. "What was it you said about original ideas, Spence?"

"I said, 'The original idea is nothing to fear—'"

"Okay, okay—we've got it," Sharon snapped, and the table went silent.

"You know, Sharon," Theresa said after a moment, "if we did 3004, you could always do a booth on Hollywood and entertainment of the future."

Sharon tilted her head and sighed. "Yeah . . . I guess I could," she said.

Theresa grinned at Anna and Carrie, who smiled back at her. As obnoxious as Sharon could be at times, she made a good ally. She was loud and convincing, and people generally listened to her. So if Theresa could get her to go for the future theme, too, there was a good chance that it would get chosen.

"In fact, we could use a lot of my ideas for the future theme," Sharon went on. "And actually, now that I think about it, I guess which theme we choose isn't really all that important. It's what we do with it that matters. And with me in charge of decorating, we're sure to win."

Theresa's eyebrows shot up. *Sharon in charge?* Theresa had kind of been hoping that she would have the chance to see her idea all the way through. After all, she'd been the one to come up with it. And it would be the perfect opportunity for her to prove that she wasn't the ditz everyone seemed to think she was.

Again she stroked her lucky bracelet. "I was kind of thinking that maybe *I* could be in charge of the decorating—you know, if my theme gets chosen."

Sharon didn't even try to hide her laughter. "You've got to be kidding," she said, holding one hand across her stomach. "You? In charge of something that big?"

"What's wrong with that?" Theresa asked.

She glanced at her friends, but they had suddenly become captivated by the contents of their lunch trays.

"Oh, nothing," Sharon said. "Except for the fact that you're one of the least organized people I've ever met. You're always dropping things and forgetting things and tripping over things. I'm not trying to be mean or anything, but do you honestly think you could organize the entire fifth-grade area without messing something up?"

"I—" Theresa began, but just then the bell rang, signaling the end of lunch. Startled, Theresa jumped, bumping her tray slightly and sending her half-eaten cherry yogurt tumbling to the floor. "Oh, no," she moaned. There was pink goop all over.

"See what I mean?" Sharon said with a smirk. Then she picked up her tray and left. "See you at the class meeting."

Carrie and Anna rushed to Theresa's side with handfuls of napkins to help her clean up the mess.

"Don't listen to her," Anna said.

"She's just jealous that everyone liked your idea better than hers," Carrie added.

"Thanks," Theresa mumbled, but she couldn't

help wondering if they were being honest with her.

Neither Carrie nor Anna had said a word in her defense—or even looked up from their french fries—when Sharon had been going on and on about what a mess Theresa was. And if her two best friends didn't have faith in her ability to organize the decorations for spring carnival, what were the chances that anyone else would?

CHAPTER
Four

"All right, everyone. Let's get started," Mrs. Wessex called to the buzzing mass of students.

For the fifth-grade meeting, she and Mr. Kane had opened the divider between their rooms, and Mrs. McGuire, the other fifth-grade teacher, had brought her class in, too.

"As you well know," Mrs. Wessex began, "spring carnival is just around the corner, and we need to come up with a theme for our area."

Immediately everyone started whispering excitedly. Things like: "Have you heard about the ice cream party?" and, "We have to win!" There was so much energy in the room, it was hard to sit still.

"Quiet down, please," Mrs. Wessex called. "We need ideas for themes, and I can't hear you if everyone is talking at once. Go ahead and raise your hand if you have a suggestion."

A bunch of hands shot up in the air, and everyone started looking around to see who else was raising theirs.

"Go ahead," Anna said, nudging Theresa with her elbow. "Raise your hand. Tell her your theme."

"Ow," Theresa hissed. "Okay, okay." She was about to put her hand in the air when she saw Sharon's arm shoot up. She waved her arm around. "I have an idea, Mrs. Wessex," she said.

"All right, Sharon," Mrs. Wessex said. "What is it?"

Sharon stood and cleared her throat. "I thought we could do a future theme," she said. "Something like, 'Welcome to 3004' or '3004: A Space Odyssey.'"

Theresa's jaw dropped. She felt her friends' eyes on her, but she couldn't look away from Sharon. Meanwhile, the other students began to whisper their reactions. All the other students who had been raising their hands to say their ideas lowered them back to their sides. No one wanted to compete with what Sharon had just said. "Wow!" Theresa heard, and, "That would be awesome!" A lot of people seemed to really like her idea. Too bad Sharon was getting all the credit.

"That's a wonderful idea, Sharon," Mrs.

Wessex said, turning to write *3004* on the chalk-board. "Anyone else?"

"Um, Mrs. Wessex?" Anna piped up, her hand raised high.

"Yes, Anna?"

"I just wanted to let you know that the future theme was actually Theresa's idea—not Sharon's."

Eyes popped all around the room, and the whispering rose in volume as everyone darted looks at Sharon, Anna, Theresa, and Mrs. Wessex in turn.

"Okay, class—quiet down," Mrs. Wessex said. Meanwhile, Mr. Kane and Mrs. McGuire moved around the room, instructing individuals who were still talking to focus their attention up front.

"Sharon," Mrs. Wessex said when everyone had quieted down again. "Is that true? Was 3004 Theresa's idea?"

Sharon smiled and nodded as though she'd done absolutely nothing wrong. "Oh, yes," she said. "It was Theresa's idea. But she was so nervous about saying it in front of everybody that I thought I'd do it for her."

"Yeah, right," Theresa muttered out of the corner of her mouth.

Mrs. Wessex glanced toward Theresa briefly and pursed her lips. "I see," she said, and

Theresa had a feeling that she really did. "Well, thank you, Sharon, for getting the idea out there, and thank you, Theresa, for coming up with it. Now . . . do we have any others?"

The room was silent for a moment. Then Billy Rafuse raised his hand.

"William?" Mrs. Wessex called.

"I was just thinking, along with the 3004 thing, do you think we could do something on spaceships?"

"Oh, well," Mrs. Wessex said. "Yes—I'm sure we could, but we haven't actually chosen 3004 as our theme yet. That's just one of the suggestions."

"It would be so perfect, though," Billy insisted. "I have this huge NASA book at home, and I could design a bunch of rocket ships that could be cars of the future—"

"Hey—there's a Web site with cars of the future on it," Jeremy Gray cut in. "Maybe we could use some of those to—"

"My brother uses this 'search for extraterrestrials' program as a screen saver on his computer," Maria Mancini added. "Maybe we could set that up somewhere." One hand after another shot into the air as people came up with more ideas for the future theme. Pretty soon everyone was talking at once.

Theresa's face lit up as she listened. Kimberly was saying something about having a future fashion show, while Lauren Graham was suggesting a scale model of a 3004 space station. Spence and Matt were talking extreme sports and hip-hop again, and Adam Kersnowski thought it would be cool to have *The Jetsons* and *Futurama* playing on a TV somewhere.

"Wow—everyone really loves your idea, Resa," Carrie said.

Theresa grinned. "Seems like it," she agreed. "Thanks for speaking up for me, Anna."

"No problem," Anna replied. "I wasn't about to let Sharon steal your glory."

Just then Mrs. Wessex raised her hands. "All right, all right," she said. "I can see you're all very excited about Theresa's idea, and that's wonderful. But we only have a few minutes left to finish our class meeting, and I want to make sure we get everyone's ideas for themes on the board so we can take a vote."

Once again the class quieted down, and Mrs. Wessex repeated her original question. "Now—does anyone else have a *theme* suggestion?"

Theresa glanced around the room and waited, but no hands were raised.

"Nobody?" Mrs. Wessex asked, her brow furrowed.

She waited another fifteen seconds, but no one responded. "All right," she said slowly. "Well, then, let me just take an informal poll. How many of you—by a show of hands—would like to go with Theresa Allen's suggestion: 3004?"

Theresa was shocked to see nearly every hand in the room shoot up. Gradually she raised her hand, too, and in another five seconds she couldn't spot anyone who hadn't.

"Oh, my," Mrs. Wessex exclaimed, smiling. "I've never had a class reach consensus that quickly. Maybe it's a sign that this is the fifth grade's year to win."

"Yeah!" a few students called out. Then, when Mrs. Wessex turned to the board and circled Theresa's theme, everyone cheered.

"Now," Mrs. Wessex said, her voice rising over the chatter, "we're going to need someone to be in charge of coordinating all of the booths and overseeing the decorations for the area so that everything fits with the theme."

Theresa's heart fluttered. She wanted to be in charge more than anything! Planning and coordinating the decorations sounded like so much fun. If only she weren't so disorganized. Then maybe people would believe that she could do it. Maybe *she'd* even believe that she could do it.

"I'll be in charge of decorations, Mrs. Wessex," Sharon called out.

"Oh, that's very generous of you, Sharon," Mrs. Wessex said, "but I thought that since the theme was Theresa's idea, we'd see if she was interested in the position first. Theresa?"

Theresa's stomach flipped. Everyone in the room was staring at her. Maria and Lauren were whispering and giggling over in the corner, and Theresa was positive they were talking about her and what a joke it would be for her to be in charge.

"Oh . . . uh," Theresa stuttered. She hadn't expected Mrs. Wessex to just offer her the position. She'd assumed the class would have to vote for a decorating chairperson, and it seemed clear from all of the shocked expressions around her that she wouldn't have been their first choice.

"Theresa?" Mrs. Wessex repeated. "What do you think?"

"Well . . ." Theresa hesitated. "I . . ." She glanced around. Carrie and Anna were staring at her wide-eyed, and Sharon was scowling. Not exactly votes of confidence.

"Theresa?" Mrs. Wessex asked again.

Theresa swallowed hard. She wanted to, but she wasn't sure she should. Or, more accurately, she wasn't sure she *could*. Then she heard her sister's voice—"*You'd lose your feet if they weren't attached to your ankles.*" Suddenly a feeling of indignation rose in her chest.

"I'll do it!" Theresa said suddenly. The words came out a little louder than she had meant them to, but at least they were out there.

"Wonderful," Mrs. Wessex said, beaming at Theresa. "I'm sure you'll do an excellent job."

Theresa smiled nervously. She certainly hoped she would, but part of her was already wondering if she'd made the right decision. Apparently her friends were wondering the same thing—Anna and Carrie were both staring at her cautiously.

"Are you sure you want to do this, Resa?" Carrie whispered. "That's a lot of . . . *work.*"

"And a lot of organizing, too," Anna piped in.

Oh, great, Theresa thought. Her friends didn't think she could do it. A sudden wave of anxiety washed over her, and she felt her palms begin to sweat. Maybe they were right. Being in charge of the entire fifth-grade area wasn't going to be easy, and being organized wasn't exactly Theresa's strong point.

Maybe I should let somebody else do it, Theresa thought. She was just about to raise her hand and bow out when Mrs. Wessex began talking again.

"All right, so that's settled. Tonight I want everyone to think about booth ideas to go along with Theresa's theme. We'll be having another class meeting tomorrow during third period to iron out all of the details. And then, once your booths have been approved, you can start working on them. Theresa, you can focus on coming up with some general decorating ideas for now, and then when we know what all of the booths are going to be, I'll get you a copy of the list so that you can check in with everyone and make sure everything gets coordinated. Okay?"

"Okay," Theresa said. *What have I gotten myself into?* she thought. What if she couldn't handle it? What if she let the whole class down and blew their chance to be the first fifth grade to win spring carnival? She pressed her eyes closed and heard Sharon's words echoing in her head. *"You've got to be kidding! You? In charge of something that big?"* And then in the distance she heard Sharon's voice again—but this time it was for real.

She was all the way across the room in a group with Billy, Jeremy, Maria, and Lauren, and she was talking softly, but Theresa could still hear her. It was like her ears had focused in on the conversation the minute she'd heard Sharon say her name.

"I can't believe Mrs. Wessex put *Theresa* in charge," she was saying. "She is so totally klutzy and disorganized. There goes our shot at winning." Theresa tried to keep listening, but she was distracted by Carrie tugging at her arm.

"Resa—come on. We have to get to science class," she said.

"Huh? Oh, right," Theresa said, gathering up her books. She wished she'd been able to hear whether or not the others agreed with Sharon, but it was too late now. Everyone was filtering out of the room to get to their fifth-period class.

"Shoot," Theresa mumbled. It would have been nice to know how the others had responded.

"Theresa—is something wrong?" Anna asked.

"Oh, no. It's nothing," Theresa fibbed. She didn't want to repeat what she'd overheard—it would only make them feel bad for her, and it would make her feel worse. Besides, what if they agreed with Sharon?

"Good," Anna said. "Then let's go."

As they walked into the hallway, Carrie turned to face the other two girls. "Hey—how did you guys do on that homework, anyway?"

"What homework?" Theresa asked.

"You know, the reading we had to do for science class, with all those questions about solar power and light waves. I was totally lost by the end of the chapter," Carrie said.

"Wait a second—we had science homework last night?" Theresa said. "When did Mr. Howell assign that?"

"Yesterday during class," Anna said. "He wrote it on the side of the chalkboard like he always does."

"Oh, man," Theresa said. "He's going to kill me. I totally spaced out. Sometimes I'm so—" Theresa stopped short, but she was all too aware of the word she'd been about to use: *disorganized.*

Jeez. If she couldn't even stay on top of her homework assignments, how was she going to keep up with all of this spring carnival stuff? Something told her she'd bitten off way more than she could chew. And when all was said and done, Amy would know she'd been right. With Theresa involved, the fifth grade didn't stand a chance.

CHAPTER
Five

"Theresa—your ice cream is starting to drip," Carrie said. "Either you have to hold it yourself, or I'm going to start licking it."

"Okay, okay. Just a second," Theresa said. "I want to show you what I got at Sara's." She opened the white plastic bag she was holding and removed what looked like a black, leather-bound book. "Ta-da!" she said, setting it on the large, round, green metal table in the middle of the mall's food court.

"What's that?" Anna asked, taking a bite of mint chocolate chip.

"My new planner," Theresa announced. She held the book at several different angles and ran her hand across the cover like a game show model.

"Beautiful," Carrie said. "Now take your ice cream."

"Fine," Theresa replied. She took the cone from Carrie's hand and began licking the nearly melted coffee ice cream all around the edges. In less than fifteen seconds she had all the drips stopped and everything under control. "There," she said. "Now—don't you want to know why I bought myself a planner?"

"Is this a trick question?" Anna asked. "Because I sort of figured it had something to do with the way Mr. Howell said, 'Theresa—you need to get a planner,' in science class today." Carrie giggled and Theresa cocked her head.

"Very funny," she said. "But that's only part of the reason." She unsnapped a clasp on the front of the planner and flipped it open. "See— it has a calendar section in the front with plenty of space for me to write all my assignments, but it also has all this other stuff."

Theresa waved her hand over the back section of the planner, which was full of different sorts of paper—lined, blank, graph, and colored.

"Maybe you should drop out of school and make a career out of modeling planners on the Home Shopping Network," Anna suggested.

"*Anna*," Theresa groaned.

Carrie pointed to Theresa's cone. "You're dripping," she said, but her warning came too late. A dark brown chocolate chip covered in light brown coffee ice cream splattered onto the paper in Theresa's planner.

"Shoot!" Theresa reached for a napkin. She dabbed at the ice cream, but while she was wiping it, more ice cream fell off her cone and landed on the paper. By the time she was done, sticky brown drips covered the back section, causing most of the pages to stick together. Theresa stared at it. "I can't believe I just did that."

"At least the calendar part is still okay," Carrie said, wincing slightly.

"Yeah." Theresa snorted. "I guess."

Anna jogged over to Ed's, where the girls had gotten their ice cream, and returned with a handful of napkins, a bowl, and a plastic spoon. "Here," she said. "Just stick your ice cream in the bowl, and then show us the rest of your stuff."

Theresa sighed. "Thanks, Anna," she said. She upended her cone and plunged it into the bowl, ice cream first. Then, after wiping her hands clean on a few napkins, she examined her planner.

"Well, a few pages are still okay," she said. "But not enough to help me keep track of everything for spring carnival." Theresa shook her head and exhaled heavily. "Maybe Sharon was right. Maybe I should tell Mrs. Wessex to choose someone else to be in charge."

"Well . . ." Anna tilted her head. "If you're not comfortable being in charge, you could always just tell her you've changed your mind."

"I didn't say I was *uncomfortable*," Theresa said. "I mean, I *want* to do it—I just don't want to mess everything up."

"I'm sure you won't," Carrie said, but Theresa couldn't help feeling that she didn't sound all that convinced.

"Did you get anything else at Sara's?" Anna asked, pointing to Theresa's bag. "It looks like something else is in there."

"Oh," Theresa said, picking up the white plastic bag on her lap. "Yeah, there is, but—"

"Well, show it to us," Anna said.

Theresa sighed again. It seemed kind of pointless now that her planner was virtually destroyed. She reached into the bag and pulled out a long black tube with white caps at each end.

"Uh, Theresa," Anna started. "Is that a magic wand?"

"I wish," Theresa said. She waved it around a few times and said, "Abracadabra! Fix my planner! Hocus-pocus! Finish my science homework!"

"That would be awesome," Carrie said. "I'd

use it to make myself an endless supply of black raspberry ice cream."

"No way—mint chocolate chip," Anna said. "But you said it wasn't a magic wand. So . . . what is it?"

Theresa popped a white cap off one end and tilted the tube until a pen slid out. It was shiny and black, just like the tube, except that it had glittery silver stars and moons all over it. Perched at the top was a silver fairy with delicate wire mesh wings and a wand with a star on the end.

"Wow, that's really pretty, Resa," Carrie said.

"Thanks," Theresa said. "I was going to keep it with my planner. See—there's a little pen holder on the side." She slid the pen into a small elastic loop, then drew her hand back quickly. "Ew!" she said, wiping ice cream off her hand. Apparently she'd missed a spot when she was cleaning up. "Great, now my pen's all sticky, too."

"I'm sure you can wash it off," Anna said.

"Yeah, maybe," Theresa said. But she was feeling pretty discouraged. It seemed like the harder she tried to get organized, the worse things got.

"Yo—ladies," a familiar voice called. Theresa looked up to see Spence and Matt approaching the table. Each of the boys pulled out a chair, flipped it around, and sat down straddling the back of it. "What's going down?"

"My self-esteem," Theresa mumbled.

"What was that?" Spence asked.

Theresa shook her head. "Nothing," she said. "I'm just trying to get organized for spring carnival, and it's not going so well."

"Oh, that's right," Matt said, turning to Theresa. "You're in charge of everything, aren't you? That's great that everyone went for your idea."

Theresa looked down at her ruined planner. "I just hope I don't screw it up."

"You won't," Spence said. "The decorations will be ill / but right now it's time to chill. / You girls up for some danger? / A game of Storm Ranger?"

Theresa smiled in spite of herself. "How do you do that?" she asked.

Spence widened his eyes. "Do what?"

"Rhyme everything."

"Oh, that," Spence said. "I don't know. It just kind of happens—I open my mouth and start rappin'. It's probably from listening to so much hip-hop, you know? It's like reading a lot of Dr. Seuss. / Pretty soon your tongue gets loose."

"And you start to sound like Mother Goose," Carrie said.

"Not bad, not bad," Spence said, giving Carrie a high five. "We'll have you freestyling in no time."

"I don't know about that," Carrie said, "but I would like to try Storm Ranger. I've heard Anna and Matt talk about it so much, I feel like I already know how to play."

"All right," Spence said. "Anyone else?"

"Anna will play," Matt said. "She has to try to beat my latest high score. I made it to level twelve yesterday and saw a completely new enemy."

"You did?" Anna said. "Who was it?"

"Mr. Feetstink," Matt said with a perfectly straight face.

"Mr. Feetstink?" Theresa repeated. "Who's he?"

"He's supposed to be a high school gym teacher who mutated when Dr. Sphere hit him with his chaos laser," Matt explained. "Now he has forty-two feet and he attacks by taking off his sneakers and blasting you with his foot odor."

"That's great," Spence said, chuckling. "I *have* to play this game. Anna, Theresa—you in?"

"I am," Anna said.

"Ohhh," Theresa said. "I'd like to, but . . ." She stared down at her sticky planner and her even stickier pen. "I can't." She shook her head. "I have to figure out some of this spring carnival stuff."

"Do you want us to stay and help?" Carrie asked.

"No—you guys go ahead without me," Theresa said.

"Are you sure?" Anna asked.

"Definitely," Theresa replied. "Have a good time—and shatter Matt's high score."

Anna laughed. "I will," she said. "And then I'll show Carrie how to do it, too."

"Oh, right," Matt said. "Like it's that easy."

"It is for me," Anna said with a shrug.

Theresa smiled as she watched them walk toward the arcade, Anna and Matt trading insults all the way. Once they were out of sight, she looked down at the table and focused on her planner. "Time to get to work," she told herself.

She grabbed her fairy pen and gave it a tug, but thanks to the ice cream spill, it was stuck in its holder. "Ugh," Theresa groaned. She gave it another tug, but it still wouldn't come loose. Frustrated, Theresa tightened her grip around the fairy and gave it one more pull—too hard a pull, as it turned out.

The pen came free right away, but Theresa had pulled so forcefully that she'd ended up pulling the fairy right off the end. "Oh, no," Theresa said. "I can't believe I just broke it!

I've only owned it for ten minutes!"

She set the fairy ornament on the table and looked at it closely. "If there ever was a sign, this is it. I should just tell Mrs. Wessex I've changed my mind. If I can't even *touch* organizing materials without messing them up, then I certainly can't do the organizing!" She reached for the small silver ornament on the table, intending to toss it in the garbage along with her now-ruined planner. But just as she was about to grab it, it moved.

Theresa gasped.

First it just sort of wobbled to the right. Then it shifted back to the left. And then, while Theresa watched, wide-eyed, the tiny fairy began to grow. Slowly at first, then faster, until she was nearly two inches tall. Her wings and wand vanished, and her silver coloring melted away.

Instead, the little sprite was wearing a white T-shirt, brown cargo shorts, a Red Sox baseball cap, and a backpack. She had thick wool socks and muddy hiking boots, and in one hand she was holding a long, thick stick that reached all the way to the ground.

"I'm ready when you—" the fairy started. Then she blinked a few times and looked around. "Wait a second," she said. "This is *not* the Missouri River, and you're *definitely* not Sacajawea."

CHAPTER

Six

"Wh-Who . . . w-what?" stammered Theresa. She had to be seeing things.

"I hate it when this happens." The little fairy shook her head. She stuffed her hand into her front pocket and dug around frantically for something. "Oh, no—don't tell me I left it at home."

Left what at home? Theresa wondered. She was too stunned to say it out loud.

Suddenly the tiny sprite clutched something in her hand and exhaled. "Phew," she said, extracting a small purple stone from her pocket. "Amethyst," she said to Theresa. "My lucky gem. It calms me—helps me to focus. If you'll just excuse me for a moment."

The little fairy turned around and hopped into the air. The next thing Theresa knew, she was hovering about a foot above the table, sitting cross-legged on a purple pillow with yellow tassels at the corners.

"What are you—?"

"Shhh," the fairy murmured. "I'm meditating."

She placed the amethyst on the pillow in front of her, closed her eyes, and rested her hands on her knees, palms up. "Deep breath in," she said to herself, "and a deep breath out. Another deep breath in. And a deep breath out. Okay—one more time. Deep breath in and a deep breath out." She sat silently for a moment, then scooped up the amethyst and snapped her fingers.

"Ahhh, that's better," she said. "I feel much more centered now. Okay—where were we?"

Theresa stared and blinked. "I think you said something about Sacajawea," she offered.

"Oh, that's right," the fairy said. "I was just about to hike out of the Missouri River Valley with Lewis and Clark when I got sent here. Oh, well. I guess I'll have to finish that trail another day."

"You were hiking with *Lewis and Clark*? And *Sacajawea*?"

"Yes. Lovely people, all of them. And so brave. I—"

Just then a high-pitched beeping came from out of nowhere. "Oh—that's me," the fairy said. She unclipped a small black pager from her shorts. "Time to find out what this is all about. I'll just be a moment, okay?"

"Uh . . . okay," Theresa replied. She watched as the fairy tossed the pager into the air and snapped her fingers. Instantly the pager was transformed into what looked like a miniature hovering computer screen.

Theresa could see that it was covered with words, but the letters were far too small for her to read. The fairy, however, was having no trouble. She kept pointing at the screen and waving her finger, scrolling through documents and muttering to herself every now and then.

"Mm-hm. . . mm-hm . . . Theresa Allen . . . right . . . *ohhh—klutzy and disorganized?* That wasn't very nice. Mm-hm . . . right, I see . . . spring carnival . . . confidence issues . . . organizationally challenged . . . yep . . . okay . . . got it."

She snapped her fingers again, turning the monitor back into a tiny pager, which she caught in her hand and clipped back onto her shorts.

"Okay," she said. "Why don't you have a nice, soothing cup of chamomile tea and tell me all about this spring carnival event." The fairy circled one of her hands in the air, and a cup and saucer appeared in front of Theresa.

"Um, I don't drink tea," Theresa said.

"No problem," the fairy said. "What would you like? Cocoa? Apple juice? Water with lemon?" With each suggestion she pointed to the cup in front of Theresa, transforming its contents into the various beverages.

"Actually, I'm fine," Theresa said.

"Suit yourself," the fairy said. She pointed one last time and the cup disappeared altogether. Theresa leaned forward and rested her head on her hands so that she was only inches away from the tiny figure.

"Are you real?" she whispered. "Or am I dreaming?"

The fairy reached forward and jabbed Theresa's hand with her stick. "Ow!" Theresa said, jerking her hand back.

"I'm real. Dreams don't leave imprints," the fairy said. Theresa glanced at the spot where she'd been hit and saw a tiny red mark.

"No, I guess they don't," Theresa said. "But still—"

"I know," the fairy replied. "You've probably never seen a magical being before, but trust me— I *am* real. I'm Isadora, by the way. Izzy for short."

"I'm Theresa," Theresa said. "But then, I guess you knew that." The small figure smiled. "So then—are you really a *fairy*?"

Izzy nodded. "I certainly am—certified by the UFC."

"The *what*?"

"The UFC—Universal Fairy College. I have an undergraduate degree in general enchantment and a master's in social work."

"Wow," Theresa said. "But if you're a—" She glanced around to make sure no one was watching or listening to her. No one seemed to be, but she lowered her voice just in case. "If you're a fairy, why don't you have—?"

Izzy held up her hands. "Wings, right? You were going to say wings, weren't you?"

"Well, yeah," Theresa said. "And a magic wand."

The fairy shook her head, swishing her long brown ponytail back and forth. "I will never understand why you humans make us look so ridiculous."

"What do you mean?" Theresa said. "I think fairies are pretty."

"Pretty? Maybe. But foolish nonetheless. We're always drawn like cute little Barbie dolls flitting about in short skirts and butterfly wings. It's really not a very flattering image."

"You mean, fairies don't fly?" Theresa asked.

"Oh, we fly," Izzy said. "But we don't need

wings to do it. Of course, some fairies do wear wings from time to time, but only for special occasions. You know . . . weddings, graduations—things like that. But not all the time—and definitely not to fly. They'd get in the way."

"What about magic wands?" Theresa asked.

"Wands are for beginners," Izzy said. "I gave mine up during my second year of graduate school. Now I just wave my hands or snap my fingers or nod—whatever I feel like doing. It's all the same. See?"

Izzy stuck out her hand and clenched it into a fist, and across the table a napkin curled itself up into a ball. Then she flicked open her fingers and it went sailing into the trash.

"Cool," Theresa said, but the fairy wasn't done.

Next, Izzy snapped her fingers, and Theresa watched in amazement as her melted ice cream formed itself into a neat scoop again. Then, when Izzy raised her eyebrows and glanced at Theresa, the ice-cream cone righted itself and floated over to Theresa, who grabbed it and took a lick.

"Good as new, right?" Izzy said, smiling.

"Definitely," Theresa said.

Finally Isadora folded her arms at chest level and nodded, changing her entire outfit from shorts, T-shirt, hiking boots, and backpack into jeans, a peasant blouse, and Birkenstock sandals in the blink of an eye. Her Red Sox cap was gone, and her long brown hair hung loosely about her shoulders and cascaded down her back.

"Wow," Theresa said. "That's amazing."

"It comes in pretty handy," Isadora said.

"I bet," Theresa agreed.

"So—let's get down to business. Talk to me about spring carnival," Isadora said. "I'm here to help you out."

"You *are*?" Theresa exclaimed. "Awesome! So then can you just, like, snap your fingers and get everything organized for me?"

Izzy tilted her head and winced. "Unfortunately that's not the way it works."

"Why not?"

"Well, have you ever heard the expression 'Give a girl a fish and she'll eat for a day; teach a girl to fish and she'll eat for life'?"

"*No-o*," Theresa said. "What does fishing have to do with spring carnival?"

"Yo, Tee—that's a good question." Theresa spun around to see Spence standing behind her. "And here's another one—who are you talking to?"

CHAPTER
Seven

"Oh, I, uh," Theresa started. She glanced from Spence down to Izzy and back again.

"What'd you do—get another ice cream?" Spence asked, squinting at Theresa's perfectly intact cone.

"My other one, uh, melted." She stared down at Izzy again and saw that Spence had followed her gaze, but he didn't appear in the least bit shocked. If anything, he seemed puzzled as to what she was looking at. Evidently he couldn't see the tiny fairy standing there.

"Who's this?" Izzy asked.

"Spence," Theresa responded automatically.

"Yo," Spence replied. "I'm right here—you got my ear."

"Oh, right," Theresa said. If Spence couldn't see Izzy, he probably couldn't hear her, either, which meant that Theresa needed to stop answering her out loud. Unless, of course, she wanted Spence to think she was insane.

"Hey, you okay, Tee?" Spence asked. "You look a little . . . spooked."

Theresa gave a nervous laugh. "Spooked?" she said. "No, I just—well, you sort of scared me before. I was, you know, trying to come up with ideas for spring carnival, and I guess I was pretty focused."

"I'll say you were," Spence agreed. "You were talking to yourself."

"Oh, I do that sometimes," Theresa said quickly. "It's sort of a weird habit, I know."

"Ain't no thang," Spence said. "I talk to myself all the time."

"I like this boy," Izzy said. "He's very in touch with his inner self. And he has unique speech patterns."

Theresa had to fake a cough to keep herself from laughing.

"Where's everyone else?" Theresa asked when she had regained her composure.

"Still in the arcade," Spence said. "Carrie's on her third game with Anna coaching, and then Anna and Matt are gonna go head-to-head."

Theresa took a lick from her ice cream. "Did you play?" she asked.

"I got squashed on level five by some kind of lizard-horse-snake thing."

"Too bad," Theresa said.

"Nah, it's all right," Spence replied, pulling out a chair. "I wanted to come back and talk to you about spring carnival anyway."

Theresa raised her eyebrows. "You *did*?" she asked. She bit off a big section of chocolate cappuccino chunk and licked her lips.

"Yeah, I need help coming up with an idea for a booth."

"Ahhh," Izzy said, smiling at Theresa. "People seek you out for advice. You're a natural leader."

Theresa snorted. "The ideas come easy—it's the organization I'm worried about," she muttered.

"Whoa—can you play that back for me one time?" Spence said.

"Oh, sorry," Theresa replied, realizing she'd done it again. "I guess I was just thinking out loud." She turned away from Spence, pretending to wipe her chin with a napkin and mimed locking her mouth shut and throwing away the key to Izzy.

"I can be quiet," the little fairy said. She snapped her fingers and went back to hovering on her pillow again.

Theresa turned to Spence. "So," she said, having another bite of ice cream, "what did you have in mind?"

"Well, I wanted to do something hip-hop related."

"That's a shocker," Theresa joked. "Are you doing it with Matt?"

"Nah—Matt wants to do some kind of sports thing," Spence said. "I'm on my own right now, which is no problem. Trouble is, I'm not sure what to *do* for the booth other than maybe play music and call it intergalactic hip-hop, you know? I mean, how do I make it, like, a *booth*?"

"Mmm." Theresa nodded. "I see what you mean." She licked her ice cream while she thought it over. A couple of seconds later the idea came to her in a flash.

"How about this—you could call your booth something like 'Spence's Intergalactic Hip-Hop Stop' and have it be a club that plays music and serves trendy refreshments—with hip-hop names, of course. *Or*"—Theresa paused to lick her cone again—"you could make it into a futuristic music store, and you could pretend to be a big hip-hop star from another galaxy who's there for some kind of promotion. You could come up with a bunch of fake album covers, and people could try to compete with you at some kind of rapping or rhyming game."

"You mean like a freestyle battle?"

"I guess," Theresa said. "Is that what you'd call it?"

"Yep. Two MCs trading phrases, trying to outdo each other—that's a battle. Cool idea, Tee. Thanks."

"Sure," Theresa said, "but I didn't really do anything."

"But you did—you gave me a place to start. And you also made me hungry," Spence added, eyeing her ice-cream cone. "I'm gonna go score a scoop—you need anything?"

"No, I'm all set, thanks," Theresa said. As Spence jogged over to Ed's, she looked down at Izzy, who was giving her a smug smile.

"That was wonderful," Izzy said. "He came to you for help, and you solved his problem. You're very good at this."

Theresa rolled her eyes. "I told you—the ideas come easy to me. It's keeping organized that gives me trouble."

"Nonsense. You just have to stay focused and trust your instincts."

"My instincts ruined my planner," Theresa said, nodding at the sticky mess of pages in front of her.

"No problem," Izzy said. She waved both of her hands in wide circles, and, right before Theresa's eyes, the planner went from stained and gooey to perfectly clean.

"Whoa—thanks," Theresa said, lifting it into the air to examine it.

Suddenly the little fairy hopped down and started glancing around. "Is it me, or did it just get really cold in here?"

"Huh?"

"Theresa!" a familiar voice called.

"Ugh," Theresa groaned. "It's not you," she told Izzy. She turned around to see Sharon approaching while Kimberly, Lauren, and Maria stayed behind chatting in a small group.

"Hey," Sharon said, "we just saw Carrie, Matt, and Anna in the arcade, and they said you were down here working on spring carnival stuff."

"Ooh," Izzy said, narrowing her eyes. "I'm getting a really bad vibe from this one—lots of negative energy. Something tells me you shouldn't trust her."

"I don't," Theresa said. Then she looked up at Sharon. "I mean, I *am*," she corrected herself quickly. "Working on spring carnival stuff, that is." She glanced down at Izzy, and the fairy sighed.

"I know. Quiet," she said, jumping back onto her floating pillow.

"So, how's it going?" Sharon asked. "Have you come up with a lot of decorating ideas yet?"

"*Well* . . ." Theresa hesitated.

"You know," Sharon went on, "at first I was kind of upset that you got picked to be in charge of our theme instead of me, but now I'm kind of glad."

Theresa narrowed her eyes. "You are?" she asked.

"Absolutely," Sharon said. "I mean, you have *so* much work to do! You have to decide how to decorate our section of the gym and keep track of what everyone's planning to do for booths. You'll need to find out how much you can spend on decorations and submit some kind of budget to Mrs. Wessex. At some point you'll have to get together a decorating committee and find time to meet to plan things out, and then you'll have to be at school early to help set everything up and stay late to make sure it all gets taken down. Phew! That's a lot of work. But then, if you weren't up for it, I guess you wouldn't have told Mrs. Wessex you could do it."

"Wow, I don't usually dislike people," Izzy commented from her pillow, "but in her case, I might have to make an exception."

Theresa scratched her head and tried to ignore her little friend. "Um . . . what are you doing for a booth, Sharon?" she asked.

"I haven't decided yet," Sharon said. "I'm having a hard time coming up with something to fit your theme."

"*My* theme?" Theresa said.

"Well, of course—it was *your* idea, right? Isn't that what Anna said? *'The future theme was Theresa's idea, not Sharon's'?*"

"Um—"

"Oh, it's okay," Sharon said. "I'm actually glad she cleared that up. I've heard a lot of people say they're having a hard time with the theme, and I'd hate for them to think it was my idea. I mean, 3004 sounded good during the class meeting and all, but no one really seems to be coming up with any good booth ideas. But then, I'm sure people will come to you if they have problems."

"Well," Theresa said, "Spence did." She nodded toward Ed's, where Spence was just paying for a huge cone with three different-colored scoops of ice cream on top.

"Hey, Sharon," Kimberly said, running up to her side. "Spence is over at Ed's. Lauren, Maria, and I are going to head over, 'kay?"

"Okay," Sharon said. "I'll meet you over there." Kimberly ran back to the others, and then the three of them headed toward Spence, giggling all the way. "They are *so* immature," Sharon remarked, shaking her head. "Well, anyway, good luck with everything. Oh—I see you bought a planner."

"I did," Theresa said. "I think it will really help."

Sharon shrugged. "Maybe," she said. "But my mother—she's a lawyer, you know—she says that I was born organized. It's in my genes."

"In your—?"

"*Genes,*" Sharon said. "You know—I inherited my ability to stay organized from her. And my dad—he's really organized, too. My mom says people either have it or they don't, and that stuff like planners and PalmPilots may make a person *look* organized for a while, but they don't really help in the long run."

"Oh," Theresa said. "Well—"

"Anyway, I have to get going," Sharon interrupted. "But hey—don't worry about your theme. I don't think it's nearly as lame as everyone else seems to. And besides, I'm sure you'll get a chance to help everyone with their problems at tomorrow's class meeting."

"That's it," Theresa heard a small voice say, and when she looked up, Isadora was floating above Sharon's head, sitting cross-legged on a big gray storm cloud. "Say the word and I'll soak her," the fairy said.

"Izzy!" Theresa shouted.

Sharon drew back. "Huh?"

"Oh, uh . . ." Theresa glanced nervously at Sharon, who was staring at her like she'd gone completely insane. "It's just . . . I was saying . . ."

"'Is he,'" Sharon said. "You shouted out, 'Is he.'"

"Right," Theresa said. "I meant, um, Spence. I think he's done getting his ice cream. I was going to say, 'Is he leaving?' Because I thought you wanted to talk to him—didn't you?"

Sharon squinted at Theresa. "Not really," she said. "But I guess I should catch up with Kimberly and the others." She nodded toward Theresa's planner and smirked. "Good luck getting organized."

"Thanks," Theresa said, forcing herself to smile. But as soon as Sharon turned to walk away, she dropped her head into her hands and moaned.

Izzy snapped her fingers, vaporized the cloud, and glided down to the table, where she stood, rubbing her amethyst in her hands. "Whoa. I don't know what got into me there. I'm usually very calm, but that girl—"

"Sharon has a way of getting to people," Theresa said.

"I'll say," Izzy agreed. She plunked the amethyst into her front pocket and stood with her arms at her sides, her feet about a half-inch apart.

"Izzy?" Theresa said.

"Shhh!" hissed the fairy. Then she took a deep breath, raising both arms into the air and bringing her palms together above her head. Theresa watched as Isadora took a big step forward with her right leg. She sank into a deep lunge and held it—her arms straight, her palms pressed together, and her gaze focused straight ahead. After about thirty seconds she stepped back, bringing her legs together again, took another deep breath, and repeated the lunge position with her left leg forward.

Theresa watched and waited until finally, after another thirty seconds had passed, Izzy stepped back, lowered her arms, and exhaled heavily. "Phew. Warrior one is my favorite pose. It always centers me and brings me back to a place of peace."

Theresa squinted. *A place of peace?* This fairy

just kept getting weirder and weirder. No wings, no wand, and now . . . *yoga*?

"Ahhh, that's better," Izzy said, shaking out her arms and legs. "I feel much more relaxed now. How about you? Do you need a little centering exercise? I could lead you through a few stretches."

Theresa glanced at all the people milling about and wondered how it would look if she stood up and started practicing yoga in the middle of the food court. "Thanks, but I think I'll pass," she told Izzy.

"Suit yourself," Isadora said with a shrug. "Just as long as you didn't believe any of that stuff Sharon was saying about spring carnival."

Theresa winced.

"You didn't . . . *did you?*" Izzy asked.

"Maybe just a little," she said with a half shrug.

"You can't," Izzy told her. "She was *trying* to upset you. That's the whole reason she came over here. I hate people like that. I mean— shoot! There I go again." In one quick motion Isadora plunged herself back into warrior one. "*Hate* is a very strong word," she said, keeping her gaze forward. "I don't *hate* her. I just—" All at once the little fairy dropped her arms to her sides and shook her head.

"Are you okay, Izzy?" Theresa asked.

Isadora stared up at Theresa, shamefaced. "I have anger issues," she said quietly.

"Anger issues?" Theresa repeated.

Izzy nodded and glanced down at the table. "Like I said, I'm usually very calm, but every once in a while someone pushes my buttons—you know what I mean?"

Theresa gazed toward Ed's, where Sharon and the others were still standing. "I know what you mean."

"One time," Izzy continued, her head still lowered, "I turned a snobby rich woman into a miniature poodle for two whole days. I thought seeing life as a lapdog might humble her."

"You turned her into a—?" Theresa began. Then she giggled. "Did it work?"

"Well, *yes*," Isadora answered. "She definitely gained a little perspective. But the UFC didn't exactly approve. Fairies aren't supposed to change people into animals—at least not without an advanced degree in transmogrification."

"Oh," Theresa said. "I see."

"Still, I think that friend of yours deserved a little rainstorm. It might have cooled her down a bit," Izzy said.

"Yeah, maybe," Theresa agreed, "and it would have been kind of funny, too."

"Well, I'll try to control myself in the future, but if she starts talking like that again, I just might have to douse her," Izzy said.

Theresa pictured Sharon getting soaked by a shower in the middle of the mall and chuckled. But when she remembered all the things Sharon had said, her smile faded.

"Unfortunately, I think Sharon's right," Theresa said.

"Are you joking?" Izzy asked.

"No," Theresa replied, shaking her head. "I mean, the planner is a nice idea, but owning it isn't going to change the way I am. I'm horrible at keeping organized. I can't keep track of all the stuff she was talking about! Budgets, booth ideas, decorations, a committee—it's too much."

"It may sound like a lot when you lump it all together like that, but trust me—you can do it," Izzy said. "You just have to take it step by step."

"Izzy," Theresa said, "you don't understand. I'm a total mental klutz. I had already forgotten that there *was* a class meeting tomorrow! I can't stay on top of all of this. Planner or no planner, I'm just not good at being organized."

"Do you know how many negative statements you just made about yourself?" Izzy asked.

"Huh?"

"Seven," Isadora said. "At least. And that's too many. Come on—grab all of your stuff and let's get out of here. We've got work to do."

"Where are we going?" Theresa asked.

"Home," Izzy said. "There are too many distractions at the mall."

"All right," Theresa said with a sigh. She stood up and stuffed her planner and her broken pen back into the Sara's bag, put on her backpack, and offered her outstretched palm to Izzy.

Izzy glanced down at Theresa's hand. "What's that for?"

"Hop on," Theresa said. "I'll put you in my pocket or something."

"Oh, that's very kind of you, but no thanks," Izzy said. "Pocket travel gives me motion sickness. I'll meet you there." And with that, she raised both arms above her head dramatically and vanished, floating pillow and all.

I'll have to see if she can teach me that trick, Theresa thought. *That way, when everyone starts blaming me for the fifth grade's last-place finish at spring carnival, I can just disappear.*

CHAPTER
Eight

Theresa climbed the stairs to her room slowly. *Izzy better have some good ideas,* she thought, *or I'm doomed.*

Secretly, she was hoping the little fairy would just snap her fingers and produce lists of ideas and then wiggle her nose and turn Theresa into an organizational genius. But something about the whole "teach a girl to fish" quote told her it wasn't going to be that easy.

"Hey, Reesie, what's that?" Amy asked as Theresa shuffled past her sister's room. "A little black book with all your boyfriends' phone numbers in it?"

"Good one, Amy," Theresa grumbled. She looked in to see her sister sprawled across her bed with her cell phone in one hand and the TV remote in the other. "No, it's a planner."

"A planner? What's up with that? Is my ditzy sister finally trying to get organized?" Amy laughed.

Ditzy. Nice. That was something she hadn't been called yet today. "It's for my homework. And spring carnival," Theresa explained.

"Why do you need a planner for spring carnival?" Amy asked.

"Because I'm in charge of organizing the booths and decorations," Theresa replied. She started to walk away, hoping her sister would leave it at that, but she could never be so lucky.

Amy sprang to her feet and jumped into the hallway. "They put *you* in charge?" she asked, her tone sounding remarkably like Sharon's.

"So?"

"It's just that . . . wow—that's a really important job. I mean, when the judges come around, that's the big thing they're looking at—how well all the booths fit the theme and how well organized everything is. At least that's what Mr. Howell told me when he was a judge my eighth-grade year."

"Mr. Howell is a lunatic," Theresa complained, remembering how upset he'd gotten about her missing homework.

"Oh, yeah," Amy agreed. "He's freakishly neat, but he was right. Amanda Klein was

super-organized with all of the decorating—
from setting up to taking down—and we won."

"Well, thanks for the pep talk, Ame—I think
I'm going to go get started," Theresa said, and
she tried to walk away again.

"What's your theme?" Amy persisted.

Theresa stopped and sighed. Why couldn't
her sister just ignore her tonight like she did
every other night? "It's 3004," she said.

"Three thousand four?" Amy repeated.
"That's kind of lame. Who came up with that?"

"I did," Theresa mumbled.

"Oh. Well, I'm sure you'll find a way to make
it work."

"Thanks, Amy," Theresa droned. Then she
plodded down the hall, wishing there was some
way she could erase the last twelve hours and
start over again.

When she got into her room, Theresa closed
the door and leaned back against it. "Ugh," she
groaned. First Sharon and now Amy. Who
would be next?

"Izzy!" she whisper-shouted into the air.
"Are you in here?"

Theresa waited a minute, then tried again.
"Izzy?" Again there was no answer.

"Great," Theresa muttered. "Now I'm imagining

that little people are talking to me at the mall."

"You didn't imagine me," the fairy called.

Theresa's eyes darted around the room. "Where are you?"

"Up here," Izzy shouted. Theresa raised her head and looked at the ceiling just in time to see Izzy floating down with a parachute. Then she clapped, and the next thing Theresa knew, the parachute was gone and Izzy was standing on her desk, dressed in a leather bomber jacket, a white scarf, an old-fashioned pilot's helmet, and flying goggles.

"What in the world are you wearing?" Theresa asked.

"You like it?" Izzy asked, flipping the scarf over her shoulder. "Amelia had an extra uniform in her cockpit, so I—"

"Amelia?" Theresa asked. "As in Amelia Earhart?"

"I had a little free time on my way back here," Izzy said matter-of-factly. "I stopped in to wish her luck on her first solo flight."

Theresa shook her head. "Wait a second," she said. "First you were hiking with Lewis and Clark, and now you've been hanging out with Amelia Earhart?"

"What can I say? I'm a history buff," Izzy said. She clapped again and transformed her flight gear into a long, flowing, patterned skirt, a white tank top, and, once again, Birkenstocks. "There. Are you ready to get down to business?"

Theresa sighed. "I guess," she said. "I just don't know how I'm going to pull this off when nobody believes that I can—including me."

"Ah," Izzy said. "I can help you with that." She clicked her heels, and suddenly a podium appeared in front of her. The little fairy was now sporting a tailored business suit. Her hair was drawn up in a loose bun, and she was wearing horn-rimmed glasses. She leaned forward and spoke into a bunch of microphones like she was giving a press conference. "First, you're going to be realistic," she said, her voice booming through the room.

"Izzy!" Theresa hissed, covering her ears.

"Sorry," Isadora said. "I've never been very good with mikes. Too formal." She waved her hand and the podium disappeared. "Let me try that again. First, you're going to be realistic," she said at a much lower volume.

"What's that supposed to mean?" Theresa asked.

"Well, you just said that nobody believes in you. Is that true?"

"Didn't you just hear my sister?" Theresa replied.

"Yes," Izzy said matter-of-factly. "And I heard that ridiculous girl at the mall, too."

"Sharon," Theresa said.

"Right—the one who needs a good drenching," Izzy replied. "But tell me . . . who else has said they don't believe in you?"

"Well . . ." Theresa said. She chewed the inside of her cheek and thought it over. "There are the kids Sharon was talking to today when she said I was klutzy and disorganized."

Izzy shook her head. "No—that was just Sharon again. You didn't hear whether anyone actually agreed with her or not."

"How do you know that?" Theresa demanded. "You weren't there."

"It was in your file," Izzy explained. "All that stuff I read on that screen?"

"Oh. Well—what about Carrie and Anna? They haven't exactly been cheering me on."

"*No*, but they haven't been knocking you down, either. They're just looking out for you— they're your friends. And if you asked for their help or their support, you know they'd be there for you in a heartbeat."

"I suppose," Theresa said.

"So then really what it comes down to is that two people have questioned your organizational skills, and you're not confident you can pull this off, right?"

Theresa shrugged. "I guess," she said.

"You *guess?*" Izzy said. "Well, I *know*. Trust me." She snapped her fingers, and Theresa's room went pitch-black. The next thing Theresa knew, she was sitting in a folding chair, with a bottle of spring water in one hand and a tub of popcorn in the other.

"Izzy—?" she started, but then suddenly a slide projector clicked on and the words *be realistic* flashed on one of Theresa's bedroom walls.

"So like I said, that's number one," Izzy announced, underscoring the words with an extra-long pointer. "Be realistic. The whole world isn't against you, and nothing horrible is going to happen if your class doesn't win."

"Except that everyone is going to hate me," Theresa said.

"Uh, uh, uh," Izzy said, waving her pointer. "There you go again. Remember—be *realistic*— not *pessimistic*."

Theresa rolled her eyes. It sounded like something her mother would say.

"Now, number two," Izzy went on. She pressed

a clicker that had magically appeared in her hand, and the projector flipped to the next slide.

Theresa read the words that flashed on her wall in bold black letters. "'Break it down'?" she asked. "What's that supposed to mean?"

"It means," Izzy said, gesturing with her pointer as she spoke, "that big tasks can seem overwhelming. But if you break them down into smaller steps and tackle each one individually, they're easier to get done."

Theresa tilted her head. "You mean like when my mom tells me to clean my room. It always seems impossible at first, but then she comes in and helps me put away clothes, then organize my bookshelf, then clear off my desk, and pretty soon it looks a lot better."

"That's exactly what I mean," Izzy said. "And that's what you need to do with this spring carnival thing. Break it down into little pieces instead of trying to tackle the whole thing at once."

"All right, I guess I can try that," Theresa said. She took a sip of the spring water. "What else have you got?"

Izzy smiled. "We're down to the big three," she said. "The most important things to remember. Are you ready?"

Theresa leaned back in her chair and

grabbed a fistful of popcorn. "As ready as I'll ever be," she said.

"All right," Izzy said, and she pressed the clicker again. "Here they are. Number three: Do your best—because that's all you ever can do. Number four," she continued, clicking to the next frame, "ask for help when you need it—because being in charge doesn't mean working alone. And most important, number five—"

Izzy waved her pointer and everything in Theresa's room returned to normal. The lights came up, the projector was gone—even Theresa's tub of popcorn had disappeared.

"Hey, I was eating that," Theresa protested.

"Don't interrupt," Izzy told her. "And number five," she repeated, waving her hands dramatically, "have fun!" On the word *fun*, Izzy pointed both of her index fingers into the air like little guns, and suddenly confetti shot from the ceiling, raining down on a little basket of goodies that had appeared on Theresa's desk.

"What's all this?" Theresa asked, picking out a pack of bubble gum.

"Study supplies," Izzy said. "I wasn't sure what you liked, so I got a little of everything."

Theresa dug through the shredded paper in

the basket and plucked out a small plastic egg. "Silly Putty is a study supply?" she asked.

"Mm-hm." Izzy nodded. "And so are Legos," she said, pointing to a small box at the bottom. "They're both excellent for plotting things out and getting creative ideas."

"And the Slinky?" Theresa asked.

"A reminder to stay flexible."

"What about this?" Theresa said, picking up a miniature satin pillow that looked remarkably like the one Izzy was always hovering on.

"Sometimes you just have to take a break," Izzy said. "That's important, too, you know."

"I guess it is," Theresa said.

"But before you can take a break, you have to start working," Izzy said. "So get out that planner, and let's figure out what you have to do. Do you remember the tips I gave you?"

Theresa closed her eyes and pictured the slide show on her wall. "Be realistic," she said. "Break it down, do your best, ask for help when you need it . . . and have fun."

"Perfect," Izzy congratulated her. "Remember those and you're golden."

Golden, Theresa thought. *Sure. Either that or bright red when I fall flat on my face in front of the whole school.*

CHAPTER
Nine

"Well, you all certainly did a wonderful job coming up with booth ideas," Mrs. Wessex said, motioning to the list that now covered three sections of the chalkboard. Evidently Sharon had been lying when she'd said that people were having a hard time with Theresa's theme. Everyone seemed plenty enthusiastic about it today.

"I told you not to trust her," Izzy said, appearing on Theresa's shoulder.

Theresa chortled, causing Carrie to give her a bewildered look. "What?" she mouthed.

"Nothing," Theresa whispered back. Then she glanced at Izzy.

This time the little fairy was dressed in a long black dress with a white apron and matching bonnet.

Theresa raised one eyebrow at the tiny sprite.

"Plymouth," Izzy said, rubbing her stomach. "Great place for a turkey dinner."

Theresa's jaw dropped and she started to ask Izzy if she was talking about *the* Plymouth—the one where the first Thanksgiving had taken place—but Izzy stopped her.

"Better pay attention," the fairy said. "You're on."

I'm what? Theresa wondered. But she didn't have to wait long to find out.

"Now, Theresa," Mrs. Wessex said. "I was hoping that you could come up front and share some of your decorating ideas with us. And then maybe everyone can help to brainstorm ways to use those ideas in their booths. How does that sound?"

Gulp. "Fine," Theresa said. She stood up and began weaving her way to the front of the class, stepping over, behind, and between all of the fifth graders who were packed into the room.

"Remember the tips!" Izzy whispered in her ear, and then she vanished. But Theresa had a feeling she hadn't gone too far.

"Okay," Theresa began. "Since the theme is 3004, I thought that to start off, we should have two big banners that say, 3004: See What's in Store."

"*See what's in store?*" Sharon sneered. "Isn't that kind of hokey?" Billy and Jeremy chortled, and it looked like Lauren and Maria were giggling, too.

"Well, it doesn't have to be that, exactly," Theresa said. "I mean, if someone wants to come up with something else, that's fine, too. I just thought it would be good to have banners over the entrances."

"To the gym?" Kimberly asked.

"We can't put stuff over the entrances to the gym," Sharon said. "Only in our area. Which reminds me—do you know which corner we're getting yet? Because if we're in the back, maybe we can use the trampoline for a moon bounce or something."

"That would be awesome," Kimberly said. "Can we, Mrs. Wessex?"

"I'm not sure about that, Kimberly, but right now we need to listen to Theresa and think about our decorations," Mrs. Wessex said. "Theresa— go ahead."

Theresa swallowed hard and tried to regain her train of thought. She didn't usually have trouble talking in front of people. But then again, she didn't usually have Sharon sitting in the front row trying to sabotage her, either.

"So anyway, like I was saying, I think we should use banners to mark the entrances to our area—I didn't mean the entrances to the gym—and we could make those entrances by setting up the booths like this."

Theresa reached into the canvas bag she had brought to school that day and removed a model she'd built out of Legos.

"Uh, hello?" Sharon said. "Legos have been around for a long time, Theresa. I don't think anyone's going to believe they were invented in 3004."

A bunch of students laughed at Sharon's comment, and it took Mrs. Wessex another thirty seconds to get everyone quieted down again. *Why can't she just let me talk?* Theresa wondered.

She was beginning to get frustrated with all of Sharon's comments, but when she looked over at Sharon, her grimace turned into a smile. There, floating just above Sharon's head, was Izzy in a miniature hot air balloon with the words *Inflated by Sharon Ross* written on the front.

Theresa started to giggle, but she managed to stop herself by taking a deep breath.

When she looked at Sharon again, Izzy's hot air balloon was gone. Instead, there were five new ones floating around the room—each with one of Izzy's tips emblazoned on its side: *Be realistic.*

Break it down. Do your best. Ask for help. Have fun.
Theresa read the words and felt her spirits lifting.

Sharon might not think Theresa could handle being in charge of spring carnival, and there might even be a few others in the room who agreed with her, but Theresa knew that she didn't have to let them get to her. And she also knew that she'd worked hard last night getting ready for this meeting. She was doing her best, and that was all anyone could ask of her. And now it was time to have fun.

She cleared her throat, took a deep breath, and got ready. "Okay, so if you take a look at the Legos," Theresa said, holding up her model so everyone could see it, "you'll understand what I mean about the banners. See—we can set up our booths so that our whole area is walled off, like this. And then there can be just two entrances—one at each end. That way it will be really easy to decorate our section and make it feel like its our own space."

"I see what you mean, Theresa," Mrs. Wessex said. "That's rather clever. Usually people just line their booths up along the wall."

"I know," Theresa said. "I was looking at pictures of spring carnival in my sister's old yearbooks last night, and it just seemed like there was a lot of wasted space in the center of the gym. That's what gave me the idea to arrange our area differently."

"We could make arches with balloons," Carrie suggested. "My cousin did that for her prom last year and it looked really neat."

"Hey," Maria said. "I've seen those before. They're really nice."

"Sure, they are—*at proms*," Sharon said.

"I think they'd work okay here, too," Theresa said. "They'd really separate our area, and they'd give us a place to put the banners. And you know—maybe the banners could just say, Welcome to 3004. Then, on the inside of each archway, we could do another set of banners that say, You are now leaving 3004—Please come again. You know, like the way they do town signs?"

"That's a cool idea," Jeremy said. "Then it would be like we had our own town in the gym."

"Hey—that gives me a whole new idea for decorating," Theresa exclaimed suddenly. "Why don't we make it like a town in 3004? All of our booths could be like separate stores of the future." She turned to the list on the chalk-board and started scanning all the ideas.

"Okay, like this. Billy—you and Jeremy are doing something on future vehicles, right? So your booth could look like a futuristic car dealership."

"Cool," Billy and Jeremy said at the same time.

"And Lauren and Maria—you two wanted to do future food, right?"

"Right."

"So how about making your booth into, I don't know . . . Café Neptune or something like that? It could be a restaurant of the future, and you could come up with weird menus and stuff."

"Yeah, I like it," Maria said.

"Me too," Lauren agreed.

"And Matt—you wanted to do something with sports, so your booth could be a futuristic sporting goods store with all kinds of freaky equipment for stuff like . . . crater diving and . . . surfing Saturn's rings."

The classroom started to buzz with excitement as everyone began coming up with more ideas for their futuristic town, and Theresa felt like she was positively glowing. As soon as she'd relaxed and started to have fun, the ideas had just come flying into her head, and now she and all the other fifth graders were really psyched for spring carnival.

"Well, Theresa," Mrs. Wessex said, walking over to her and touching her shoulder gently. "I can see I put the right person in charge. You've done a wonderful job getting us started. Look at how excited everyone is."

Theresa glanced around the room to see everyone smiling and talking about things they could add to their booths. It was so cool to know that she'd been the one to come up with the idea they were all so pumped about.

"Thanks, Mrs. Wessex," Theresa said.

"No—thank you. You've put in a lot of work already," Mrs. Wessex said, "and it shows."

Theresa stared down at her feet. She knew she must be blushing, but it wasn't because she was embarrassed. It was because she was proud.

"Mrs. Wessex? Can I go to the bathroom?" Sharon asked. And that was when Theresa realized that Sharon was the only person in the room who wasn't smiling.

"Certainly, Sharon. Just grab the bathroom pass off my desk," Mrs. Wessex said.

Theresa watched as Sharon plodded over to get the pass and then walked out the door, dragging her feet all the way.

If only there was a way to get Sharon to help instead of trying to make things difficult, Theresa thought. And then, just as one of Izzy's hot air balloons came floating by, she realized that there was.

CHAPTER
Ten

"Theresa—you had such awesome ideas at the class meeting this morning," Anna said as Theresa sat down at the lunch table. "Everyone's been talking about it all day."

"You were so great, Resa!" Carrie agreed. "I can't believe you were worried about being in charge."

"I can," Sharon muttered without looking up from her salad. She'd been sulky and quiet most of the morning, Theresa had noticed. But now it sounded like she was ready to give Theresa a hard time again, which was fine. This time Theresa was ready.

"What do you mean, *you can*?" Anna asked. "Theresa's doing a great job."

"She has good ideas, I'll give her that," Sharon said. "But there's still a lot of work to do, and if Theresa is her usual disorganized self, she could still blow it."

"Sharon!" Carrie said.

"Yo, girls, let's keep it positive," Spence said. "No need to complain, let's refrain from disdain."

"Just say the word and I'll turn her into an emu," Izzy said. She had appeared out of nowhere, this time wearing a suit of armor and riding a black horse—fresh from the Middle Ages, no doubt. As her horse reared up, Izzy pointed her sword toward Sharon, ready to work her magic.

"No!" Theresa shouted, sending everyone at the table into shocked silence. "I mean, no— don't get upset with Sharon. She's right."

Carrie and Anna gawked at Theresa like she was crazy. "She is?" they said.

"I am?" Sharon asked.

"She's what?" Izzy demanded, whirling around on her stallion.

"Sharon's right," Theresa repeated. "There's still a lot of work to be done to get everything ready for spring carnival, and I'm not the most organized person around, so—I'm going to need a lot of help staying on top of stuff."

For a second everyone just looked around

the table, not quite sure what to say. Then Spence leaned forward.

"Okay—shoot. What do you need? You got your posse right here, ready to pitch in."

"My *posse*?" Theresa asked.

"Sure," Spence said. "Me, Matt, Anna, Carrie—just tell us what you need."

"Okay," Theresa said. She flipped her planner to one of the back sections, where she had made a neat list of all the things that needed to be done right away. "I need someone to check on the cost of making those balloon archways," she said.

"Got it," Carrie said, raising her hand. "My mom's taking me to get new sneakers this afternoon, and the party store is right next door."

"Great," Theresa said. "All right. I also need someone to see if the local grocery will donate paper cups and napkins for all the people who plan to serve food."

"I'm there," Matt volunteered. "I can stop in on my way to the skate park this afternoon."

"Excellent. Thanks," Theresa said, penciling Matt's name in next to that task. "Okay, the next one's a big one. Sharon," Theresa said, turning to face her, "I'd really be psyched if you could do it."

Sharon drew back slightly and scrunched her eyebrows together. "What is it?" she asked a little suspiciously.

"It's the decorating committee. I need someone to make sure there are plenty of people to help put up all the decorations in the morning, and then I need another crew to help take them all down at the end of the day. It's really important that I have someone organized and responsible in charge of this, and, well—you were the first person I thought of."

"Really?" Sharon asked.

"Yeah, really," Theresa said, and she meant it. As mean as Sharon could be when she didn't get her way, she really was one of the most organized people Theresa knew. And she took her responsibilities seriously, too.

"Well . . ." Sharon looked around at all the others, who were anxiously awaiting her answer. "Okay. I guess I could do that."

"Awesome!" Theresa said. "Thanks, Sharon. With you in charge of getting stuff set up, I just know everything's going to run smoothly."

"I'll make sure there aren't any problems," Sharon said.

Perfect, Theresa thought. *Just what I was hoping for.* She shot a smug smile at Isadora, who had lost the knight costume and was now sitting cross-legged on Sharon's dinner roll.

"Nicely done," Izzy said. "But I still think she'd make a good emu."

For the next week and a half everyone worked tirelessly on their booths. The decorating committee had met several times to work on the large banners welcoming everyone to the fifth-grade area and signposts to point people to all the different "stores." Lauren and Maria said they'd stayed up until midnight one night working on the menus for their space café. And Matt Dana had held a pizza party over the weekend and invited a ton of people to come help him turn used sports equipment into revolutionary new gear for sports like galaxy surfing and black-hole diving.

By the night before spring carnival, Theresa could barely contain her excitement.

"There's going to be a clothing store called Universal Cool that Kimberly and a few others have been working on," she said as she piled salad onto her plate. "They've been to every secondhand shop and fabric store in the state, picking up weird stuff to use—old prom dresses that they've altered to look like clothes you'd see on *Star Trek* or something."

"That sounds interesting," Mrs. Allen said, passing the potatoes to Theresa.

"Yeah, and Ryan Woods and Melissa Stone painted this space scene on a huge piece of plywood and cut out two circles so people can stick their heads in to make it look like their faces are on the bodies of astronauts floating outside a space station."

"Jeez, Theresa, take a breath," Amy said.

"She's just excited, Amy," Mr. Allen said. "Your sister has been working hard, and all her hard work is about to pay off."

Theresa shot her sister a smug look while her parents weren't looking.

"You're still not going to win," Amy said.

"You don't know that," Theresa retorted. "We've got all kinds of fun booths—Jessica Foster made a game called 3004: What Would You Be? where people throw darts at balloons, and inside each balloon there's a little card describing a career in the year 3004. She has everything from Milky Way movie star and prime minister of Venus to lifeguard at Club Mercury and celebrity dog walker on Pluto."

Amy rolled her eyes and shrugged to show

just how unimpressed she was.

"That's what I'd want to be," said Theresa's little brother, Nicky. "I like dogs."

"You'd be an excellent dog walker, sweetie," said Mrs. Allen. "Amy—take some salad. You haven't been eating enough vegetables lately." Theresa plunked a bite of salmon into her mouth and watched as Amy once again rolled her eyes. "Irritated" seemed to be one of the only expressions she could manage since she'd turned sixteen.

"Look, Reesie," Amy said as she began scooping lettuce and cucumbers onto her plate. She avoided everything else in the salad—tomatoes, yellow peppers, carrots, anything that wasn't green. "I'm not saying that your class hasn't worked hard or that your area won't have cool booths—I'm just telling you not to get your hopes up. Fifth graders are the bottom of the heap, and heap bottoms don't win spring carnival."

Theresa snorted. "That shows what you know," she said. She sat silently for a few minutes, picking at her food, then finally tossed her napkin onto the table. "May I be excused?" she asked, turning to her parents. "I still have to check on a few things for tomorrow."

"Theresa—you've barely eaten," Mrs. Allen protested.

"I know, but I'm not hungry." She glared at Amy and added, "I've lost my appetite. Besides, I need to call the party store to make sure they're all set to deliver the balloon arches, and they close at six-thirty."

Mrs. Allen glanced at Theresa's father, who frowned.

"Please," Theresa begged, giving them her best smile. Mr. Allen held his frown for a few more seconds, then cocked his head and shrugged.

"All right," Mrs. Allen said. "But just this once. And I expect you to have a healthy snack before bed."

"I will," Theresa said, rushing over to her mother and wrapping her arms around her neck. "Thanks, Mom. Thanks, Dad." Then she scurried out of the dining room and up to her bedroom.

"You really should eat more, you know," a small voice said when Theresa reached for her planner. "Big day tomorrow."

"I know, I just—" Theresa stopped short. Izzy was standing on her desk wearing a tattered white silk shirt with billowing arms and black pants with torn cuffs. She was barefoot, and she had a bright red silk scarf tied around her waist and a short black one on her head. Large gold hoop earrings dangled from her ears, and in her hand she brandished a short sword.

"Nice outfit," Theresa said. "But I didn't think pirates let women on their ships."

"Some did," Izzy answered. "Ever hear of Anne Bonney or Mary Read?"

"No."

"Well, then, you should look them up sometime. Remarkable women, even if they were criminals. I was just chatting with them about what it was like to be a woman pirate—interesting stuff. So what are you up to?"

Theresa chuckled. "Nothing that adventurous," she said, unzipping her planner and flipping to the page where she'd copied down the number of the party store. "Just making sure everything's ready for tomorrow." She punched the numbers on the cordless phone she'd snagged from the hallway table and waited. As she did, Izzy was advancing and retreating across her desk, practicing various fencing moves she'd picked up on one of her journeys.

"Parties Unlimited, this is Beth speaking, how can I help you?" a voice finally said.

"Hi, my name is Theresa Allen, and I was just calling to check on some balloon archways that I ordered."

"Hold on one minute, please," the clerk instructed her. "Ah, yes. Theresa Allen. Two ten-foot archways, silver and white balloons . . . mm-hm. Everything seems to be in order. Those will be ready for delivery next Friday."

"*Next* Friday?" Theresa asked. "You mean *this* Friday, right? As in tomorrow?"

There was a brief silence on the line. "No, I mean *next* Friday—as in the twentieth. That's the date they were ordered for."

Theresa's jaw dropped. There had to be some mistake. "Are you sure?" she asked the clerk. "Because I placed that order myself, and I can't imagine I gave you the wrong date."

"I'm looking at the original order slip here," replied the clerk, "and it clearly says you need them for the twentieth."

Izzy had stopped practicing her sword fighting and was now staring at Theresa. "What's wrong?" she asked, but Theresa just waved for her to be quiet.

"Well," Theresa said, her mind reeling, "can you change that? Because I need them for a spring carnival competition that's happening tomorrow—not next Friday."

At the other end of the phone the clerk laughed. "Oh, sweetheart. I'm sorry. Balloon arches take at least a day to put together, and yours haven't even been started."

"But there's been a mistake," Theresa said. "I ordered them for the thirteenth—I know I did. Can't you rush them or something? Or, I don't know, get someone to come in and put them together tonight?"

"I'm sorry, but—"

"Isn't there *anything* you can do?" Theresa pleaded.

The clerk paused. "I can cancel the order so you won't have to pay for it," she offered. Theresa's mouth hung open. This couldn't be happening.

"But you're the ones who made the mistake," she protested, "not me."

Theresa flipped madly through her planner, searching for the calendar section, where she'd written down the confirmation number for her order. *February, March, April—there.* All at once, Theresa's eyes popped. The space for Friday the thirteenth was blank. One row below it, however, in the box for the twentieth, she had written the word *balloons* with a confirmation number and placed a little check mark next to it.

"Oh, no," Theresa moaned. "It *was* my fault."

"Excuse me?" the clerk asked.

"I'm sorry," Theresa said. "You're right. But please just . . . go ahead and cancel the order. If I can't get the archways tomorrow, I don't need them."

"Okay. I'll take care of that for you right away," the clerk said cheerfully. "Is there anything else I can help you with this evening?"

Sure, an escape plan, Theresa thought. "No, no thanks," she said. Theresa hung up the phone and felt her heart sink to the floor.

"What's going on?" Izzy asked. She put her sword back in its sheath, then snapped her fingers and lost the pirate gear altogether, changing into slightly more casual clothing—a pair of tan drawstring pants, a crocheted top, and her faithful Birkenstocks.

"I've ruined the spring carnival," Theresa said, dropping her head onto her desk.

"What do you mean?" Izzy asked.

"The balloon archways," Theresa groaned. "The entryway to our area. I messed it up. Now we don't have anything. No place to put the welcome signs, no way to make our area stand out, and no chance of winning. And it's all my fault."

"What are you talking about?" Izzy asked.

"I ordered the balloons for the wrong date," Theresa said, her head still resting on her desk.

"Sharon was right—Mrs. Wessex did blow our chances of winning when she put me in charge. Now we're going to lose, and I'm never going to hear the end of it from Amy. Even worse, no one in my class is ever going to trust me to be in charge of anything important ever again. I wish I could disappear from the face of the earth."

Theresa had lain there on her desk wallowing for another thirty seconds when suddenly it occurred to her that Izzy was being uncharacteristically quiet. She raised her head ever so slightly to see the tiny sprite standing there with her arms folded across her chest, glowering at Theresa.

"What?" Theresa asked, uncertain what she'd done to earn such a harsh look.

"Are you quite finished?" Izzy asked. "Anything else you want to throw in there? Maybe, 'The world's going to end, and it's all my fault'? Or how about, 'I'm the worst person on the face of the earth and no one's ever going to talk to me again. I might as well find an underground cave and live there for the rest of my life.'" Isadora shook her head. "I should turn *you* into an emu."

"*What?*" Theresa demanded, sitting up straight.

"At least Sharon doesn't give up. She didn't get to be in charge of decorations, but she's been busting her butt just the same. But you—" Izzy stared at the ceiling in frustration. "One little thing goes wrong and it's, 'Poor me, nothing ever goes my way, blah blah blah.'"

"I don't sound like that," Theresa said.

"No—you sound worse," Izzy replied matter-of-factly.

"Well, what do you want me to do? Jump up and down and cheer about the fact that I've messed everything up?"

"*No,*" Isadora said. "I want you to deal with it."

Theresa slumped forward again. "Oh, I see," she said sarcastically. "You want me to be realistic, break it down, do my best, ask for help, and have fun, huh? Fine. Here goes—realistically, I've messed up, and there's nothing to break down because we have no archways. I've been doing my best, but it obviously isn't good enough, and nobody can help me now because it's too late. As for having fun, it's hard to do when I've just proved to my sister and the rest of the world that I really am the disorganized idiot they all thought I was."

Isadora shook her head. "An emu would be too good for you."

"Aaargh!" Theresa roared. "Don't you get it, Izzy? It's over. I messed up, and there's nothing I can do about it."

"Nothing, huh? Do you suppose that's what Lewis and Clark said when they were cold and hungry and stuck in the middle of a mountain range? 'Gee, we've really messed up, and there's nothing we can do about it. We might as well quit right here.' Do you think that's what they did?"

Theresa sighed.

"Of course they didn't!" Izzy answered herself. "They kept going, and eventually they made it through. And what about Amelia Earhart? When people told her aviation was for men, did she give up? No way! She proved them wrong. She saved up enough money to buy her own plane and flew it right across the Atlantic Ocean!

"And how about the Pilgrims? Their first winter in America was really tough, but when spring finally came, did they just hop back on their boat and sail away? No—they dug in and prepared themselves better the second time around, and the next winter was a little bit easier."

Theresa folded her arms across her chest and scowled at the little fairy. True, none of those people had given up, but none of them had been dealing with balloon arches, had they?

Izzy took a few steps closer to Theresa and looked her in the eyes. "You say you're being realistic when you say there's nothing you can do, but it doesn't sound very realistic to me," Isadora said. "You still have fourteen hours before it's time to set up for spring carnival, which is plenty of time if you break down what you need to do and ask for help from—what did Spence call them?"

"My posse," Theresa grumbled.

"That's right—your posse." Isadora smiled. "I do like that boy. He has a way with words."

Theresa chortled in spite of herself. "He does," she agreed, almost smiling. Then she remembered the archways. "Look, Izzy, I know you're trying to help me out and everything, but I just don't see what I can do at this point. It's too late for the party store to make our arches, and that's not something I can do on my own even if all my friends do pitch in and help."

Izzy jumped into the air and glided to the top of Theresa's lamp, perching on the rim so that she was face-to-face with Theresa. "You remember those tips I gave you?"

"Yes, but—"

"Well, I left one out."

Theresa narrowed her eyes. "What is it?" she asked wearily. She was pretty sure Izzy didn't have a tip that would help her now unless it was: *Ask your magical fairy friend to whip up a few balloon archways out of thin air.*

"Capitalize on your strengths," Izzy said.

Theresa craned her neck to lean in closer to the fairy. "What does that mean?"

"It means that everyone has something they're good at—a strength of some sort. So when you're working on a project like this, you should always find your strengths and use them."

"I still don't see what you mean," Theresa said. "I don't even know what my strengths are."

"Yes, you do," Izzy said. "You already told me once."

"I did?"

"Mm-hm. At the mall. When Spence came to you for advice. Do you remember what you said to me?"

Theresa squinted, trying to remember. "Be quiet?" she guessed.

"No-o," Izzy replied. "You told me the organization was hard for you, but the ideas came easy."

"Oh, right. I guess I did," Theresa said. "But how's that supposed to help me now? I don't need more booth ideas—I need a balloon archway."

"So come up with a way to make one," Izzy said. "Or come up with another idea for an entryway. You said it yourself—*the ideas come easy.* You're creative, Theresa—and you're a quick thinker. So stop whining about the archways that you're not going to get and come up with something else."

Theresa sat back in her chair and folded her arms across her chest. Everyone was expecting balloon-lined entryways. They were bound to be disappointed with anything else she came up with at the last minute. *Unless . . .*

"Hey, Izzy—pass me that pencil," Theresa said. The fairy waved a finger and floated the pencil over to Theresa. "Thanks," Theresa said, snagging it out of the air. "I wonder," Theresa muttered, making a quick sketch on one of the pieces of graph paper in her planner. "If we had Ms. Gilbert let down a few of the rings and tied a rope here. . ." She made a few more lines on her graph paper, then sat back to look at it.

Slowly a smile crept onto Theresa's face. "You know, Izzy, that just might work. But it's going to take the whole posse to pull it off."

CHAPTER
Eleven

"There—how's that?" Sharon asked, stapling the last of the silver balloons onto the makeshift archway Theresa had designed just last night.

"It looks great, Sharon," Theresa gushed. "Thank you so much for getting everyone here early to make this work."

"No problem," Sharon said. "It was easy. Everyone was willing to come in when they heard what happened with the order."

Theresa pressed her eyes closed. "I still can't believe I had the wrong date," she said.

"Don't sweat it," Sharon said. Theresa stared at her, wide-eyed. She'd expected Sharon to make a snide comment about how disorganized she was or what a ditz she was, but she certainly hadn't expected Sharon to be supportive.

"Really?" Theresa asked.

"Sure. I mean, it wasn't the smartest thing you've ever done. . . ."

That's more like it, Theresa thought.

"But still, you did a good job pulling everything together. The fifth-grade area looks great, and you know—" Sharon stepped back to admire the entryway. "I actually think this looks better than the one we would have gotten from the party store. The streamers make it look more complete."

Theresa gazed at the curtain of white streamers dangling from the ceiling, each one with a shiny balloon attached to the end. She and the other members of the decorating crew had created entryways by suspending ropes like clotheslines at each end of their area. Each rope was about fifteen feet long and hung about ten feet above the floor.

Once these "clotheslines" were up, Theresa and the others had cut lengths of white streamers to hang straight down from the ropes. The streamers at the outer edges hung all the way to the floor, but as they worked their way inward, the decorators had made each successive streamer a little shorter so that the ones in the middle were only about a foot and a half long. The overall effect was that of an archway, and to finish it off, they'd attached silver and white balloons to the ends of the streamers, turning it into a balloon archway.

"It does look pretty good," Theresa agreed. "How's everything else coming along?"

"I think we're all set," Sharon said, "but I'm going to walk through one last time just to be sure."

"Good idea," Theresa said. "Thanks again, Sharon."

"Anytime," Sharon called over her shoulder. Theresa took a few steps back to admire both entryways. Across the top of each were huge banners that read, Welcome to 3004. It really did look incredible.

Theresa sighed. Izzy had been right. Once she'd stopped whining and started focusing, she'd been able to come up with a solution to her archway problem. And by breaking down the tasks and asking for help from her friends, she'd managed to make it work. Carrie had scored the extra streamers and balloons, Spence had come through with the ropes, Matt and Anna had each brought stepladders, and Sharon had called everyone on the setup crew to get them in a half hour earlier. The whole posse had come through.

And the fifth-grade area, with its enclosed futuristic town, really stood out. All of the rest of the classes had set up their booths the traditional way—backed up against the walls. A few booths in each section were set in closer to the center of the floor, but the fifth grade was the only class that had turned their area into a contained space, and the effect was amazing.

Theresa walked through the rear arch and found herself facing the Astro Gym. As it turned out, Mrs. Wessex had been able to arrange for the fifth graders to use the trampoline after all.

Sharon had worked with Lesley Fine to decorate its edges with gray moon-rock pillows. They'd also created a storefront made from cardboard and streamers and a big sign inviting people inside to try the most technologically advanced exercise machine of 3004—the moon bounce.

The next store in their futuristic town was the W^2 Music Emporium, where people could check out bands in the year 3004, as designed by Spence and Carrie, aka W^2—for Willis and Weingarten.

"This looks great, you guys," Theresa said as she checked out some of the weird album covers Carrie had designed and the phony song titles and lyrics that Spence had come up with. "And I love your alien costume, Spence."

Following Theresa's suggestion, Spence had come dressed as a famous alien rapper who was getting ready for his first Earth concert tour. He had two heads, five eyes, and a spiked, dragonlike tail. All day long he planned to challenge people to freestyle battles. Carrie was ready to hand out candy and dollar-store prizes to anyone who could outrhyme him.

"Yo, Theresa—you want to be my first opponent?" Spence asked. His voice was muffled by his costume, but it didn't seem to affect his ability to rhyme. "We'll have a freestyle battle. / You can shake, roll, and rattle / and I'll rap until the cattle come home."

Theresa laughed and shook her head. "I think you just won, Spence. Carrie, you're going to be holding that loot all day, you know."

"I know," Carrie said. "Maybe I should just give it out to anyone who dares to challenge him."

"That might be a better idea," Theresa agreed.

As she continued her walk, she passed Todd Metcalf's Surreal Estate, where people could view models of rental condos on Mars, and Billy and Jeremy's Used Car Lot, where people could test drive a "space car" that Billy and Jeremy had built from spare wood and old appliance parts.

Theresa had been a little wary when they'd

first brought it in, but it actually worked really well. It had a wooden frame with wings and all kinds of dials and controls on the inside. Then Billy and Jeremy had set up a big TV in front of it and put in a video with footage taken from a helicopter camera so that it seemed like the car was actually flying through the sky.

There were tons of other booths, too, like Lauren and Maria's Intergalactic Café and XTreme Planet, the sporting goods store Matt had set up with a couple of his buddies. Anna was running a bakery, where she and a bunch of others were holding cakewalks, only they were calling them "moonwalks." And instead of walking away with a cake, the winner received a MoonPie.

Overall, the fifth-grade area looked amazing. There were silver and white balloons everywhere, and everyone had done a great job making their booths look futuristic and cutting-edge. Theresa was psyched. It felt like they actually had a shot at winning.

"Hey—have you checked out the other areas yet?" a tiny voice said in her ear. Theresa turned to see Izzy wearing astronaut gear and hovering next to Theresa's head in a mini space shuttle.

"I thought you said you were a *history* buff,"

Theresa said, keeping her mouth as still as possible when she spoke.

Izzy tapped a patch on her bright orange uniform, which bore the initials *S. R.* "I borrowed this suit from Sally Ride, the first woman in space," she said. "She was a very important part of history indeed. Besides, I wanted to support your whole future theme, so showing up in a stagecoach or a Model T didn't seem appropriate."

"Good point," Theresa said.

"Thanks," Izzy said. "So—have you checked out all the other classes' themes?" she asked for the second time.

"No, but—"

"Well, I have," Izzy said, "and you have absolutely no competition. The eighth grade did Hollywood, yawn, and the sixth graders just have a whole bunch of carnival booths and a couple of bales of hay. I think it's supposed to be a county fair."

"What about the seventh grade?" Theresa asked.

Izzy pressed her eyes closed and shook her head. "That one you have to see for yourself. Come on!"

"Izzy, I—" Theresa started, but it was no use.

Izzy's spaceship had already whizzed ahead and out through the far archway. *"Oo-kay,"* Theresa said with a sigh. "I guess I'll go check out the other areas."

She followed Izzy's path out of the fifth-grade section and across the gym to where the seventh grade was set up. "Uh-oh," she said as soon as she saw their sign.

"Can you believe it?" Izzy said, pointing to one of the booths. "They're all over the place."

Theresa gazed at all the booths. The seventh grade had chosen fairy tales as their theme, and as a result, there were little pictures of fairies on just about everything in their area. But they weren't fairies like Isadora, with baseball hats and hiking boots and astronaut suits and Birkenstocks. No—they were all glittery, winged fairies with short skirts and magic wands. They were—

"Cute little Barbie dolls flitting about in short skirts and butterfly wings. Your school is infested with them," Izzy groaned. "But that's not even the worst part."

Theresa was sure she was going to regret it, but she had to ask. "What is?"

"The stories!" Izzy shouted directly in Theresa's ear.

"Man, it's a good thing no one else can hear you," Theresa muttered, rubbing her temples. "You're not going to transmogrify anybody, are you?"

"Of course not," Izzy said. "Not that they don't deserve it."

Theresa coughed to suppress a smile. Then she cleared her throat. "Wait a second—I get why you're upset about the fairies, but what's wrong with the stories?"

"Isn't it obvious?" Izzy asked. "Look around. What do you see?"

Theresa scanned the booths. They looked fine to her. There was one based on Little Red Riding Hood, one next to that about Snow White, and one farther down with Sleeping Beauty. Theresa also saw the Three Little Pigs, the Three Billy Goats Gruff, and Goldilocks and the Three Bears, among others.

"Well?" Izzy demanded. "Don't you see?"

"See what?" Theresa asked.

Izzy shook her head. "I'll spell it out for you—they're calling these stories *fairy* tales, right?"

"Right."

"So where are the fairies?" Izzy demanded. "Not one of these stories actually has *a fairy*!"

"They don't?" Theresa glanced at all of the nearby booths again and thought it over. "Wow, you're right—they don't. Huh. That's weird. I wonder why we call them fairy tales."

"I have no idea," Izzy said, "but these drawings must be dealt with."

"*Izzy,*" Theresa said, "what are you planning to do?"

"Improve them," Izzy said.

"Izzy—you can't," Theresa told her. "You may not like the booths, but the seventh grade worked hard to make them. You can't just change them around. And besides, they have to be judged for the contest—*without* your improvements."

"Fine," Izzy said. "So I'll wait. But mark my words—those butterfly-winged babes are going down." She glanced at something over Theresa's shoulder. "And soon, too," she added.

"What do you mean?" Theresa asked.

"I mean, here come the judges. They just finished looking at your area."

"They—*what*? How do you know?"

"Because," Isadora said. "They just came out through one of your archways smiling and taking notes, and they're headed this way next."

"Smiling? They were smiling?" Theresa said. "I have to go find out how it went."

Theresa started running toward her class's area, then stopped and turned back to the fairy. "Don't touch anything—okay?"

"I won't," Izzy assured her. "I promise." But there was something about the smile on her face that made Theresa just a little bit nervous.

CHAPTER
Twelve

"I'm so nervous, my knees are shaking," Theresa said.

"Me too," said Anna.

"Me three," added Carrie.

The three girls clasped hands and stared at the front of the gym, where the three judges—Mrs. Hendrickson, the music teacher; Ms. Hamlin, the art teacher; and Mr. Howell—were getting ready to announce this year's spring carnival winner.

According to Carrie, Spence, Anna, Matt, and Sharon, things had gone really well with the judges. They'd stopped at nearly every booth in the fifth-grade area to tell the students what a nice job they'd done, and Mr. Howell had even taken a minute to try to outrhyme Spence.

Of course he'd lost—he'd gotten stuck trying

to rhyme his own name, at which point Spence had jumped in with, "Yo, Mr. Howell / don't throw in the towel. / Your name rhymes with *owl* and *dowel* and *foul*."

All three judges had laughed and congratulated Spence on his victory, and Carrie had offered them all lollipops just for stopping by. They'd declined, saying they weren't accepting candy or prizes from anyone until the judging was done, but Ms. Hamlin, the art teacher, had said she'd be back later to win one from them, which seemed like a good sign.

Anna said Ms. Hamlin had even commented on the archways, saying they were "much better than those gaudy ones people buy at the party store." And according to Sharon, all three judges had told her that "Welcome to 3004" was the best fifth-grade area they'd ever seen.

Now that it was time for the judges to announce their decision, Theresa found herself replaying that comment over and over in her head. It sounded promising, but then again, the fifth grade had never won spring carnival before. So being the best fifth-grade area ever might not mean all that much.

"Could I have everyone's attention, please?" Ms. Hamlin said into the microphone. She didn't have to ask twice. As full of excitement as the gymnasium was, everyone had gone silent the moment she'd started to speak.

Theresa gripped her friends' hands tighter, and they both squeezed back.

"Thank you," Ms. Hamlin went on. "On behalf of Mr. Howell, Mrs. Hendrickson, and myself, I'd like to say that we were impressed with all of your hard work. I think you all deserve a round of applause."

On the word *applause*, the gymnasium erupted with shouts, whistles, and tons of clapping. Everyone was obviously pretty wound up about the competition—so much so that Theresa could almost feel the tension flowing through her veins. She stopped applauding and reclasped Anna's and Carrie's hands in order to keep her own from shaking.

"All right," Ms. Hamlin said as the noise died down. "This is the moment you've all been waiting for. Choosing one winner is always difficult—especially when everyone has put in such a good effort. But there was one class that really stood out this year, and that class was . . ."

Ms. Hamlin paused for dramatic effect, smiling out at the crowd. Theresa felt her heart pounding in her chest and her mouth going dry.

"Who?" she murmured quietly, unable to contain her excitement. "Who is it?"

"For the first time in ECS history . . . the fifth grade!" Ms. Hamlin finished.

A roar went up all around Theresa as her classmates began jumping up and down, screaming and high-fiving one another.

"We did it!" they were yelling out. And then people started congratulating Theresa personally.

"Awesome theme, Theresa!"

"You rule, Allen!"

"Go get the award, Theresa! Go get the award!"

Theresa looked up at the stage, where all three judges were applauding and Ms. Russell, the principal, was holding a plaque and eyeing the fifth-grade group expectantly.

"Theresa," Mrs. Wessex called from the side of the gym. "Go ahead—go up and accept the award."

Theresa's eyes bugged out. Mrs. Wessex wanted *her* to go up there?

"Yeah, Theresa," Anna said. "Go get it."

"Go, Resa!" Carrie called, grinning and clapping excitedly.

Theresa could hardly believe that everyone wanted her to be the one to accept the award for the fifth grade. But after being told so many times, her legs began to move automatically, and she found herself moving toward the stage as if she were in a dream.

She was halfway to the stage before she even realized what she was doing, and it was then that a thought occurred to her. She glanced up at the stage, where Ms. Russell was patiently waiting, and held up her index finger. "Just a minute," she called, although it was doubtful the principal could hear her over all the applause and chatter that was still going on. Even so, Theresa knew what she needed to do.

She ran back to the fifth-grade group and grabbed Carrie and Anna, Spence, Matt, and Sharon. "You guys come up, too," she said. "None of this would have happened without all of your help."

"No way, Tee," Spence said. "This is all about you—it's your moment of glory."

Theresa put her hands on her hips and grinned. "I want you to come, too, and that's the end of the story," she said.

"You go, Resa!" Carrie giggled, and everyone else laughed, too. Then, with a little more coaxing from Theresa, they all headed up to the stage together.

"Nice work, ladies and gentlemen," Ms.

Russell said as she placed the plaque—which had yet to be engraved—in Theresa's hands.

"Thank you, Ms. Russell," Theresa said. Then she hoisted the plaque above her head for the whole fifth grade to see. Once again the crowd exploded with clapping and cheering, and Theresa couldn't help laughing out of sheer joy.

She looked out at all of her peers, so thrilled to become the first fifth grade ever to win spring carnival, and smiled. Then she scanned the rest of the audience and was surprised to see that people in all the other grades were still clapping and cheering, too. Apparently everyone thought the fifth grade had deserved to win, and as Theresa examined the other areas from the vantage point of the stage, she could see that their area truly did stand out.

She was just about to lower the plaque and turn to leave the stage when something in the seventh-grade area caught her eye. *Oh, no,* she thought, squinting to get a better look. There, floating on her pillow in midair, was Izzy. And behind her was a construction crew, complete with scaffolding, working on the seventh-grade sign that stated their theme: Fairy-Tale Land.

Theresa forced one last smile to the crowd, turned around and shook Ms. Russell's hand, thanking her again, and then walked off the stage. As she and the others returned to the fifth-grade area, everyone began giving Theresa high fives and congratulating her, but all Theresa wanted to do was check on Izzy.

"Could you take over for me here?" she asked, handing the plaque to Sharon. "I need to . . . use the bathroom."

"Sure," Sharon said. She gladly accepted the plaque and held it up again so that the whole fifth grade could get a look at it. And as all of her friends started cheering again, Theresa rushed away, booking it to the seventh-grade section of the gym.

When she got there, Izzy, the pillow, and all the scaffolding was gone. "Izzy?" Theresa whispered. "Where are you?" She hunted around for the fairy for a moment, but her eyes stopped when she saw the seventh grade's sign.

At first Theresa gasped. Then she clapped a hand to her mouth and laughed out loud. True to her word, Izzy hadn't touched a thing, but the construction crew she'd conjured up had altered the image of the fairy completely.

Instead of the wispy winged creature with the short fitted dress, star-tipped wand, and cute blond ponytail, the fairy now looked remarkably like . . . Izzy. The way she'd looked when Theresa had first met her.

She had long brown braids, a Red Sox cap, cargo shorts, and hiking boots, and now the sign read: Fairy-Tale Land—Where Fairies Are People, Too.

Theresa shook her head and grinned. "Okay, Izzy," she said quietly. "You can come out now. I'm not mad. I think it's a big improvement." She stepped closer and looked all around the sign, but there was still no Izzy. Then she saw it.

Down on the floor, just below the spot where Izzy had been relaxing on her pillow, Theresa saw something silver and shiny. She stooped to pick it up and realized that it was the fairy ornament from the top of her pen—only now, instead of wings, the fairy was wearing a baseball hat. And the wand that she'd been holding was gone, too. In its place was simply a small silver hoop. Theresa smiled when she saw it, knowing immediately what it was meant for.

She brought the little fairy charm to her lips and gave it a quick kiss. "Thanks, Izzy," she whispered. "I'll remember all of your tips."

As she was attaching the fairy to her charm bracelet, Theresa noticed that something was written on its back. She flipped it over and read: *Ask for help, do your best, and have fun.*

"Especially the big three," she added. Then she clipped the fairy onto her bracelet and headed back to the fifth-grade area to find her friends. They had an ice cream party to prepare for.

"Well, you did it," Amy said later that night. She was standing in Theresa's bedroom doorway.

Theresa looked up from the book she was reading. "I told you we could," she replied with great satisfaction.

"What did you do, bribe the judges?"

"Amy!" Theresa said. She closed her book and sat up on her bed.

"I was only kidding, Reesie. Jeez."

"Maybe you were this time," Theresa said, "but you weren't before. All those times that you said we didn't have a shot and that I'd mess everything up if I was involved, you meant it."

"I meant *some* of it," Amy admitted.

Theresa scowled and folded her arms across her chest.

"Come on, Reesie, don't take everything so seriously. I'm your big sister. I'm supposed to give you a hard time—it builds character."

Theresa remained silent. She cocked her head and continued to glare at her sister.

"And besides, I really didn't think you had a shot at winning. The—"

"See!" Theresa shouted. "There you go again. You think—"

"Dial it back a notch, Reesie," Amy interrupted. "If you'd let me finish, I was going to say that I didn't think you had a shot at winning because the fifth grade never does."

"You mean the fifth grade never *did*," Theresa corrected her.

"Whatever," Amy said, but she was smiling just a tiny bit. "Look, I came in here to say congratulations, but now I'm not so sure I want to."

"So don't," Theresa said, giving her a tiny smile back.

"Fine, I won't." Amy turned and walked away.

Theresa pulled her legs underneath her and sat cross-legged on her bed for a moment, her hands resting on her knees, palms up. *So Amy came in to congratulate me,* she thought, her lips curving into a smile. *Maybe I'll meditate about that for a few minutes.*

She was just beginning to understand why Izzy enjoyed sitting that way so much when something hit her on the side of the head. It was Amy's pillow.

"Amy! What are you doing?" Theresa asked.

Her sister stood a few feet away from her, grinning. "Pillow fight?" she asked playfully.

Theresa smiled. She and Amy had had pillow fights all the time when they were younger, but it had been at least two years since their last one. "You're on," Theresa said. She rolled back on her bed, grabbed her pillow, and walloped her sister on the side.

"Ooh—I'll get you for that one," Amy said, giggling, and then she and Theresa proceeded to thwack each other until they both fell on the floor, laughing.

It's not exactly "Congratulations," Theresa thought, lying in a heap with her older sister, *but it will do.*